I0637761

The Waterboy

Joe Moore

Published by Kimber Moore & Associates, 2025.

Table of Contents

To Janice, for enhancing the book with every read and for everything.

Acknowledgement.

For their encouragement and thoughtful observations on iterations of The Waterboy, Al Ruskin, George Manojlovic, Bob Gray, Andrew Newman, and for profound background on the Murray-Darling Basin, Peter Redfearn.

Edited by Linda Godfrey who does a wonderful job with skill and candour.

Michelle Moore who designed the cover which defines the book with creativity and grace under pressure.

The Waterboy

A dry bed.

'Water,' Mick Darby paused for it to sink in, tried not to laugh, 'safe, clean, drinking water for families, water for cultural reasons, environmental reasons, recreational uses, water for industry, farms, mines, factories. We don't have it. And the secrecy,' he continued, 'secrecy about ownership of that water feeds conspiracies. There's a water register but it's voluntary.'

Darby thumbed the remote to show a picture of the Darling River, dry, a car halfway across a bridge gave the river's width, crumbling banks showed depth. He zoomed in on a toddler in the middle of the photo, both feet in what water there was not even covering her toes.

The Prime Minister had appointed Darby Commissioner for Ecological Intelligence, Security and Terrorism. The Riverina was his focus, and he needed cooperation. Mick Darby was with the Intelligence Committee. A small group of high-ranking professional intelligence officers formed the Committee out of despair with governments whose response to crisis was to announce a new agency, and then not fund it. The Committee concentrated on those few critical, cross-agency security briefs too important to leave with those who squabbled for their country. Its current focus, water.

With the Committee's research Darby convinced the Prime Minister that the integrity of Australia's ecosystems could no longer be guaranteed. He'd argued that the megadrought, water shortages, water theft, and a bull market for shares in water rights and entitlements created conditions ripe for civil unrest. He concluded the Riverina threatened the Murray-Darling Basin.

'We can manage,' he closed his argument, 'conspiracy theorists, extremist groups, environmental activists, community activists, mercenary industry associations and self-interested politicians. What we cannot manage is if they act together. A dry bed, if you will, of alliances.'

One of the Prime Minister's advisors looked up, looked around, 'a dry bed? Profound. Unlikely isn't it, conspiracy theorists, greenies, the CWA, a rabble of self-interest, coalition of incompetence.'

Darby wondered if he was talking about the government.

His office had lined up meetings with water regulators, government agencies with some responsibility for water, state water authorities, private sector agronomists, water researchers, he got nowhere. On second visits he met their lawyers, there were no third visits. All he had was a clearer idea of the scale of the threat to water security, mostly government-funded threat.

Darby had decided to go local, to police districts dealing daily with the fallout of megadrought, increasingly unruly queues for bottled water, unsafe playgrounds fenced off, play equipment left unmended, businesses closed. He got nowhere in his meetings with police chiefs. The older guard were professional bullies, and Darby knew he couldn't provoke or force them. They asked for evidence; he came back with intelligence. A concept foreign to most of them. The younger chiefs were careerists and assured Darby they'd have to consult, widely, that'd take some time. It'd be a question of resources, they said.

Sandy Pelham was Darby's last meeting. Darby tried to keep an open mind, but he'd heard that Pelham owed his job to the Wiggles, and that the local State and Federal parliamentarians, and the district's former police superintendent had complained about him. Not necessarily a bad thing.

Chief Superintendent.

Sandy Pelham, on his way out of his office, half-closed the door and used a finger to wipe dust off the name plate, *Chief Superintendent*, when his office landline rang. He walked back in.

'You've got your op, code name, Operation Marinya.' His boss was on the line. 'You run it, but you get no relief from running your District.'

Pelham had expected nothing less, but bellyached a little for form. He moved around the desk and sat.

'You're sure you want to reopen inquiries into meth overdoses in your District? Some of them go back years. I've read the reports, all of them, your predecessor's, coroners' – conclusion in every case is overdose.'

'Did you notice there were no investigations, no follow up of where they got the drugs from, no crime scene. They were just addicts,' Sandy paused, 'to my predecessor, not victims of crime.'

'OK, not on overtime though. Marinya's a big op,' said his boss, 'liaison with neighbouring Districts, it'll be more a test of your leadership, Sandy, than a test of your policing.'

Sandy sat up straighter in his chair and reached for a pen.

'Leadership,' said Sandy.

'Precisely,' said his boss, 'no getting lost in the weeds. One more thing.'

Sandy spun the pen over his fingers, 'only one?'

'Your good work has attracted the interest of Canberra. Liaise with them directly. I'll let you know when they want you.'

'Yes ma'am.' No choice.

He went home, changed, and sat at his computer, opening files, folders, rearranging the contents of physical files and scribbling in his notebook. He picked up the phone to let his team know the op was on, but glancing at the time thought it better left for morning.

Sandy had spent months poring over District files of meth arrests. He correlated them with meth-related hospital admissions, psychotic episodes, sewage analysis reports. For at least four years meth use had ravaged the Riverina, running because of minimal police attention, leadership - corrupt or inept. And then eighteen months ago, a boost in use, and a steady increase in arrests for cocaine and weed, and not meth.

And five deaths by meth overdose in the recent four years. Sandy knew he'd not get far with reopening the overdose cases, any evidence would be long gone, some of the buildings where the victims died had since been demolished, phone records may be available. But Sandy wanted to signal that where drugs killed people, he wanted to prosecute the suppliers for causing death. He'd start with the most recent crimes.

What was it? A new meth manufacturer, dealer network, protected?

When police busted a lab, seized a few kilograms of meth, arrested cooks, dealers and a few users a local spike in the price of meth and a cut in quality followed. After a few months of no busts nor arrests prices and quality stabilised. Competitors of those taken out of business moved in, crims had budgets too. Taking a few criminals off the streets made a fleeting difference to serious crime rates. Start all over again.

Sandy'd been told that policing was like dipping your foot into a bucket of water. Your foot made a splash, caused some water to spill perhaps. Then seconds after you withdrew your foot, there was no evidence of it having been in the bucket. Would that happen with Marinya.

Time to walk.

First though, Sandy ordered his notes, locked them away, checked his doors, windows, went out the front door, pissed on his lemon tree, ducked back inside to pocket his smokes and a lighter. He chose the streets parallel to Wagga's main, then headed for the darkness of the racecourse. He skirted it and took the highway out of town, stopped on the bridge across the Murrumbidgee to North Wagga, lit a smoke. Glad now he'd remembered them.

The river had shrunk, river in name only. In the darkness he could make out more of the pale sandy bed than the black strip of water reflecting the streetlights. Smoke drifted from him, settled, then vanished. He shuddered and turned for the walk home.

Sandy was puzzled by shadows splintering from the bitumen footpath onto the dirt, until he tripped, not shadows but cracks in the footpath and the verge. How much of Wagga was now cracked and ungrassed he wondered. Smaller towns in the Riverina had run out of water, Wagga city relied on bore water.

Megadrought they were calling it on the news. Intransigent, even the police station toilets boasted the reminder to save water, 'if it's yellow let it mellow, if it's brown send it down.' The sign over the sink in the station kitchen warned of violence if the dishwasher wasn't full, and then some, before it was turned on.

More than blog?

Three days. A fit human could go without water for three days. On the fourth day, death. Lucas had his summary of two years' research on how to make clean water available within three days to Australians dying of thirst or ill from using unsafe water.

He stood at the lectern, looked down at his laptop. With a double degree in chemistry and politics, studying for his PhD on water security in Australia he was not sure why he needed notes, he knew it all off by heart - especially this version. The last of the five speakers had all drawn a muted response from the audience. Lucas slipped a USB into the laptop. He'd had to submit his slides to the organisers so that all five presentations had the same look and feel. His had come back sanitised, 'you don't want to lose your funding,' his supervisor had lectured. Lucas knew he wouldn't change his thinking to fit in with the donors represented in the room.

He realised he was at war with himself and not the university. Lucas wasn't sure what he wanted. For his work to be taken seriously? In a way it was taken seriously because everyone who read it wanted him to change it. Part of him wanted the room to burst into spontaneous cheering while part of him wanted it to self-combust. He didn't know which he preferred.

His topic today, 'Water – a natural resource unnaturally managed' presented to a water industry symposium. A few smokers shuffled back into the room of suits, skirts, professors and students. Lucas waited, still, his opening slide displaying 'three days'. He began, audience quiet, a bit bored until, when presented with a slide, under the heading 'Mismanagement', that listed Australian water companies along with research labs and authorities, their employers. The audience gasped, mouths opened, heads flung back, Lucas, blonde, pale, broad-shouldered, chin with more bum fluff than beard, black jeans failing to hide stick-boy legs poking out of Doc

8

Martens, looked around the room, took a sip of water, tapped his satchel with his boot. Derision may have not been what he wanted but he knew he needed it. The prompt to get out of there.

A suit shouted, 'fuck off waterboy'. It was picked up as a chant and swelled, followed by laughter, jeers, boos, threats to sue and walk-outs. By the end of his presentation five out of eighty-three attendees remained. His peers, he thanked them, they clapped him.

A few suits had talked themselves into waiting for him at the exit, talked up what they would do to him. They saw his face in the light and moved aside to let Lucas walk right through them. They may have been suits but even they knew to let him go.

He walked to his one-room flat, packed a duffel bag and the charger for his laptop and took the next train to Broken Hill.

He bought a van kitted out for life on the road from a pair of backpackers who were over it. He camped throughout south-eastern Australia. No alcohol, enough food. Walked fire trails all day, out and back to his rough camp.

Lucas put his years of studying to use. He wrote draft blogs at night and posted them when he went on-line at libraries and trawled environmental activist sites. He blogged about corrupt water authorities, legislative loopholes and water mismanagement. A question popped up on his blog. Anonymously, he was asked if he was prepared to do more than blog?

Could he do more than blog? He'd scrapped his career, was that not enough? Without an answer, he logged off, sat with face in his hands scratching his thin beard.

Always a smart kid, doting parents, no school task, or university assignment a challenge. Nothing at which he couldn't and didn't excel. An anonymous post, 'Could you do more than blog?' Six words, six nails.

Lucas was drawn to the Murray-Darling Basin. Australia's largest water system. He knew the numbers by heart. A beast at one million square kilometres; three times the size of his native Germany, two and a half million people, forty percent of Australia's agricultural produce, key cultural and spiritual connection for forty First Nations communities. Highest number per capita in Australia of people dead from thirst and ill from toxic water.

He camped in free sites all over the Basin, from St George in the north, to Seymour to the south, west to Wilcannia, east to Goondiwindi. He saw funerals, dry riverbeds, dead fish, dead trees, private dams brimming with water, irrigation systems half a kilometre long and watering fifty-hectare cotton crop circles - mechanical triffids force-marching the Basin to an early collapse. Broken, mauled, crushed beyond recognition.

Now he was beginning to learn the heart behind the numbers.

Could he do more than blog? He got the message implied in that question. Doing more than blogging begged Lucas to find a way to resuscitate the Murray Darling Basin, bring the beast back to life.

The question nagged him as he prowled the Holbrook grocery store shopping for his next camp, a few days of fresh food and ten days of tins. Holbrook was a joke, renamed in 1915 to cover up its German heritage. His father would have lamented long into the night about that, 'Germanton, a fine name.'

Lucas scowled at the checkout's 'how're ya love?' and scurried to his truck to drive to Livingstone National Park on the road to Wagga. He nearly missed the turnoff, the blog question a head kick of expectation. He stopped inside the park entrance and opened his phone to check the map, more texts, the same question. He deleted the texts and chose a campsite. The track was a nightmare as he dipped into ruts and ploughed out of the sand. Other than blog what could he do? There was water in the Basin, but it was privately stored, not available for anyone but its owner. If water was to be available inside three days, it had to be bought from the hoarders. He could talk, write, march, sit in, protest - the pace of his truck and his thoughts didn't match. He'd do better off the track and swung the wheel to his right and after a hundred metres braked hard. There was his answer. A faded, bullet-holed sign, 'Unexploded ordnance safety warning.'

If he was going to free water in the Basin, return water to the people, revive the environment, he needed a three-point plan. Focus, money, and people.

Focus first. He settled on the Riverina, middle of the Basin. Lucas's plan was to fund his passion by putting his chemistry degree to good use, to cook meth. He had cooked it to pay his first university fees when his father stopped his allowance. His father had been so proud that Lucas had made money, although he didn't know how, that he'd reinstated monthly payments. Lucas knew the equipment he needed and found it in op shops, kitchen shops and hardware stores. What he couldn't get there he sourced with ingredients from his former suppliers. They'd want a cut - the cost of doing business.

He went to Wagga, where the major court cases were heard, searched for lawyers who socialised with senior police. Only one lawyer drank regularly with the police superintendent.

Lucas phoned the lawyer; they agreed on a retainer. When Lucas suggested to the lawyer that he admired the District Superintendent, Clive Baxter, the monthly retainer fee doubled, 'Clive and I,' the lawyer explained, 'need to understand the value of your admiration.'

Now Lucas could protect his business, and Clive had a regular supply of arrests - drug users, low level dealers, petty thieves, the occasional thief with a warehouse of cheap counterfeit goods. Lucas refined his recipe and recruited women as cooks.

Lucas knew women were the invisibles of the drug industry, victims of abuse, not organisers, users, not cooks. He paid them well, kept them off their product, encouraged them to keep working their part-time jobs, hiding openly in and around Wagga.

Turn the pressure up.

Sandy's direction to focus on dealers improved his arrest stats, but only a few cases had made it to court so far and he was yet to secure a conviction. Delays caused by Covid meant that arraignments prepared eighteen months ago now needed more planning. Interviews were a nightmare with suspects schooled in 'no comment'. Doubts about the security of evidence chains had been nurtured, prosecutors had been outgunned on technicalities by defence lawyers, police evidence ruled inadmissible, juries seduced by charming young defendants with expensive suits and impeccable character references.

His management team added to Sandy's findings about the effects of meth use and swore at the skill of defence lawyers. 'You know,' said the detectives' chief, 'the people these lawyers defend don't have the money to pay them, so who's paying? There's no way we can get close to the lawyers, without digital forensics there's no way we can directly trace who pays them.'

'Koen Barrett,' said Sandy, 'where are we?'

'Still trying to get the evidence and the records together,' said his detectives' chief.

'I want your report for COB,' said Sandy.

'Chief, it was an overdose, overdose of an addict, in and out of rehab, not exactly a surprise ending.'

'Someone supplied him with drugs that killed him, I want that someone. Report for COB.'

'Current cases,' risked one of the management team, 'you mentioned digital forensics,' she gestured to the officer opposite, 'what are you thinking?'

'If we could get data from smartphones, devices, computers and the cloud for our offenders,' he held his hands up wriggled his fingers, 'alleged, then among their secrets we might be able to find and follow the money.'

'Fishing,' said Sandy.

'Occupational hazard,' said the detectives' chief.

'Let's take a break, coffee, back here in ten, short presentation and then let's see about warrants for devices.'

Sandy had taken on a couple of interns, postgraduate students from the Criminology Faculty at the nearby Charles Sturt University. They fossicked socials, Facebook, Instagram, Snapchat, X, Vine, and YouTube of all those caught up in meth related offences in the Riverina police district.

'Most of your offenders are freelancing,' the interns concluded their presentation to the Marinya team, 'buying, using, selling, day-to-day, no big plan, not organised, unknown to other offenders, social supply out of where they live. Money, disrespect, abuse - sexist, racist, homophobic, and violence are all over their socials. They hang out together, post pictures of themselves at parties, pubs, raves, use hashtags and emojis to meet up.'

'But four of them have a different profile,' she used the laser to highlight her talking points. 'Five big differences - they have no posts about money, abuse, disrespect, or violence, yet almost everyone they are linked to has. These four don't post names, places or even dates, well not that we can recognise, we think they use codes, and we'd expect them to use encrypted apps. These four use privacy settings on every app. The others we have looked at, they don't worry about privacy, everything posted is public.'

'Codes? Why?'

'The absence of names, place, and dates, so very unusual to hang out online and not mention one of these. And we think they already use some kind of code, their texts use no numerals, maybe they use one-time pads, sophisticated. There are no photos of them, and they're recruiting on socials,' continued the intern.

'What do you think we have here?' said Sandy.

'These four fit a profile of an organised gang. We've only reviewed the data for this district. Printed copies,' she said reaching over to hand them out.

'We have the phone data for these four and at least some,' Sandy shuffled through the printout, 'of their contacts, don't we?'

'Thing is,' said the financial crimes head, 'we examined the phones to help build cases on the drugs charges. We easily found enough evidence, thought we had, we had no reason to look harder. Now we want financial data, contacts with the four, ah, main guys. The warrant, Sandy, does the warrant cover what we want to do now?'

'No, the warrant doesn't cover the four,' he gestured to the interns, 'you found. So, let's get a warrant for their phone records, we have enough justification don't you think?'

'Yes,' said the finance head, 'and I'll give you a form of words to add to it as well.'

'OK.' Sandy said, 'thanks, let's get our heads around the warrant when we're done.'

The intern's work lifted the team and in an hour the meeting was done, tasks divided and assigned.

Sandy stood, 'a few closing thoughts. Join me in thanking our interns,' applause and a few shouts, 'and a couple of changes to how we're going after dealers. I want to turn the pressure up. No more charges of social supply. I don't care how small the amount of meth you find, charge them with possession, intent to sell, if you suspect they're using, charge them with self-administration of a prohibited drug. Let's get among them, I want everyone selling, dealing, making to think they're living in an open prison.'

'Sure Sandy? This'll clog...'

'Sure,' said Sandy, 'lawyers, magistrates, court clerks, will all complain, launch legal challenges. Thing is, I'm not sure they're working for us anyway, not saying or thinking they're corrupt, just that they don't share our obsession, maybe getting them get a bit busy will help them focus.'

The Head of Rural Crime shook her head, 'Sandy, there's another reason behind the social supply charges,' she folded her arms, 'the charge is not heavy for the simple reason that it encourages offenders to seek help, rehab. Youths and adults charged with more serious offences – don't do rehab, they do more drugs.'

'Charge them with self-administration and drop it to social supply after they've signed on for rehab, will that do it?'

At eighteen hundred hours Sandy heard the knock on his door and looked up to see his Chief of Detectives holding open a device.

'The trail on Barrett may not be cold,' he said sitting opposite Sandy and turning the device to face him.

'What do you have?'

'His phone, the stuff we found with him at the crime scene, we still have it. Barrett had no relatives, no partner, no-one has claimed his stuff.'

Sandy picked up the device, 'these are screenshots, from his phone?'

'Texts, all to the one number. Hours before he died, he was arranging to buy. And then, assuming he bought ten minutes before time of death estimates, he called the same number. We're onto Optus about it, we rang it and it's no longer in use.'

Sandy handed back the tablet, 'what are you thinking?'

'Ah, that you were right to go for this.'

'Don't get used to it,' Sandy said.

Too much going on.

Hardyn Brack took his shoes off, raised the blind on the aircraft window, lingered on his reflection, opened a sparkling water. He reached for the buckle and racked the seat back for he stood two metres and couldn't straighten his right leg. A football accident, a motorbike accident, diving, climbing, a gunshot, accident at birth.

The pilot's flight path from Wagga to Sydney took them over part of Brack's land, some cotton rich, most of it water, great squares and rectangles of water, and wasteland. Hectares of pale trunks and limbs of dead trees reached out to Brack like so many children wanting to be picked up, lost on Brack.

Exhausted by drought and Brack's chemical waste, much of his land deteriorated daily. He'd had to deal with that yesterday. Brack replayed the conversation, adding to his notes for his lawyer.

'Environmental crime, Hardyn this is serious, I wouldn't be doing my job if I didn't take this up the line,' the Riverina head of the Pesticides Authority held up a field report.

'Up the line,' said Brack.

'There's more,' said the bureaucrat, 'not just the chemical spills. Your employees have destroyed a freshwater midden, bulldozed it, buried it.' He held up another file, 'witness report. Nothing I can do except send it.'

'Yeah, I know, "up the line".' Brack sat back, hands resting on his lap, right heel tapping the carpet.

'Thanks for asking me to come in,' said Brack, 'appreciate the opportunity to work something out with you.'

'No, you've got it wrong, Hardyn,' the bureaucrat leant forward, licked his lips, 'this is different, a heads-up, there's nothing we can work out here.'

'How much? That's the question, isn't it?' said Brack, 'the detail of working something out, again.'

'I can't bury this; it can't be buried. I need to report it.'

'Your chain of command,' said Brack, 'it leads to me. I am,' he tapped the desk with one finger, 'the end of the line. You need to read your agency's annual report. Seventy two percent of your budget,' Brack pointed, 'your budget, comes from me, Chair of the Cotton Federation.'

Two years ago, Brack had convinced multinational pesticide companies to wash their government donations through the Federation, industry bodies not needed to register as lobbyists, meetings raised barely an initial in a Minister's diary.

Brack reached for the two documents, 'so,' he said, 'job done, you've taken the reports up the line.' He weighed them, 'thirty-five million dollars' worth of reports.'

Brack stood and shoved the paper in his satchel, 'destroy every trace of this bullshit.'

He drafted thank-you emails to his lawyers. They'd litigated and won against a small class action by farmers claiming water theft, floodplain harvesting by one of his southern cotton farms. He instructed the law firm to seek damages. He emailed another 'thank-you etc etc' for two federal politicians and a retired police superintendent, Clive 'Ankles' Baxter.

Brack'd left them drinking on his tab after lunch. The pollies and the cop had once been very useful to him, thwarting amendments to water regulation, harassing protesters and arresting trespassers seeking evidence of water theft.

And the ex-cop was moaning about his replacement. Over lunch he told them how incompetent this new guy, Sandy Pelham, was, not a patch on his chosen replacement, the young bloke who'd been recalled to Sydney after a month, an argument with a journalist, Brack recalled. The two pollies had signed the ex-cop's complaint where Pelham's leadership style was described as incommunicative, distrustful of his management team, and unable to let go of even the most minor tasks.

'Prick even impounded my Mercedes,' said the ex-copper, 'had it towed and locked up, even had to pay to get it back.'

'What?' said one of the pollies, 'in Wagga, didn't know they did that. Where did you leave it?'

'Outside the station, not the point though, is it? It's about respect, twelve years I ran this District.'

'Best get this off now,' the ex-copper stood, 'might not remember to do it tonight,' folded the complaint into an envelope, excused himself for a few minutes to drop it in the post box on the pub corner.

The old copper didn't bother Brack too much, he'd been worth every cent. Brack had asked him about getting a new contact, his replacement. The old guy had grinned, 'let's keep to the current arrangements.' Brack doubted that, figured the new superintendent a risk if he'd stirred Ankles into a complaint.

Heavy turbulence woke Hardyn, he buckled up, let his mind wander. The Cotton Federation pitched cotton farming as small, family owned, no dominant companies, little concentration. Brack knew this was inaccurate. Using proxies, nominees, intermediaries, trusts, and tax haven registrations, Brack had been able to disguise from the ATO the extent of the holdings he had increased with his backer's money. He wasn't the only one, all the Federation directors were in on it, although only he had the Texan backing, the others had Chinese or Malaysian patronage.

He had too much going on. You could have anything you wanted Brack knew, if you were prepared to risk everything. It was all a bit of a juggle, too much up in the air. He knew the secret to juggling was invisible threads, or threads only visible to him.

I'll call him at ten thirty.

District Superintendent Sandy Pelham's bad day began like all bad days begin, no coffee. He took the delivery box off the kitchen door and centred it on the stone bench, unpacked the groceries he'd taken inside the night before, no coffee. He checked his order against the packing list, touched each item as he read, he'd ordered coffee beans and had been rewarded with two five kilo packs of lite spuds.

He packed away the groceries, wiped the bench clean, bent down to check for smears at eye level. With no coffee beans in his house, an early morning phone call left him riffling drawers, cupboards, bedside table, pockets, scanning bookshelves, table, desk, coffee tables for the cigarettes he'd given up over dinner. The calm of his night walk through Wagga city had dissipated.

'The Feds want to talk now,' said his boss, ending the call. 'Mick Darby, he's expecting you to ring on this number.'

At least his boss hadn't sounded happy about running Darby's errand. Pelham hadn't planned to be at the station until later in the morning. He rang his EA at home.

'Change in plan?' she asked.

'No,' said Sandy, 'got another job for you though. I need anything you can get on a Mick Darby, a Fed, he's in Canberra. I'll be calling him when I get in, ten thirty.'

'And if he calls you before then?'

'What?'

'Well, he's a Fed, you know what they're like. I'll get a call saying, "Mr Darby's on the line". So, if he calls before you call him, what'll I tell him?'

'That I'll call him at ten thirty.'

21

Pelham remembered to water his lemon tree and the two roses in pots near his front door with the water he'd saved from his shower. It was the only water they'd had since he'd been in Wagga, aside from pissing on the lemon tree.

Sandy drove out to the saleyards for the seven am start and saw few stock for sale and fewer still bought. He liked spending time at the sales, lowing of cattle, smell of feed, shit, thought it helped him to understand what some were going through. He wasn't bothered there; locals appreciated his increasing the numbers of the Stock Squad. Farmers were unhappy, not the Hanrahan of old unhappy, really pissed off.

This time of year, usually saw farmers rebuild their stock. They weren't doing that today unless it was all online. He joined a group of heavy men with thermos flasks and thick sandwiches, declined their offers, just sat, and heard about water prices.

'Really? Thought there was plenty of water in the river, heard it was running well further up, not here though.'

'River levels? The Murrumbidgee, Sandy, not a useful indicator,' he was told, 'it's fed when the winter snow melts, the others rely on rainfall. Thing is it's getting dry too, fuck-all snow for two years in a row and not much rain. And the chemicals in artificial snow - poison, that's what they use, so you can't feed animals where that shit's concentrated in the water. Murrumbidgee supplies a quarter of Wagga's water in normal times, now the city's on bore water only and we'll see heavier restrictions soon.'

'You used to be able to trade water with your neighbours. Now, there's a water market, whatever the fuck that means,' said one pouring black tea into a battered mug, although Sandy smelled more than tea.

'What it means is that no one knows who owns the water and no one knows who's selling it,' said another, pushing the brim of his hat off his forehead with one misshapen finger which he now pointed at Sandy, 'you trade through your broker, but it's not his water, he's just the broker. You got a stock squad, Sandy, now you need a water squad, mate.'

Stock prices were high too he'd noticed, buyers, live and online, were few, but it was the water that bothered people. He'd ask some of his local officers whose families farmed, see if there was more to know.

Pelham's EA googled and found Darby's title, which turned out to be wrong anyway. Sandy called the number his boss had given him and arranged to meet Mick.

Sandy had his EA make a dinner reservation. 'And book him a room for a few nights, starting a week today.'

'The Houston?'

'You think he'll be a problem,' said Sandy.

'We'll see if he has a sense of humour,' she laughed.

'He'll be here around two-thirty,' said Sandy, 'so shift everything I have next week please. Same for the Marinya team leads. I'll want the Marinya files in here too. Something else, know anything about local pollies pissed off with me?'

'Well, the ex-super's pissed off with you and he's still close to the local Nats, State and Federal. He's pissed with you so, stands to reason his mates might be. Why?'

'Oh, something this bloke Darby said.'

Bushwalking.

Lucas's battered Hilux was at the campground, a shade more faded, annex stretched taut so leaves wouldn't pool. And here he was, opening the door of Bertoldo's Bakery to let a woman in. Past the Post Office, turning left, crossing to the library, texting as he walked.

Harry met him on the Griffith library steps and both headed for shade and no listeners. Lucas, blonde, broad, baby-faced with a wispy beard, pierced, tattooed, restless, favoured black jeans and army disposal shirts. Still the trace of a German accent.

Harry, Wiradjuri, tall, thin, jeans faded, blundstones scruffy, rarely seen in the same messaged t shirt, more than twice Lucas's age and fitter.

When they'd first met Lucas had talked about walking trails as a kid in Germany, how much they were like fire trails. Harry introduced him to bushwalking and Lucas was up for it. Lucas got confident in the way of all those who underestimate the bush and those who know it, went on his own. Harry found him with no water and a day's walk to his truck in forty degrees.

'What the fuck are you doing', said Harry bending down, waking him and loosening Lucas's shirt.

'Bushwalking,' Harry could barely hear him.

'No, you're not, you're dying,' Harry tipped a little water into Lucas's mouth, Lucas grabbed at the bottle, 'hey, not so much.'

'Take a look at these,' Lucas passed over his phone, 'scroll through. I wanted them more out of sight. Look,' he laid a finger on the screen, 'threatening people, showing off.'

'Can't stop all of them and besides, they keep the cops busy, and happy. Take these away and the cops'll look harder,' Harry handed the phone back.

'If you run too many dealers, you risk losing discipline.'

'What?' Harry pointed to Lucas's phone, 'discipline these kids? Mate, parents tried,' Harry counted off on his fingers, 'uncles and aunties, school, some of their mates, juvie. They buy from us, they don't work for us, let 'em grow out of it.'

'No,' said Lucas, 'that's not what I meant. The group around you and me, tight. They don't slip up, that's where the discipline is. But these,' Lucas scoffed, 'they're being noticed, more of them picked up, charged. We need to quieten them down. The more the cops scare them the more likely they'll talk, drop a name. They need to stick to 'no comment', no need to panic, they'll be bailed, there's no room in any of the lockups. We need to change how we work, split things up again.'

Lucas explained he had a new lab, smaller, 'using more labs to cook...'

'Won't that mean a bigger operation?' said Harry, 'didn't think that's what you meant.'

'Yeah, no it's not what I meant. I want more smaller labs, and more but smaller teams selling.'

'What brought this on?'

'Couple of things,' Lucas stretched and reached for his smokes, 'cops are not as friendly as they were under Ankles, six months he's been gone and this head cop, Pelham, proving to be a fucking nuisance, I can't get to him so no more friends there.'

Harry thumbed his phone, 'seen this?'

'What is it?'

'Your mate, Pelham.'

Lucas took the phone and started the video, 'a car crush?'

'Yeah, one of my blokes, down the food chain, was pulled over for speeding. He had a bag on him. He admitted personal use when he was interviewed. Cops were not interested, charged him, impounded his car, said the car was illegally modified and crushed it that night. Videoed the crushing, it's up on Facebook as a warning.'

Lucas handed the phone back, 'this Pelham's more of a nuisance than I thought.'

'Most of the boys have souped-up cars and trucks so they're jittery. Question being asked is do we pay for his car?'

'Your guys,' said Lucas.

'When he gets out, he'll get an old Camry and a hiding,' said Harry.

'Not in that order,' said Lucas. 'Do you know Pelham even impounded Ankles' car? New Merc.'

'Maybe he's not all bad,' said Harry.

'Yeah, well you won't be saying that if he catches you. We need to be extra cautious, so smaller teams, moving smaller amounts, I'll keep their cut the same, though.'

'More teams,' said Harry, 'smaller target, yeah, I get that. Increases the odds one of them will be caught but.'

'Yeah, well that's a risk, not as big as fewer, bigger loads,' said Lucas, 'we can take small hits but five, ten kilos - we'd lose too much. No, I think the guerilla way is right.'

'OK,' said Harry, 'see the logic in that, no big busts, flexibility.'

'Well, it'll be too much - we need another bloke to join us, you, and me, and he'll need a small team. So, can any of your guys step up? None of mine could.'

'No,' said Harry, 'but I know of a bloke who'd be useful.'

Harry knew of an ex-Navy diver. After the Navy the diver drifted, had his mother sign over her house deeds and put her in a nursing home, and lived with a succession of ever-younger girls.

Whelan the Wrecker.

Sandy's boss sat at the polished wooden table, a half-full jug of water leaving shadows under the glare of hot fluorescents, no glasses. Someone cared for this table, outsized, glossy, still with the fragrance of a citrus polish. The chairs were unmatched, tops of armrests scrubbed from being pushed under the table. She made no move to shake hands, gestured to the chair opposite. Sandy sat, noticed the shallow drawers set under the table, parallel to inset green leather squares, he counted twelve, wondered what was in them.

'Heard of "Whelan the Wrecker?"' she paused, there was no way he was going to fill that gap. He had no map for this conversation. Only his boss had any idea what it was to be about.

She tilted her head to one side, light reflected off her black-rimmed glasses hiding her eyes, 'Sandy, perhaps I could ask a different question?'

She sounded amused, reclipped her ponytail. He searched for an exit.

'Disrupting criminal activity. Let me quote you,' she said. '"Operation Marinya is a creative, problem-solving methodology to disrupt illegal drug markets." Now,' she sat back, 'I understood you to mean that you and your officers would be disrupting the family lives, friendships, relationships, school runs, shopping, watching kids play sport, playing sport,' she shrugged, 'fucking up the day-to-day lives of criminals or at least suspects. Today, Sandy, you will convince me I heard you correctly because your criminals seem to be suffering no discomfort, far less disruption.'

There was a knock at the door and an officer came in set a pile of folders on the table.

'Thank you,' his boss said, and she rested one hand on the pile, 'these are not reports of disrupted illicit activity, Sandy.'

Sandy could feel sweat at the back of his neck and soon his shirt back would darken. Hadn't felt this since he was undercover. Four years on a mission to catch those running drugs from Pacific islands into Cairns and smaller towns along the coast, Cooktown and up around the Cape to Seisia. The difference was he'd enjoyed being scared there, part of the test, the tunnel vision, pumped, would he make it. But in a fucking office, not outnumbered, no guns, no drugs. Just his boss. He flinched.

She misread it, 'take your time,' she said.

Sandy pointed to the pile, 'I had a few calls from magistrates moaning about workload, staff shortages...'

'And you thought, "oh heads up, I'll let my boss know"', she touched the pile, 'but no. I get the heads up direct from judges, magistrates, sheriffs, court attendants – you are wrecking their lives. Victims of spousal assault, muggings, burglaries – all their cases pushed back, some for two years or more. Again, lives disrupted by you, and for what? No results, no busts, no drug seizures, criminal activity disrupted? Not so much.'

'So, our learned colleagues missed a few bowls sessions,' Sandy scratched his head, 'we changed much of the way we did courts during Covid, there's no point going back to the old ways. They're assessing backlog using a hundred-year-old justice system, not using technology we have today, proven over the last couple of years; virtual courts, online streaming, digital lodgement of evidence.'

'You can offer those suggestions when you meet with them. They're keen to hear your thoughts.'

'Meet with them?' Sandy ran a palm across the nape of his neck.

'Followed by a phone hook up with the Superintendents of Districts you wanted included in Marinya, feeling left out. Also, suspicious of the time you're giving to Mick Darby. Remember they all knocked him back and they're keen to know why you haven't.'

'Yet,' said Sandy. 'I've agreed to meet him, have not said yes or no.'

'They're all very senior and experienced coppers. Sandy, you've booked him into the Houston for three nights.'

Sandy shifted in his chair, 'they're complaining, they want to see me fail, so why did they sign up for Marinya?'

'Complaining? No, "bringing a matter to my attention", you know how it works.'

She folded her arms, 'get them inside your tent Sandy.'

He sat straight, knuckles on knees.

'You spent four years undercover getting a commendation while they spent four more years developing alliances, contacts, refining networks of informants. They don't want you to fail, the Riverina's an embarrassment to them what with the idiot you replaced, and Ankles before him.'

Sandy slumped in his chair, 'I'm finding this very confusing.'

'Your proposal for Marinya correlated a steady stream of arrests for mainly small-time crimes, compounded with the growth in meth supply. In your six months in Wagga the arrests have dried up and the meth is still there, increasing. So, initial thoughts?'

'Well, the usual suspect,' Sandy leaned forward, 'is Ankles. He kept the peace, was fed crumbs to ignore the meth operation.'

'We have the meth operation still in play, and you have no crumbs, as you call them, no warehouses of counterfeit, no illegal cigarettes, no grow houses on your watch. Ankles goes and the busts stop, on your watch. Conclusion?'

'I'm now the usual suspect.'

'Impounding Ankles' Mercedes? Look at me, I'm the boss? And now a complaint against you made by the good ex-superintendent Baxter.'

Sandy, voice raised, 'is this you officially informing me about a complaint?'

'If you want official, Sandy, let's go back ten minutes in this conversation and make it all formal, official, recorded.'

Sandy shook his head, 'took me by surprise that's all.'

'Look, for some reason you have gotten under Ankles' skin,' she looked up eyes wide, 'he's raised his head. And he's fucked up the complaint form, so we have a way now to investigate him.'

'How? From a complaint?'

'Well,' she sat back, 'vexatious complaint? Complaints Commission would have to review Ankles' service history to see if you two ever served together, crossed paths before to rule out a suspected vexatious complaint. Ankles' mates in the Force won't be able to protect him from Complaints.'

'I don't know how he fits in,' said Sandy, 'only that he's now coaching suspects how to get through our interviews.'

'Don't you worry about Ankles, leave him to others. Worry about these people,' she slid a file across the table.

Sandy opened the folder, took his glasses off to scan the top page, 'background on judges, magistrates, summaries of my District peers' careers...I shouldn't have this.'

'And yet you do. Collaboration, these people,' she tapped the table, 'they can be convinced of your approach, they want in, let them. Do your homework, get them onboard, you have a month. Marinya must work.'

'A month?' said Sandy, 'that means we'll have to be more relentless, more disruptive. There are a few tactics I'm planning.'

'Tell me.'

'We're working with business licensing, and how many of them are there,' he shrugged, 'to close a business where we arrest an employee for drug offences. Nail salons, auto spare parts, tyre shops – can't afford to close for a month so the owners might give us something to avoid the hit.'

'How will this work?'

Sandy rested his hands on the table, 'let's say we arrest a nail salon employee for meth possession, we have twenty-seven business licences and permits we can cancel, forcing the nail business to close and reapply, a lengthy process,' Sandy smiled.

'You arrest an employee, and you go after the business owner?'

'Yes,' said Sandy, 'cancel the licences, close the business while we investigate if the owners were involved in selling meth. The owners will appeal of course but meanwhile we've searched the premises and put pressure on the meth sellers and dealers, made it harder for them to hide in plain sight.'

'OK, nail salons,' his boss made a note, 'fallout?'

'We did some scenario planning with post grad students at Charles Sturt...'

'Maybe not those words Sandy.'

He nodded, 'residents feel safer and there's a small increase in trust in police. I'll need the PR unit to dress it up and use it like a firehose on social media.'

'You don't have the staff for all these checks and closures.'

'Services NSW, Fair Trading – there's a long list of departments keen to be in on this. Their staff are locals, pissed off at the crime rates, their kids in trouble and not being able to do anything about it. We've shown them what to do about it – go to work and do your job.'

'I need a report on these tactics for my boss, and any results, forget the uni students and their scenarios, write it up differently. The attraction of Marinya is it goes beyond taking a few criminals off the street leaving their businesses exposed to competition. It's good work, Sandy.'

'It's my whole team.'

'Speaking of which,' she pointed to the folder in front of Sandy, 'make sure it is. There's a one pager for you in there too, plan on a page - a reminder, do what you're good at, and delegate.'

She stood and Sandy came around the table, she shook his hand, 'all you'll remember on the way home is perfectionist and not consulting. Don't beat yourself up.'

After taking the wrong exit at the confusion of roundabouts leading to the freeway at Gwynneville Sandy threaded his unmarked through the trucks struggling to make it up Mt Ousley and took the Picton Road exit to the M31.

Sandy checked his speed, set the cruise control and went over the exchange with his boss, starting with don't beat yourself up. Don't beat yourself up, it's like trying not to think of a polar bear.

They used to hang thieves in Texas.

Brack was met at the airport by his driver, the only person Brack knew who stood up to him. After all, he reasoned, how could you trust someone you could bully? After being manhandled by farmers he'd sued in the southern Riverina, there'd been some nasty, graphic threats, his car blocked at protests about water wasted on cotton had convinced him that he needed a driver who doubled as his bodyguard. Driver, bodyguard, the perfect cover for counsellor, advisor, especially one who'd been fined for insider trading. Brack bought him, paid his near million dollar fine.

They'd first met outside Bankstown airport. Brack hired cars then, insisted on the same driver, who this time wasn't at the car. A stranger had the door open.

'Mr Brack, I've not driven for you before. It'd be good for both of us if that were to change.'

'Only beggars like change,' said Brack.

The bloke talked a great story, insider trading conviction, bailed, a near million dollars fine, jail threatened. 'And the reason you're telling me this?' asked Brack.

'Trading water. Now, water is separate from the land it's on. Trading is something I know how to do, and I can do it for you.'

'Yeah, 'said Brack, 'but why would you? There are plenty of blokes who would want to get into water.'

'Sure, but you're the only one who needs to.'

Brack walked away, got out his phone to call for another car, the bloke called after him, 'they used to hang thieves in Texas, maybe still do,' he said and opened the rear door of the limousine.

'OK,' said Brack, 'how did we get here?'

'Quickly,' said the driver, 'too quickly, Mr Brack. Delaney Holdings, the name of your property was the clue, it was easy from there. When you came back from Texas the only way to get more water in the Riverina was to buy more land. You bought in at the top of the market, subsidised with the money from the Texans, but they're about to find out where their money has gone.'

'Let's say you're right.'

'Mr Brack, my proposal depends on trust. I know I'm right. Let's start from there?'

'OK, I'm fucked. What can I say.'

The driver nodded, 'the water market in the Murray-Darling Basin, since water is separate from the land it's on, the value of the water rights is over twenty billion dollars, trades each year of up to a billion.' He looked in the rear vision mirror at Brack, 'thing is there are no rules in this market. And I can get you out of the shit with the Texans.'

Brack took him at his word and risked Texan money set aside for fertilizer. Doubled his money in one trade. He paid for the fertilizer, plus rewarded his trader and now that he had a stake, they kept trading.

Half an hour off the plane Brack was with the chief executive of Cotton Federation, the industry lobby group for Australia's cotton farmers. Liz Evans had been a journalist for a NSW rural magazine, had run for and lost preselection for a Federal seat when the aging National's sitting member had retired. Brack had met her the night the preselection was decided; dissuaded her from turning on the Nats, play the long game, he'd convinced her, and coaxed her into his bed for a shorter one.

She'd started working for the Cotton Federation two months later. She had surprised Brack then by insisting they no longer sleep

together, 'we've got enough to hide with cotton,' she'd said, 'you can't
hide what's between the sheets forever.'

'Have you caught up with those demonstrations, demos around the
Riverina. You know more are planned?'

'Yes,' Liz said, 'this Sunday, Lockhart. "Lockhart says NO",
Sunday after that there's one advertised for Temora. Free buses are
listed. Why? Why bother? They're conspiracy freaks; anti-vaxxers,
getting messages from their toasters, on about drop bears, 5G and
Bill Gates. You're not that rich yet, are you?'

She was getting cheeky. 'I pay you to pay attention. The recent
two marches had people holding banners and talking about cultural
flow, they can't even fucking spell, black spelled b l a k. Shouting
about water theft, specifically irrigation, more specifically cotton
irrigation. Banners with Big Cotton, in red. Get back to Wagga, I
want that stopped.'

NASA.

Downstairs called Pelham's office just before one o'clock, his visitor, Mick Darby.

'He's nearly two hours early,' said Sandy's EA.

Sandy said nothing, just opened his right hand, palm up.

'I'll expect he'll be gone two hours quicker,' she said.

Sandy got to the bottom of the stairs and saw a tall, heavily built man standing at the front desk talking to the duty constable. Sandy opened the door to the right of the desk.

'Here's our boss now, Mr Darby,' said the constable. Sandy wondered why his constable was so much at ease, why not Superintendent? The two men shook hands, not a contest, a handshake. Darby turned and thanked the constable, and Sandy keyed the numbers for the door.

Sandy took Darby to the office he'd had rearranged, asked about tea, coffee, water.

Darby's phone rang, 'I'll need to take this,' he said looking from the phone to Sandy, 'excuse me.'

Sandy shut the door, went to his own office, answering emails, reading the final paragraphs, and signing reports. The meat in a police report, like a conversation, was at the end.

Three hours later Sandy looked up to see Mick Darby.

'Sandy,' he said, 'I apologise. This is not where I wanted to start. Looks like your afternoon was better than mine,' said Darby as he took in the desk, bare except for mobile phone, neat stack of paper, laptop, and tablet, arranged side by side.

'If you're done with that for today then, I'll show you where we've got you staying, meet up for dinner later. I'm done here, Mick, so whatever suits.'

'You know what,' said Mick, 'I could do with a good walk. You up for that?'

'Suits me,' said Sandy.

'I can find the Houston OK, so where's the best place to meet? I'm in your hands, Sandy.'

'Why don't I meet you outside the Houston in an hour? There's a good walk along the river. We can start there.'

Sandy locked away his devices, pocketed the phone and left the office. His EA looked up as he gave her the paperwork to file, shook her watch, 'bloody thing, stopped, cost me a fortune too,' she said.

'Canberra hours,' said Sandy over his shoulder.

'Oh, and can you let Tassie know where I'll be please, and I'll call him tonight?' Tassie, his Senior Sergeant, confidant.

Sandy Pelham walked the kilometre home, changed into running gear, old clothes, and nearly new sneakers. Just in case, Darby looked fit, sort of bloke who might run not walk. Dressed, he drank some water, filled two bottles, and headed for the Houston.

It'd taken six months to get this far, he didn't need Feds to fuck it up. Finally getting somewhere and now the Feds, or whatever Mick Darby was, were interested. If they were that interested, they could have come along a bit sooner. What did Mick Darby want?

Mick was outside the Houston, stretching. Fuck, bastard does want to run.

'Up for a run,' said Sandy handing over a bottle of water.

'No way,' said Mick, 'long drive today though and ther. that phone call, gotta shake out some of the tension. I'll tell you about it as we go,' he said, 'the river this way?'

Darby turned and headed to the river, Sandy beside him. 'Can I ask you one question first?' asked Mick.

Sandy looked at him, 'expect there'll be more than one.'

'They tell me you're here because of the Wiggles.'

Sandy laughed, 'keeps on coming up. Bloke who'd been here for years retired. Replacement was a young bloke, from a family of coppers, career fast track. Silly prick arranged for his photo in the local papers with the District's new vehicles, unmarked cars included. The unmarked were purple, red, green, and yellow. We've still got them. The story came out under a headline about the Wiggles settling in Wagga.'

'Seriously,' said Mick, laughing, 'shitcanned for that?'

'It got ugly, or rather he did. Tailed the photographer and the journalist, harassed them, had guys park outside their houses. He's on leave still. So, yeah, the Wiggles got me this job. Plus, a few station and residence doors got resprayed in their colours too, kept the story going.'

'You get the painters?'

'No, got poor footage of a tattoo though, so we've been around to all the tattoo shops.'

'Great story.'

'Yeah,' said Sandy, 'kind of yarn that gets around. Much like you, been all over the country I hear, talking NASA to hillbillies, and now you're here.'

Mick Darby talked his way along the river walk and almost all the way back again, Sandy with a few questions here and there, content with his company. It meant he wouldn't walk away the evening

'It's a fucking nightmare,' said Mick. 'I'm being taken to the cleaners everywhere I look. Take the legislation for example. Murray-Darling Basin, five states and territories all with their own legislation. Leave the Commonwealth out of it for now. Let's take just one state. New South Wales? There's the Water Management Act, the Water Act, Water Management Plans, Water Sharing Licence, Water Access Licence, Water Management Work Approval Plan (submitted in triplicate), Water Entitlement Licence, Water Allocation Licence, Development Approvals needed for dams, weirs, pipelines and bores, and a Water Distribution Allocation Licence.'

Sandy stopped, took off his cap and brushed his hair back, replaced the cap, 'so, each act, licence, approval covers a different piece?'

'Be easier if that was the case,' said Mick, 'no, they overlap, contradict, and are silent. Every person I speak to quotes different paperwork to tell me why they can't do anything, which means really, why I can't do anything.'

'Silent, I don't get that.'

'It's probably not the right word,' said Mick, 'take water trading. There are no laws governing the water market, no license needed, ASIC doesn't regulate the market. So, you can do whatever you want with water, you get away with it, and if you get ripped off, there's also no protection. So, yeah, silent in that there are no laws.'

'But haven't a couple of big irrigators been fined? So, there must be some way to get a handle on it.'

'Yeah,' said Mick, 'fined. No money's been paid yet. The prosecutions are being appealed. The appeals will take years, jurisdictional claims, evidence custody methods and procedures. One of the problems with satellite imagery is the technology to capture data on water is way ahead of government agencies' technology to license, protect and store these data. Lawyers are all over that. We know for one of the cases on appeal the lawyers will argue the satellite imagery was corrupted.'

'So,' said Sandy, 'is that where NASA comes in?'

'Back to NASA, I need a license to use their satellite data,' Mick said, 'Ecological Intelligence, Security and Terrorism, that's my agency. NASA satellite images come with their own secure documentation, unbroken chain of evidence. What we've learned from the UK and Belgium where ecological terrorists have been charged is that without NASA evidence custody protocol lawyers get satellite data ruled inadmissible. Threats from ecological terrorism now attract the same interventions as any other domestic terrorism threat. So, the NASA dispute is not about the license, it's a factional fight between my Minister and Defence. Defence won't let me have a licence.'

'Same interventions, what does that mean?'

'Well, the best example is my Minister could call in the army to protect water assets, dams, pipelines if there were a terrorist threat.'

'The army, domestic protection?'

'Yep, been done before. Hilton bombing 1978, heads of state here for CHOGM, officials were staying at the Hilton and were due to leave for Bowral to continue their fine dining and drinking, croquet, whatever they do. The Army and the Air Force provided security from Sydney to Bowral. So, yeah, done before. So, the funny thing is my Minister can call out the Defence Minister's troops. Another reason he doesn't want to hand over the licence.'

'Toys out of the sandpit,' said Sandy.

Homework.

Lucas met Harry's contact in a Wagga suburban pub. The Turvey Tavern boasted a concrete parking area for its regulars' mobility scooters. The drinkers paid no attention to Lucas and his companions. They paid little attention to anything outside a schooner glass.

'Mike Nelson,' said the diver, putting his hand out, calloused and confident.

Lucas shook his hand, 'Lucas.'

'Harry.'

'So, how'd you two meet up?' Nelson looked from one to the other.

'Bushwalking,' said Lucas.

Lucas talked about the money in selling meth, talked about setting up distribution networks, laundering arrangements. It would make money. Lots of easy money. Just ask Harry.

'I've got the stuff we need,' said Lucas, 'the cooks and the places to do it. Where you fit in is moving it and selling it, and of course, making money. You'll never know anything about how the stuff gets to you, you do the transport from there, and the selling. It can't be traced. The less anyone knows, the lower the risks. Money'll come back to you.'

'Clean, laundered? How?' asked Mike.

'I'll look after that.'

'Yeah mate,' said Mike leaning back, 'whatever, how will you look after it?'

'Whatever?' said Lucas. 'What does that mean? What do you mean?'

'Nothing, Lucas,' said Mike, 'just that you have an answer for everything.'

Lucas stayed still, said nothing.

'Lots of talk so far, Lucas. Talk, not money.'

'Tell you what,' said Lucas, 'Mike, you could have something I need, then I'd count you in. Otherwise...'

'Otherwise, what?'

'Otherwise,' said Lucas, 'Otherwise. Fuck off.'

Mike Nelson stood up.

Harry thumbed his phone, 'if you decide you're in, then this won't get to anyone else,' he held the phone in front of Nelson.

'How'd ja get that?'

'Homework,' said Harry.

Lucas sipped his beer and said, 'sit down. You're ex-Navy, right? Know any explosives guys, experts? You must have worked with them?'

'I might know someone,' said Mike, sitting down, 'what's it to you?'

'More about what's it to you, Mike,' said Lucas, 'find me someone and you're in.' Lucas looked up, signalled three more to the barman who scowled and started pouring.

'Bloke have a name?' asked Harry, 'why would he be interested?'

'Money,' said Mike, 'he's interested in money, mad punter and bad at it. Name's Gino, lives out at Cookardinia.'

'When can I meet him,' asked Lucas, 'Run a few things past him?'

The MENSA dealing meth.

Two of Sandy's officers intercepted him at his office door. For years hospital emergency departments had worked with police, so a call from Griffith Base Hospital in the early hours reporting a young and fit man who presented stabbed, bashed and unconscious was no surprise. Stitched, mended, and medicated he was interviewed routinely, at first. When he told his interviewers of being beaten up by his girlfriend who had been using ice, the drug team was contacted.

The drug team profiler was intrigued. Female drug abusers are most often victims of assault. Meth users don't discriminate. Now, meth abuse and heavy drinking seemed to have increased the risk of women being violent.

They'd found the woman; she hadn't left the flat and wasn't really with it. Scratching at open sores, missing some teeth, she was held in a secure bed, to be interviewed as soon as she was able.

She slept, and two days later, sweating, shaking, and vomiting she gave up the guy who introduced her to ice when she was at high school, later dumped her because she was too old, at eighteen. An ex-Navy diver who used to do some diving in the irrigation canals for the police.

'He said he'd found a few dead bodies, that they didn't bother him,' she told them.

Sandy's officers wanted to get her moved to Wagga, interview her again.

'Wagga?' said Sandy, feeling his way, 'or Griffith? Your call, she's talking in Griffith, at the hospital, is she?'

'Yes Boss, but won't you want to talk to her?'

'Guess she must feel she's been looked after if she's saying so much. If you have her brought in here,' Sandy looked around, 'where're you going to keep her? In the cells? Taking her away from people who she must know saved her life...what do you think you might do?'

'Go to Griffith, Boss. it'll be late though, we're OK to stay a night?'

Police of all ranks captured by budgets, Sandy waved them away. 'Tassie'll sort that. You get packed.' They got up to follow Sandy out when he turned and stopped them, 'what else do you know about the bloke she beat up?'

'Not much,' they admitted to being caught up with the woman's story.

'OK, get the Griffith guys to bring him in, and interview him again while you're there. We need his name to run past the interns on the social media profile.'

Sandy watched from the end of the front row of the briefing room as the two interns got out devices, charts of paper, posters. High windows to one side of the room allowed for natural light and denied the view of the carpark. The two side walls held a collection of material for Operation Marinya. The front wall faced a bank of interactive whiteboards under more high windows. Any one of the team members could display information, photographs, data, text on the boards from their devices. And information on the whiteboards may be accessed by devices too. All dated and timed stamped electronically to preserve the integrity of the documentation.

As members of the team arrived well before the start time, Sandy met briefly with each one, sometimes in pairs, not saying much, leaving them to it, knowing that these informal catchups and chats before, during and after formal briefings helped sustain a team.

Sandy stood, stepped straight ahead from his front row seat to the lectern, put his glasses on, took command of the room.

An image of a diver appeared across the whiteboards, mask, wetsuit, goggles, flippers, and tanks. Followed by another image, blurred and without the mask.

'Our ex-Navy diver calls himself "Mike Nelson". He's not. We don't have his name, yet.' The false name appeared under the image. Sandy continued, 'Mike Nelson, lead character, a diver, in Sea Hunt, an early television show. This Mike Nelson,' Sandy glanced at the image, 'he's a smartarse.'

The room was silent, the group's attention on Sandy, the images of the diver getting barely a glance.

Sandy continued, 'you'll find this background,' the screens filled with text, 'on your devices, Nelson gave a false name and address to police at Griffith while he worked with them diving for bodies. The address is wrong by one letter and could be dismissed as a typo if his name weren't false too. It's a clever typo, you can see it here,' he used a laser pointer to highlight it, 'I appreciate Mr Nelson's wit, because I know that it will catch him out. He thinks he's quicker than all of us put together. The Mensa dealing meth to teenage girls. One hypothesis is that he's connected to the gangs with the different social media profiles that these young folks,' he pointed to the interns, 'got for us last time we met. And thanks to these guys,' he pointed to two officers sitting midway down the room, 'who convinced Nelson's ex to talk.'

'For more on that and other developments, let me hand you over to our colleague skilled in the world of meth gangs.'

Sandy left the room, and the session settled into the routine of an investigation; developments, data, evidence, intelligence, informants, assumptions, hypotheses, witnesses, names, patterns, observations, progress, all the while building lists of action items to be prioritised and assigned.

Fireworks.

A caller who left no name and no number with Triple Zero alerted the operator and asked for the fire brigade. The operator put the call through to Fire and Rescue and despatched appliances to the accurately reported location of the remote property, off the Tallimba road about halfway between West Wyalong and Tallimba.

Fire, ambulance, police, and the local journalist raced to the fire ground. They found it easily enough as the flames were visible from kilometres around in the flat desert. The fire appliance easily navigated the gate adorned with corrugated iron 'frack off' signs and rattled as it crossed the ramp.

Timers were started, and watchers with radios mobilised as soon as the triple zero call was answered, giving Lucas exact records of the time taken, travelling speeds on macadam and dirt roads, the storming of the two gates, and the number of vehicles and people attending.

'They just crashed through the COD gate,' Lucas heard from the watcher at the entrance to the property.

'What?'

'A COD gate, C for carry and D for drag, carry or drag gate, looks like they're doin' both anyway.'

First on the scene secured the ground, noted the absence of any vehicles. Outbuildings were engulfed in flames, and the derelict house already embers.

'Not water, don't waste it out here,' the captain alerted his officers, 'foam, only foam.'

More vehicles arrived. As the firies went to work the journo took photos and recorded her thoughts. Ambulance and police officers helped, chatting up the journo, keeping her out of harm's way.

The fires were going nowhere as other than the lit buildings there was nothing flammable, no winter grass, no shrubs, no trees. Then shots rang out from a blazing outbuilding.

In the scramble for cover men and women tripped over each other, stopped, helped each other up, some falling again, mouths and eyes wide open and in shock, legs knew what to do but struggled with the effort. Rapid, intense explosions replaced the sound of shots fired, and, adding to the flames set against the black sky were cascades of sparks, waterfalls, exploding stars, illuminating the groundswell of disbelief, quickly followed by anger.

'Fireworks,' said the fire station captain, 'buddy up and check each other, then let's put this bastard out.'

Police officers secured the fireground and set up a wide perimeter. Detectives and forensics were on their way and wanted as much of the crime scene as possible preserved.

Sandy Pelham was alerted when chemical analyses of the fire ground showed the fireworks had been remotely detonated. Sandy had every building on the property searched.

By dawn Sandy was on the property to be told, 'every building has been checked, we have nothing.'

Of the properties adjoining the fireground three were occupied and the residents were being interviewed. 'The next property to the east is vacant, I'll take a look, follow me,' he said.

Sandy pulled up in a puff of dust and started to walk a track to a row of trees. He walked through and then up a gully, and there, roof level with his head, remains of a house. It sat on uneven piers of bricks, car tyres, some stumps, enjoyed weathered timbers, windows free of glass, rusted iron roof, downpipes that either didn't make it to the ground or didn't make it to the gutter, or where the gutter would have been.

He stood on a truck tyre and peeked in a broken window, inside wasn't just rotting, it had been smashed, every wall, floorboards, split mattresses, pipes, and broken bongs, they'd even tried to pull the ceiling down.

Around the back he was thankful there was no wind - thick, black slime seeped from an outdoor dunny. Piles of rubbish cans, torn black plastic bags, poisoned grass, evidence of fires, glass everywhere and nearer to him dozens of punctured anti-freeze cans.

Sandy called it in and waited for the specialist team to come over from the fireground.

'It doesn't make sense,' said Sandy. 'Sophisticated fireworks display and next to it an abandoned meth lab, hasn't been used for months and so primitive it's a wonder it didn't catch fire or worse.'

'Called forensics?' asked the fire captain.

'No,' said Sandy, 'I think what happened here is that a stray firework found its way in and burnt this dump.'

'I can manage that.'

'Thanks,' said Sandy, tapped the captain's shoulder, 'we're being played here, someone's trying to distract us.'

He's a smart bloke.

Lucas's first test, redecorating police station doors - was to find out if some of Harry's group could plan and finish a raid in a few hours, keep it secret, and not get caught. The second test was to find out secrets of first responders; time to respond, who would respond, would gates slow them down, and their reaction to fireworks. That's what he pitched the group who set up the fire, he wanted them to focus on emergency responders, assured them that what they learned would be useful.

Gino trained three women and two men to work explosives. They'd spent every day and some nights for a month practising with different speed fuses, making, and setting up DIY mortars, plugging tubes and preparing their cakes, a mix of mortar tubes fused together to create a series of explosions. All five could do this at night, without lights. A few practice runs and they had set their display in the run-down shack.

'Nice work, Gino,' said Lucas, 'you all did well. You need to get them setting up underwater explosions now. Just tell me what you need,' said Lucas.

'Water? Underwater? How about a swimming pool?' said Gino.

'Private ones,' said Lucas, 'owners away for a few days, nowhere near here though.'

'I need a truck with pool maintenance logos. I'll write down the materials,' Gino took a small notebook from his pocket, held it up, 'where I used to write my bets.'

'How you're going with that?' said Harry.

'I'm going OK mate, thanks.'

'When do you want the truck?' said Lucas, 'a van's easier, white, big false logos. I'll find the vacant houses for you, on a hectare or two, north-east?'

'OK.'

Gino left to meet his group; a small celebration planned.

Lucas turned to Harry and Mike, 'off the punt and the grog, he's a smart bloke,' said Lucas. 'I'm pissed off about our people missing on the cotton farms. What do your guys say?'

Harry had heard from his police informants about the van, stripped and burnt, other than that, nothing. Police thought the van had been burned and stripped somewhere other than where it was dumped and scorched again, there'd been nothing lying around where it was found. There was no trace of the couple who Lucas had sent to find and map water storage on Brack's land.

Coming back for more?

A parent complained to police that the Cootamundra tattoo shop, the Ink Well, had inked his seventeen-year-old daughter. Although the sergeant would have preferred to talk to the girl, the father said she was away at a school camp, and that he'd seen her photo on her Facebook page, showing off the tattoo. He sent one of his constables around to talk to the tattoo shop owner.

The owner was helpful, obliging, offered the young constable a discount, 'something discreet, butterfly on your ankle perhaps?'

She declined and waited for the guy to open his file. He had the schoolgirl's picture, original and a copy of the letter her father had signed over an image of the tattoo to which he'd consented. All perfectly legal, the girl was under eighteen and needed parental consent. The young constable figured the kid had forged the dad's signature for the tattoo, just as she and her mates had done the year before they'd finished high school.

The owner was relaxed, atypically on the right side of a police enquiry, attractive young interviewer, so he said to her as she stood opposite him at the counter closing her notebook. 'You know when I saw the car, the uniform, I thought you lot were coming back for more.'

The constable waited.

The owner realised his mistake, blushed, stepped back and blustered, 'well if that's all, I've a business to run.'

'Don't close early,' she said, pulling out her mobile phone, 'my sergeant will want to know,' she paused, 'more too.'

'Shit, well, you caught me off guard., No harm no foul, eh?'

'He'll definitely want to talk to you now, here if you like or at the station, in which case you will be shutting early.'

The sergeant took her call straight away and was at the Ink Well in ten minutes. While she waited for him the constable looked for a camera, the tattooist was sure to use one. If this went further, her interactions with the guy would be scrutinised. She found it and asked the owner for it.

'I'll want the computer the images are stored on too, please,' she said.

'You'll need a warrant for that.'

'Ahhh, thought the images would clear you over the girl's tattoo.'

'In the back, second drawer in the desk,' he looked at the officer as she made no move, 'OK, OK I'll get it.'

He came back with a laptop. The door opened and the sergeant walked in as the shop owner said, 'I'll want my lawyer with me.'

'OK,' said the sergeant, 'tell her we'll be at the station.'

Back at the station, the sergeant, the young constable, and the duty detective for the night sat around the sergeant's desk.

'Just take me through this, from when you got to the Ink Well?' the sergeant asked.

She reported the banter, scrolled through the photos she'd taken of the paperwork - the girl's father's letter. 'It was all wrapped up,' she said, 'I said we might be back for a statement if needed. And then, he dropped this on me.'

'He said,' she checked her notes, '"thought you were coming back for more." I said you'd be interested in that. It was all good until then. There's something about the camera, Boss, too. I called the station for you, and then you walked in, and he wanted his lawyer.'

'Nice work,' said the sergeant, 'his lawyer will be a while, not answering the phone. We've a bit of time. You two get me everything you have on him. We went through his shop seven months ago, confiscated a camera, found cash, fifteen grand, I think. We charged this guy,' nodding to the cells, 'he's on bail, not sure if his case is scheduled yet. He must be worried about more than that though.'

He looked across his desk to the constable, 'good thinking to take the camera. His lawyer will be unimpressed, but he showed you photos of the kid with the tattoos, so he was happy to have you in there. You got the camera, laptop with you?'

'Yes,' she said taking them out of her backpack, 'I hadn't had time to lock them away, but didn't want to leave them lying around.'

'No,' he said, 'you did right, I'll log them while you two get on with it,' and he reached across for the gear.

The sergeant continued, 'I'll get a warrant for any footage stored on his computer, I'll get that as soon as you have the paperwork for it. Come right back in when you're done. Check out the girl's father too, family, bit unusual for a dad to access his daughter's Facebook, have her password.'

The tattoo shop owner's lawyer arrived, objecting all the way to the interview room, demanding time alone with her client. The interview established nothing the officers did not already know. They released the shopkeeper, kept his belongings. As his lawyer stood around talking to the station sergeant, two professionals catching up, the shopkeeper turned his phone on.

He called out, 'Hey, I'm not finished here.'

His lawyer turned to him, 'what?'

'Not you,' he said, 'I need to talk to you,' he said moving towards the sergeant.

The detective who'd been part of the interview stepped in front of the sergeant, 'you need to calm down, sir,' he stood up to the shopkeeper.

'No, fuck, I really need to talk to you,' he peered around at the sergeant.

The sergeant turned and led the way back to the interview room.

This conversation lasted a lot longer and the shopkeeper signed another statement prepared by the detective. He told them everything his lawyer had advised him not to and added that this German guy Lucas had got his contact to leave a text for him to deliver the computer to a bloke who'd collect it from the parlour early the next morning. The Ink Well owner was panicking.

'Sounds a bit convoluted,' said the sergeant, 'show me the text.'

'This guy Lucas,' the tattooist said, 'he only sees the worst. The bloke who sent the text will tell him he couldn't talk to me. Lucas will find out where I've been. There's no secrets in Coota. I need the camera and the laptop. Can't you just copy it, the footage?'

The Ink Well owner had gone over the footage with the sergeant who had poor stills now of the guy calling himself Lucas as he closed the door to the back room of the shop. But excellent stills of one of his own pocketing cash.

The footage was recorded, logged, signed by the owner, and returned. They would follow the bloke who picked up the laptop and rehearsed the story the shopkeeper would have for Lucas's collector, the allegations about the underage high school student.

A couple of hours later Sandy Pelham got a text from the Cootamundra sergeant asking if the two of them could talk. Now.

Sandy let him talk over some old ground as he worked up to the tattoo shop owner, the money, footage of one of his detectives, and the German bloke, Lucas.

'I rang you about letting him go and the plan to follow the bloke who'd collect the camera,' said the Cootamundra sergeant.

'Yeah,' said Sandy, 'got my notes right here.'

'An hour after I let him go, he rang me. Said he was frightened, scared shitless. Things had happened in the last hour, he had to meet me, not at the station, though. Now this guy's not too bright but he doesn't scare easily, used to run with a bikie gang, don't know that he doesn't now.'

'Doesn't scare easily,' said Sandy.

'No. So I was interested, thought it was a con, too. So, three of us went, two cars, arranged to pull him over, just a random drug and alcohol test. He and I stood outside the light; my video camera still got the lot. He said he got a call from a bloke call Harry, black guy. Wanted the names of local blokes who are FIFO miners. There're not many from here and the tattooist knows them all, love their tatts these blokes. Thing is, this Harry wanted explosives experts, said you need experts when you're dealing with bombs.'

'Did the tattoo shoppie say if Lucas and Harry worked together?' said Sandy.

'Said he's never seen them together or heard them talk about each other.'

'What did the shoppie make of Harry?'

'Reckons it was a warning, that when he ran with a bikie gang it was one way to deliver a threat, letting him know he was at risk of being blown up. Never heard of that, you?'

Sandy had heard of it, he'd done it.

'What do you know about the bloke calling himself Harry?' asked Sandy.

'First I've heard the name. Why?'

'Because he could be saying the blokes he's in with already have explosives.'

'Have you heard of him?' Sandy shook his head, 'no.'

'Dunno, Sandy, can't make the pieces fit.'

'Well, early days. Our job doesn't come in an Ikea flatpack, mate. Thanks for calling me.'

Sandy handed an envelope to the Cootamundra sergeant, 'this is for the tattoo parlour owner, make sure he gets it this morning, and complies.'

'What is this?'

'A get out of the coffin card, I'm closing his business, cancelling his license. He has twenty-eight days to appeal and then we'll take forever to respond. He'll go broke, but he'll be alive and another pest to Lucas. I want photos of the Ink Well chained up, boarded up by morning.'

Cindi, Cindi, Cindi.

'Get me all you can on Cindi Rios,' Hardyn Brack had said, 'better yet, get a copy of her file. Her email doesn't say much, enquiry, scope, consultation blah blah blah. She must be federal though, water, agriculture, environment, who can keep up with their departments these days?'

Brack looked down and continued reading, 'oh shit, what's this bullshit? Town hall meetings, search traffic, social media, canvass the widespread community interest. Bastards, trying to outnumber us.' Brack screwed up the printout, threw it at the bin and left the room.

Liz pressed her hands against the edge of her desk and pushed her chair away. The email thanked Brack for his time and attached consultation details about a parliamentary committee into water entitlements in the Murray Darling Basin.

'Cindi, Cindi, Cindi,' Liz talked to herself out loud alone in her office, 'who are you, where are you?' Nothing in the government directory, national archives, no social media, one three-year-old media release from the Law Society congratulating Cindi on her appointment as the International Criminal Court's ecocide specialist. Not listed with the ICC. Back in Australia now? Hansard, I wonder. There she was, Senate Estimates on the Riverina. Liz read.

The Minister, 'for good reasons, water in Australia is highly regulated, it's more regulated than our nuclear power industry.'

'God help the nuclear industry,' said Cindi.

'Order,' called the Chair, 'the orderly process here, Ms Rios...'

'It's Professor.'

'I'm sure you would agree, Professor, that it's quite a task to navigate the different, sometimes competing, regulations.'

Cindi again, 'you couldn't float a leaf down the Darling because the only government response to unregulated irrigation, unrestricted groundwater use, and illegal floodplain water harvesting - especially

58

in the north - has been inquiry followed by political donations, followed by education, followed by self-monitoring.'

'Order, order.'

'Education. Millions in last year's budget, granted to the peak industry association, the Cotton Federation, to develop an online education program. They can't tell us how many hits it got, we're not even sure the money went to an education program, regulation honoured in the breach, and not in the observance.'

'Order, order.'

Liz reached for her phone, pulled her hand away from it as if it were a black snake, no, not Brack, not yet, she had nothing, would need more than Hansard. Brack had the money, she was certain the Federation had not seen it. She did some digging.

She spent two hours on the minutiae of office administration, the accounts, correspondence. Nothing about a grant. Checked the date of the Hansard record. No, she was in the office at the time, no in fact, she was on leave. She had to find Cindi.

We need a distraction.

They were at 'the Point', Darlington Point, on the Murrumbidgee. Lucas, Harry, and Mike camped near the national park in a disused hay shed, corrugated iron on two sides, trampled dirt floor, decades of cobwebs clung to rafters like old man's beard, otherwise exposed to the north and to the east. Their four-wheel drives inside the corrugated roof, facing out.

They talked through their numbers, sales, logistics, any weaknesses in their operations, any police interest, any of their people caught, any of their people needing attention. Notes made; encrypted messages sent in Signal. The business discussions over, Lucas refocussed.

'We need a distraction,' he said, 'we're three blokes travelling around, with bullshit FIFO jobs. We need a story. We won't be caught with meth, but we might get caught out on something else, driving, an accident. Something innocent, police look at us, get a bit suspicious, dig deeper.'

'Never happen,' said Mike, 'don't worry about it,' he finished his beer, 'three more?'

'Thanks,' said Lucas, 'but I'm thinking we need something more than optimism. The people here, in the towns and the farms, they're curious and are into conspiracies, they're used to them, so we hide in a conspiracy. We get pulled up. What's our cover?' Lucas looked at Harry and Mike who stared back, saying nothing.

'Water,' said Lucas.

'Water,' said Mike, 'water? What? Hide ice in water?' His laugh failed to release the tension.

Voice mild, soft, Lucas, continued, 'we already do that sometimes, it dissolves in water, you boil the water off. I was thinking that we hide behind water. We're doing research on water, taking photos, talking to people about water, taking the pulse.'

'Takin the piss more like.'

'We set it up,' said Lucas, 'we're studying water in the Riverina, it's our passion. Easy to believe. Water, what there is of it in the Riverina is a disaster. People will wish us well and leave us alone to run our business.'

'I don't know much about this. I couldn't talk about it for more than a few minutes,' Mike again.

'Mate,' said Harry, 'I don't think we have to, we ask people questions. I've been hearing all about no water, failed crops, fish kills and selling breeding stock from the blokes in the pub. All I did was say g'day. Didn't get a word in after that.'

'OK,' said Mike, 'we're all quick enough, we can ask questions and we can learn some shit about water. It's a good cover, there are plenty of cranks in the bush. You'll fit in very well,' he said, laughing and pointing at the others. 'Question is how we gunna do it?'

Lucas stood and said, 'We're in?' they nodded.

'Time for lunch, and then a few plans.' He held up bottles of water, 'figure we toast with this,' he said.

Harry noticed the dust first, a vehicle, 'wonder what that guy wants, he'll be with us in twenty minutes, there's nothing else here.'

'She wants us,' said Lucas, 'I asked her to meet us here, she's going to fix our cover story.'

'A sheila? Gotta be joking,' said Mike.

'I'm not.'

Mike sat back down.

Hair in a ponytail, hot and worried by the track, Chip peered through the dust-streaked windscreen, no water in the washers and she'd tried the wipers with the sun in her eyes, the streaks made it worse.

Lucas waved her into the hayshed, opened her door and introduced her to Harry and Mike.

'Drink?' asked Harry.

'I have some.'

'Where do we start?'

'With a reason I should trust you,' said Mike.

Chip took her keys out of her pocket and walked back to her truck, 'I know the way out,' she said, opened the door and started up.

'You have ten seconds to fix this,' said Lucas.

Mike walked over to the truck, poured water over the windscreen, 'try it now,' he said.

Wipers cleared the dust and grime.

'So, Chip, this is us,' said Lucas. 'Mike, you've met, and this is Harry. We need a cover for our interest in water. Something where people can check us out, and be happy with what they find, and leave us alone, that's where a website comes in.'

'How do you see it working?' she asked.

Chip talked them through, asking, taking their suggestions. They agreed they could hide behind a website documenting the disintegration of the Riverina. That would be their excuse for checking out places, talking to people, taking photos, talking to farmers, all the while doing business.

'Is there to be anything on the site you'd want hidden?' she asked.

'Like what?' asked Harry.

'Encrypted messages to each other, message boards, subscriber details, planning to ask for donations like every other green group?'

'No,' said Lucas, 'none of that.'

'Makes it a lot easier then.'

'I do want other people to be able to put photos up, videos, maps too.'

'Why would you want that?' Chip looked up, 'it's not that it's hard to do. If I know why you want to do that, I can get you the best result.'

'We had a couple of our people killed on a cotton farm. They were using drones to find illegal water storage, so I want to use the website as a place where anyone can post pictures of illegal water. Going onto properties is too dangerous. Bloke, a water officer, was shot at a few days ago, so this is much safer.'

Lucas paced the hayshed as he talked, 'we'll put what we know about water storage, pipes, bores, earthworks, everything in the Riverina on the website. We'll put the maps up. Then crowdsource. Put the map on the site so it can target individual properties, and ask for information about water storage, water use, location of dams, pipelines, reservoirs, tanks, movement of mobile irrigation systems, irrigation run times, pumps size, location, earthworks. Anything to do with private capturing, storing, and using water.'

'You'll get all sorts of crap up there,' said Chip, 'everything from missing pets to bucks nights.'

Lucas snorted, 'I don't care. The idea is to make a shitstorm, we're not teaching geography. It doesn't matter if it's correct. Let's get it out there, push it out, flog it on social media and mainstream. It's the cotton guys we're going after. I figure one of them killed our people Crowdsourcing costs no-one, and everyone can pile on. The site will get thousands of hits and put the big guys on the backfoot. A real David and Goliath. How long to get the map up, and be ready for people to upload whatever they've got?'

'Two days, and I can buy you a hundred thousand subscribers, so it looks like you're already a success,' Chip closed her device, opened it again and scrolled. 'Got a name, this website?'

'First Water. firstwaterdotcom,' said Harry, 'all lowercase.'

Harry handed around beers, 'Chip,' he stood beside her truck, hand on the bonnet, 'antique?'

'Close,' she smiled, getting up, 'classic, 1968 F100, big V8. Best of all no black box, can't be tracked. Your trucks, you know when your mechanic hooks them up to a computer and does the fault-finding thing. He's getting into the black box, which will also show where your truck has been. Not for me.'

So, what is ecocide exactly?

Mick Darby had listened twice to Cindi's last appearance in a Senate estimate committee.

Darby phoned, 'Professor Rios, Mick Darby, with Ecological Intelligence. Is now a convenient time to talk?'

'No,' she said, 'I'm in my office packing up, I'll be outside in ten minutes, thirsty. It'd be convenient to talk then if you'd like a drink.'

'I'll make an exception for you,' said Darby.

Mick Darby walked to a tall woman, messy hair, ill-fitting clothes, no makeup, coming through the revolving door of Canberra's newest government building. Darby smiled. She balanced a satchel and a cardboard box as she looked around.

'Professor Rios,' said Darby, 'how can I help?'

'I could do with a job,' she smiled, 'it's their loss,' flicked her head over her shoulder, 'drink first.'

Darby took the cardboard box, 'nothing says you're fired like walking out with one of these,' he said, 'do you have to return it?'

'I think I might keep it,' she said, 'I seem to need one regularly.'

'How regularly?' said Darby.

Cindi stopped, went to take the box from Darby, 'strikes me,' she said, 'you already know the answer to your question. I don't need to work for, with, anyone who does that.'

'Twelve jobs in fifteen years,' said Darby keeping hold of the box, 'longest stretch was two years in The Hague and including a year of not working to write your book. Dream jobs. Now, expert witness, one of three, to a parliamentary enquiry into water, and you threw that away three hours ago.'

She let go of the box.

She walked alongside Darby to his car. A good thirty centimetres taller than him she shortened her stride from habit, then had to skip to catch him up. Cindi talked most of the way, in the car, walking into the empty pub. Now, she took her glasses off, brushed hair from her face and leaned towards Mick.

'Ecological Intelligence etcetera etcetera. Where have you been hiding?'

'Exactly,' said Darby. Darby explained what he needed, what the agency did, and the security nightmare.

'So,' she said, 'You want me to be Chief Scientist Water Security? Small team, unlimited computer power. You'll let me use this app I've developed.'

'Your full title is Chief Scientist Water Intelligence and Security,' said Darby.

'And my law background?'

'I've got to get a bunch of lawyers untangling all the regulation duplication you know so well. I don't want you on that. When they're done, and you'll be the judge, you get to draft the legislation we do need,' said Darby,

'Ecocide?'

'Exactly,' said Mick.

'OK,' Cindi sat back, hands around her glass, 'so talk to me of your definition of ecocide, exactly?'

'Crime against the environment, deliberate destruction of an ecosystem, like the Murray-Darling Basin. Laws where company directors are personally liable.'

'Mice plague?'

'Mice plague?' said Mick.

Cindi leaned forward and laughed, 'we seem to be repeating ourselves! Not seen the results of a mice plague? Destroys an ecosystem, so does a kangaroo mob cleaning out hectares of paddock. What will you do? Box them?'

'See where you're going,' said Mick, 'not deliberate though is it? We're talking wanton destruction, ecological destruction. You've seen it, criminal flooding. Flattening thousands of hectares to harvest rainwater, prevent it reaching natural watercourses, destroying wetlands, disrupting environmental water flow, and wrecking culture.'

'You've done your homework,' said Cindi.

'We have draft legislation, testing it now.'

'Testing it? How?'

'Two examples, one we're testing the definitions with insurance and corporate liability, including directors' liability. No use leaving loopholes for them to make money. Second test is we're looking for environmental damage events that could be test cases to prosecute ecocide.'

'Unusual approach to drafting legislation.'

'I wouldn't know. I know that's what we're doing with this. Our Minister saw the legal confusion played out in Europe, burning through euros on fees. Suits both sides, of course. She wants them, insurance, directors' liability inside her tent. Laws prohibiting ecocide won't be enacted quickly, she wants them firmly on the horizon though with a well-defined approach.'

'Try before you buy?'

Cindi took her drink, light beer, looked over Darby's head; Darby dressed more carefully than she did, wore smiles like costumes, didn't seem fussed by her height, not frightened by her intellect, I could be frightened of his she thought, and his cunning.

'Your call,' said Mick casually. 'The job appeals to you. Let's say, you take it, who would you tell first? Who would you like to know about it?'

'No-one.'

Darby sipped his beer, put it down.

'Well,' Cindi said, 'that'd be the point. You're the Commissioner for Ecological Intelligence, Security and Terrorism. Can't imagine you'd want your friends and enemies knowing anything about you. Same goes for me.'

'I'll have a draft contract to you tomorrow, mark up your changes, get it back to me.'

'I've got a few things in mind,' said Cindi, 'need your assurance on them before we get that close. The heart of anti-ecocide legislation is protecting nature from harm. So, grounds for criminalisation; harm-based criteria along with legal requirements.'

'Harm, I could get my head around,' said Mick, 'it'd go to nature of the harm, extent, criteria, gravity, numbers. The legal requirements, what do you mean by that?'

'No matter where you look, the consistent thing about environmental law is that it's complex, inconsistent, piecemeal, and ineffective. The requirements are buried. I'd want them out in the sunlight.'

'Why you left the ICC,' said Mick.

'Words,' said Cindi shaking her hair, 'words under a microscope. Like frogs, words are to the ICC. Lobotomised, dissected, weighed, leaving useless strings of vowels and consonants, reassembled to stand for something else, until the scalpels come out and dissection starts again.'

Darby nodded, 'so, who blinked first?'

'They did. Comfortable payout, not so comfortable non-disclosure.'

'You signed it, though.'

'I did sign it. Why not?' She shrugged, 'I could have a gap year.'

'Touche,' said Darby.

'Where were we,' said Cindi.

'Water, you've shifted the goals to environmental law,' said Mick. 'We've nothing to do with its wider brief, biodiversity, heritage protection, extinction of flora and fauna, wildlife trade, threatened species.'

'Think again. Water cannot be separated from the environment Mick. The compartmentalisation of nature, of ecosystems is a major contributor to the failure of our environment laws now. The draft ecocide legislation we're testing?'

Cindi held her hands out, 'the tests can't be constrained. You mention insurers, corporation law. No mention of indigenous communities. Huge omission.'

'OK,' said Mick, 'I'm good with that, it's what we'll do, expand the scope. Agreed?' he held his hand out.

'Two things,' said Cindi, 'the laws and regulations around ecocide are to be drafted in Plain English.'

'Is that even possible?'

'Yes.'

'Secondly?' asked Mick.

'My app, my app for water testing. I want it used by your agency and freely available to all mobile phones, Australia wide.

'OK, I'll want it tested first,' said Mick.

'Let me look over the test criteria and the app is yours. If it meets the criteria then it's a go?'

'The app,' said Mick, 'why is it so important to you. Money? My agency hosts it and you get paid for it?'

'Not money. It's personal. For me, testing whether water is safe is personal, on your phone, as easy as using your phone. Water is personal to me. In Portuguese my family name Rios means rivers. When I look at the rivers in the Murray-Darling Basin they're shrinking and filling with dying fish - I don't want my name to be Cindi Toxic.'

'Personal,' said Mick, 'OK. I put my trust in personal.'

'And thirdly, I want the Plain English and the app – what you've agreed to, written into my contract.'

'Sure,' said Mick.

Liz Evans' search for Cindi was tracked live by one of Mick Darby's team. Darby knew it was impossible to keep secret every member of his team, so he invested in technology. He wanted to know who was trying to find them. The team worked a series of triggers and an IP address in Lake Albert had searched for Cindi on WhatsApp, reddit, Facebook, LinkedIn, Instagram, even TikTok.

The team assembled the data, threaded their way through the cubicles and knocked on Mick's door.

Mick looked up, 'Cindi's email?'

The team leader nodded.

'Better get her in then,' said Mick, picking up his phone

'You were right, Mick,' said Cindi.

'Didn't take him long, did it? So, Liz Evans, CEO of the Cotton Federation, up half the night looking for you. He's using Liz, so your email's got to him, Cindi.'

'Invitation to appear before a Parliamentary Committee along with conservationists, who could refuse?' she shook her head.

Forty dollars an almond.

Directors of the Board of the Cotton Federation, five men; all sleek skin and luxurious suits and shirts expensively tailored to mask the body corpulent. Their three-hour lunch, littered with soliloquies about their possessions, cars, boats, wives and girlfriends, and the bull cotton market. Lunch finished, adjourned rather, the eating and drinking and monologues to resume after the Board meeting. They were chauffeured to Federation offices.

Liz Evans welcomed them to the offices, took their coats, dodged their hands, checked all had their papers, knew they were unread. The meeting, time suspended she thought, lost really.

Cotton Federation offices were cheap - threadbare carpet, poorly airconditioned, no lift and the directors hated the two flights of stairs. Brack had to constantly remind them that the Federation represented family farmers, battlers. Shabby offices key to their image. Media conferences were held there, politicians feted there, growers met there.

'You see,' Brack would say in his worn RM Williams, 'not a cent of your membership fees wasted here, lucky to get it at these rates.'

Hardyn Brack, Chair, holding court; the one to whom the other four owed their wealth and the only one who did not grasp they would never forgive him for it.

'Item six on the agenda,' said Brack.

'I don't have six,' mispronounced one of his dozing peers. Brack laughed at Liz who chose to walk around the room with a copy of item six, rather than reach across the table.

'Maybe, take a minute to read it through,' suggested Brack.

Two of the four reached for their glasses, picked up the paperwork, one of them asked Brack, 'perhaps a summary, recap, main points you understand.'

'Thank you for the suggestion,' said Brack who was interrupted.

'Forget the summary, get to the point. Giving money to politicians, item four on your agenda,' the speaker began, 'what do we get out of it? What's the ROI?'

'I think a quick review will help answer that,' said Brack, 'we need some background to give your question the attention it deserves.'

'Ballpark number?' Insisted the speaker.

'Ten percent,' said Brack.

'Ten percent of what? What does that mean? Can it mean anything? Ten percent of a politician...'

'Precisely,' said Brack, 'if I may turn our attention to the summary.'

'Hardyn,' said one, 'not on the agenda, should have raised it earlier. Slipped my mind.'

'Sure,' said Brack, 'what's on your mind?'

'These anti-irrigation demonstrators, putting notices up on some of my fences, bailing up my workers, lucky their English is not that flash,' he chuckled, 'but can't we stop them? That's what we're paying the pollies for isn't it?'

'Pay 'em for results,' said another, 'happy to pay them, donate, if they get these idiots stopped.'

Brack shook his head, rolled his eyes at his CEO.

'If I could make an observation,' she said, 'there's to be another water inquiry.' She waited until the noise subsided, 'our position has been to support all the uses of the Riverina waters, the demonstrators are not arguing against irrigation, just the amount of water. If we are seen to be against the demonstrations, we will draw attention to ourselves.'

'She's right,' said Brack, 'these people attack anything in their path. I've been thinking about this for a while, maybe it's time for cotton to stand alone.'

'What does that mean? I've not seen anyone rushing to help.'

'We have always promoted the economic role of the Riverina. We've not gone out specifically about cotton, at least in public. Let's change that, present a reasonable way ahead. We grow cotton only when there's water. Let's distance ourselves from the nut growers, pistachios, almonds, hazelnuts. Those crops need water all year round. Let's see if we can get them in the frame for uneconomical use of water, and not us.'

'How would we do that? There's a lot of money in those farms, all along the rivers, not just where there's cotton.'

'Exactly,' said Brack nodding, 'all year long, all along the rivers of the Riverina. If we're agreed they're a threat, I'd say we leave the details to,' he nodded at the CEO, 'to the two of us. Maybe get you guys to get to work on your local members, state and federal, quiet dinner, farm tour? We'll get speaking points.'

'You got anything in mind?' said one.

'I do,' said Brack, 'takes twelve litres of water to grow one almond. One. Now, buy twelve litres of water, three bucks a litre, thirty-six dollars, call it forty. Forty dollars of water to grow one almond. Now, in a shop, forty bucks buys you two and a half kilos of almonds, that's a lot of fucking almonds.'

'Seriously?' said one.

'Do some research and come back if you get a different answer,' said Brack, 'thing is, they get that water for next to nothing by robbing indigenous communities, small farms, towns, stealing water from fish, frogs. Time to get that message out there.'

At the break for coffee one of the directors complimented Brack, 'good idea, Hardyn, to give us a chance to put our views, may not be on the agenda, but important stuff all the same.'

Brack laughed, turned to Liz, 'you've got this for the minutes?'

'Are you going to bring up that website,' she asked, 'First Water? Some of these guys own the properties photographed. Thousands of hits on YouTube too and all-over social media. The media will be on to it.'

'What do you think?' Brack nodded to the four men. 'Too pissed to deal with it?'

'They are,' she said, 'but when are they not? Maybe one-on-one, not here as a group. Want me to handle it? I could see them tomorrow, they're all local, and it'd be their farm managers who would handle it.'

'OK, that'll work for me. I'm calling the Minister about the site, get him to have it taken down. It's a cybercrime, posting pictures for which you have no permission on a website. Illicit data stolen from private property, published. Talk-back clowns'll run with it. Interview? Letters to the papers? What about our social media too?'

One of the directors approached, 'Hardyn, the boys and I have talked this over. We're in good shape, thanks to you. Let's leave this,' indicating the papers strewn over the Board table, 'to you. We know it's in capable hands. Not quite in the Paris end of town this place. We'll leave you to it, get out of your way.'

Hardyn shook hands, thanked them, saw them out of the building and ducked into a lane to the back of the building where he could not be overheard.

Brack was bothered by media coverage of police reporting a burnt-out campervan just outside the entrance to one of his farms. He'd been assured it would not be found. Brack knew the bodies of the man and woman were kilometres from their van. The couple hadn't had time to send the videos the drone had collected. He didn't know why they were gathering the data, nor for whom. Was the couple connected to that Water First website, he didn't know. His people had been not as patient as he would have liked. He called security at the farm near where the van was found.

'Yes, Mr Brack.'

'Any news on the police inquiries about that van?'

'No, sir.'

'What does that mean? There is no news, or you don't know of any. Don't bother! Forget it.'

Brack ducked into the street, no one around and moved back into the lane, phone ringing for his security chief.

'Hardyn, didn't expect your call, thought the meeting wouldn't finish till five?'

'There's a website, Water First, or something like that. They want people, tourists, locals, anyone with a phone to take photos of water, dams, streams, tanks, canals, rivers, horse troughs for all I know. Lefties up to no good. I want you to deal with any one of my workers who meddles with that shit, don't want photos of my land anywhere. Not Facebook, not WhatsApp, not Linked up...'

'It's LinkedIn,' said the chief.

'Whatever. Take their fucking phones off them if you must!'

Brack closed his phone, stuck it in his pocket, turned around, headed back up the stairs to grab his coat and bag.

'I'll be in touch,' he said to Liz.

Brack walked out into the street and got in the front passenger seat of his BMW.

'They buy the idea of going after the nut farms?' said his driver.

'Totally,' said Brack, 'with a bit of pressure they'll drive the price of water right up,' he said laughing.

'Well, they've got deep pockets, I've already bought up the cheapest water I can. Soon as those giant farms get any attention, they buy water. There are some other trades too that I'm on to, some more licences, sleepers and dozers that'll come onto the market, we can get there before that.'

'Sleepers? Dozers? You talking about my directors again? Maybe it was the wine over lunch, sure you've told me before.'

'Sleepers are water licenses where no water's been taken in a year, dozers where bugger all of the water's been used. These licenses are new to the market, never been traded before, the owners have no idea of their value, happens they're selling them for their retirement, too easy.'

'You're sure?'

'Hardyn, of course, I'm sure. The stuff I was busted for, insider trading, is fucking legal in the water market. Can't lose,' he pumped the horn at the car in front, 'as long as we're quick.'

Another podcast.

Lucas used firstwaterdotcom to post voiceovers, explained the devastation of the Basin featured in photos and videos. Drug, extortion, and prostitution income rose as despair grew from apprehension over water and the growing uncertainties of rural life. Lucas exploited anxiety by forecasting federal government plans to privatise water which he claimed would mean ruinous price hikes.

Another podcast, a record number of hits and shares.

Lucas sat up tall in his chair, looking straight at the microphone clamped to the wall. He finished his voice stretching exercises and began talking, the unhurried voice of conviction.

'Listen to this,' said Cindi, thumbing her phone to get the podcast. Cindi slowed, bent her head to the car's screen, 'it'll play through here,' she said, 'just turn the volume up.'

Mick Darby looked at her as she drove, 'part of my education is it, this podcast?'

'First Water, First Nations. Traditional owners viciously kicked off their land, their water stolen. The same thing happening to you now, over two hundred years later. You too, will be the people who used to farm this land. Used to and used too.'

'Got a way with words, hasn't he?' said Mick, 'This Lucas?'

'The government is privatising water, they don't deny it. Let's look at what this means,' Lucas invited, 'to make a market attractive for the private sector – especially foreigners like those owning your water now – they say that the water market needs to be free. Free of what? Well, for starters free of the obligation to supply schools, churches, hospitals, aged care places with water at a 50% discount.'

'We're not even thinking about this,' said Mick, 'well not out loud anyway. Where's this coming from?'

Cindi stopped the podcast, 'come on Mick, the water market, water traders, brokers, it's a shambles. Common knowledge, your office has been quoted on traders, and for a government whose holy grail is privatisation, next step water. It's not even a big leap, just the next step.'

She turned Lucas back on.

'Subsidies for water coming out of the kitchen taps for pensioners to enjoy a cup of tea and maybe a biscuit, gone. If the government privatises water, your mum and dad won't be able to afford a pot of tea. Your kids in childcare, or at school won't get a drink. You'll need to pack a bottle of water in their lunch box, and guess who owns the bottled water?'

'Now, let's talk shit, I know you'd rather not, right? But here's the thing. Now the federal government subsidises sewers, and they use a lot of water. What do you think a free-market sewer would look like? Think about that next time you sit on your scheisshaus.'

Mick turned the volume down, leaned back in his seat for a few minutes, 'how many podcasts has this guy put out?'

'Twenty so far. They're changing,' said Cindi brushing hair from her face, 'getting more serious, shorter, punchier. He's amped up. And they're working, some clever IT in there too, all his social media talk to each other, starting to get quoted in the local papers. Some of the signs at the demonstrations carry his one-liners.'

'And that's all we know about him?' said Mick.

Having Harry's youths at demonstrations guaranteed an arrest – usually not one of Harry's. Their task was to get a pensioner, mother of young kids, a quiet Australian arrested.

'You want ordinary people, safe, predictable,' said Lucas, 'comfortable Australians thinking, "shit, these people, they're just like me, kids and a shitty job, what's happening to them - could happen to me."'

In Collarenebri, a librarian was arrested for not moving her car from blocking the entrance to the Optus office. She was part of a crowd of forty or so in a 'Collarenebri says No' street protest carrying signs protesting electromagnetic radiation from the 5G network, and vaccination; 'Fuck the Vaxx' and '5G comes too fast'.

A real estate agent from Dubbo was detained for public urination. At the front of a crowd protesting 'big irrigation' he pissed into a metal bucket. When he finished, he held the bucket up, yelling it would be purer than the water in the river after it comes off the cotton farms. There was a lot of interest but no takers for his offer of pesticide-free piss as he was bundled into the back of the police wagon.

A nurse was arrested at an anti-vaccination rally in Tooleybuc. He'd turned up in uniform and got heated when confronted by a cameraman questioning his anti-science stance while nursing.

'Glad I'm not your patient, mate, you're probably still using leeches,' said the cameraman.

Egged on by a few youths the nurse shoved the camera, police intervened, the tattooed teens slipped away.

Got another way of looking at it?

'So why do you want to buy me dinner?' said Sandy.

'Who says I'm paying?'

'Well, you need more time to let me know why you're here Mick, what you really want from me, and I'm not walking any further. You're staying just around that corner and two blocks down. I'd like to bring my sergeant with me, not a showstopper, be useful though. Seven o'clock?'

'Seven's good. So's your sergeant. Be a pleasure.'

'So, is this a date?' Sandy's sergeant had asked.

'Make sure you get a kiss first,' laughed Sandy.

'Want to give me a heads-up on Mick Darby?'

'No,' said Sandy, 'I'll want to know what you think.'

Dinner was easy for the three men, after they'd ordered fish and salad, Mick Darby said, 'I know I'm a guest here, the paying one at that,' he laughed, 'but I'd like to have dinner first and then get serious. Suit you both.'

The restaurant emptied. Meals finished, tables cleared, they allowed themselves a small port.

Mick Darby outlined his concerns, 'the threat is the growing unrest and opposition to water theft and degradation, and the lack of any regulation. Unrest needs money to get organised, money raised by crime. Water theft and getting away with it means protection, regulatory capture by big players, again money.'

'Go back a bit,' said Sandy, 'opposition and unrest? The demonstrations, funded by crime, I don't get it.'

'What if the demos get violent,' said Mick, 'then to keep them going you need money for bail, lawyers. If you want to keep the pressure on exposing illegal activity against the big water users the irrigators, you need money, lawyers.' Mick sipped the port, 'And then there's money for expertise to destroy or damage heavy water users - rice and cotton farms, equipment, mills, gins.'

'That's not going on,' said Tassie, 'so, what are you thinking?'

'I'm thinking,' said Mick, 'that around the world peaceful protests came before every eco terrorist act. Usually starts with teachers, bookkeepers, librarians, yoga therapists, bumper stickers, and banners. Then, escalation to more violent protests with groups of young women and men, and so on to the exclusion of almost anyone else. Now, am I saying that every car with a ban fur bumper sticker becomes a bomb for animal liberation? No. But every bombing on a fur farm started with a bumper sticker.'

Sandy daubed his mouth with a napkin and rearranged the glasses in front of him.

'Sure, you're not missing a piece, Mick? I buy the play,' Sandy said, 'water,' he counted on his fingers, 'quality threat, scarcity, insecurity.' He looked to Tassie, 'growing civil unrest, maybe this firstwaterdotcom stirring things up, conditions ripe for attacks on infrastructure, and the ready money from...'

'From?' said Darby.

'Basis for Operation Marinya is our research, some intelligence, that we have a professional gang maybe making, certainly selling high quality meth throughout the Riverina, some preliminary data and along the Murray-Darling. Doesn't seem to be running along the coast or in Sydney, tight geographical distribution.'

'Maybe a territorial carve up?'

'Thing is,' said Tassie, 'none of the trimmings that go with a dispute over settling territory.'

'Maybe it was a peaceful settling,' Mick laughed, 'like a business deal'.

'Yeah right, like an AFL player transfer, no hard feelings there,' this set them all off.

'If the money from meth is being put aside to fund some of the stuff you're taking about, well that might explain why we've seen no trace of the money anywhere, no flash houses, no big spendups, nothing here got the attention of the unexplained wealth unit,' said Sandy.

'There might be a connection, but you need to remember you don't need a lot of money to destroy a regulator, jam a pump, disrupt a plant. Still, could be the missing piece,' said Darby.

Sandy shook his head, turned to Mick, 'I'll tell you what's missing. What are you doing about the water market, it's unregulated, regulate it. Secret trades, I mean, get a register. Unlicensed traders, get a licensing system. None of this shit you're so bothered about will go away if these conditions don't change. It's the kind of bullshit policing we used to do, arrest drunk drivers while letting publicans sell booze to kids and people who can't stand up.'

They drank their port. Sandy organised refills.

'Look,' said Darby, 'it's, ah ...'

'It's not on, mate,' said Sandy, 'that's what it is. You go after the hard targets here, the parasite layer; ministers, senior bureaucrats, lobbyists, lawyers, accountants, brokers, foreign investors, silent investors, political party donors?'

'Not many socialist coppers left,' said Darby.

Sandy got up, pushed his chair back under the table, Tassie a second or two behind him. Darby stood too, 'of course we are,' he said, 'there's no need to rush off. Can we,' he gestured the chairs and signalled the owner, 'a cleansing ale, fellas?'

'All the groups you mentioned, among them we suspect are those who have made millions out of water, cornered the water market. The draft ecocide laws, with those laws, will be as powerful as any anti-terrorist laws. What it means is that we can cut right through the parasite layer, as you called it. Without those laws, it's not a clean cut.'

Darby took the three beers and handed them over, 'thanks mate,' he said to the owner.

The three men sat, not drinking much more, satisfied all the elephants were out. Mostly they were silent, studying each other, looking up if one shifted in his chair.

'Not often that police are interested in enablers Sandy, getting criminals locked up is usually enough. So, why?'

Sandy sat back and explained the problem and his strategy, 'we need to seriously disrupt criminals' businesses, otherwise it's just business as usual in a few months or less,' he sipped his beer.

'This new approach, is it working?'

'Early days,' said Sandy, 'we've closed three pubs while their compliance with all the permits and licenses are audited.'

'Closing country pubs! Coppers?' Mick toasted Sandy, 'blowback?'

'Some, but the appeals courts are clogged, and the shutdowns continue until the appeals are heard. Not just in the Riverina District,' said Sandy, 'the other supers are into as well.'

'How did you get that going? The bastards knocked me back,' said Mick.

'Had to do a bit of digging,' said Sandy, 'homework. Some of my peers are happy to have some other state departments to boss around, and the younger ones see the method as a way back into the city.'

'And the audits?'

'Slow,' said Sandy, 'staff shortages, limited overtime in state agencies, paperwork getting lost. What can you do,' he shrugged. 'We close the businesses and make it hard for them to reopen, it's on their lawyers to challenge.'

'OK,' said Mick, 'assume this works, what do you think will happen?'

'At worst a few criminals close their businesses and open another one and carry on. At best they retire, shut up shop or move somewhere else. Either way, we've challenged the status quo for serious crime. That's why I'm interested in enablers and why I think you should be too.'

'There are two elements to this, this whole thing. Ecoterrorism, violence, including threats of violence against people, corporations suspected of destroying the environment, so this guy Lucas, new player in climate activism, focused on the Riverina,' Darby covered the ground again.

'The second element is ecocide. Few countries have legislation for that, now we're this close.' He held up almost pinched fingers. 'We could have the legislation under which we could go after the people, the corporations, lobby groups, enablers like brokers, lawyers, and accountants, those who have devastated the Riverina. Worse than parasites, they've cornered the water market, created the host the parasites feed off.'

'So, we,' said Sandy, looking at Tassie, 'we're going after the eco-terrorists, suspected anyway. Brack, and his enablers, suspected of ecocide, down to you Mick?' Darby nodded, 'and where they overlap,' said Sandy, 'we need to sort that out, but not tonight.'

'Yeah, we do,' said Darby, 'and also,' he drew a Venn diagram, pointed to the intersection of three circles, 'this third circle is crimes other than these two, the missing couple, assumed murdered for example, meth manufacture and selling. Related but we don't know how."

'I've got enough resources to cover the corruption and the water theft, well almost,' said Darby. 'I'm asking for your bumper stickers. From all through the Riverina. This Operation Marinya, going after the meth dealers, you've set that in motion already,' he raised his glass to Sandy and Tassie. 'What I can do for you, to help in a big way, is that I have a scientist who created an app to test what's in water, creeks, sewage, rivers, dams. It'll tell you if there's meth or meth-related waste in water. It's yours, app on every phone, as many as you want. And we'll analyse the data for you, secure custody chain, more than good enough for court. Look, it's yours, whether you come in or not.'

'Let you know in the morning,' said Sandy, 'thanks for dinner, and your company.' Mick shook hands with them, went to the register to pay.

'We walk?' said Tassie.

'And maybe a roadie along the way.'

'Bumper stickers,' said Tassie, hands in pockets, shoulders hunched, small steps.

Sandy found his smokes, offered one, gave his lighter to Tassie who lit his own and then Sandy's, 'thanks, mate.' Got his lighter back.

'Believable,' he continued. 'you can see why he's such a heavy, Sandy.'

'What are we looking for?' asked Sandy. 'Now we have two targets, we're focused on meth, who's selling, dealing, cooking, importing. We might also be called in to go after Brack. Darby's question is much bigger, what's the change behind this huge increase in meth, and therefore easy money. One of the changes is the water or lack of, right throughout the Riverina, and the increased unrest that's causing. Is that the only change, though? I mean it's the one he's paid to find, isn't it? Anti-terrorist laws, that's what it's come to, to get control over the water market.'

'I like the app he talked about,' said Tassie.

'The app! The fucking app,' Sandy laughed, clapping Tassie's shoulder, 'haven't seen it yet though. If there was no app, would you be in or not?'

'You don't think there's an app? Or not as good as he reckons?' asked Tassie. 'Well, shit, it just means more work for us, that's his offer.'

'What if he's right,' said Sandy, 'and in a year Sunrice mills go up, Leeton and Deni. The Advertiser runs a front-page story saying you and I were warned, in time to stop it and we ignored the warning. We didn't even try to stop it.'

'Well, when you look at it like that.'

'Got another way of looking at it?' said Sandy, standing still, hands in pockets, tracking a light, low in the sky, sunlight half a world away illuminating a satellite.

We're a bit old for secrets.

Sandy and Tassie discussed the fate of the world over a few beers. The publican knew them and knew to take their money, she and her staff were delighted with the new arrangements; 'if they buy their own drinks,' she said, 'you trust 'em to be fair all round. Well, I do anyway.'

'Couple of schooners of Old, please,' said Sandy.

'For two youngsters? I'll bring them over with your change,' she said, taking his money.

'Sandy,' said Tassie, 'times are changing, force is looking up.'

'How's that?'

'The interns, the uni students, we'll be in good hands when they take over the joint. You know, they're here on their holidays, want to work for us, for you mate, for nothing.'

Sandy waited until coasters arranged their drinks set down, his change in his hand. 'Thanks,' he said to the publican, 'how'd you go with that horse, Maclaren Vale, you were saying she likes a heavy track?'

'Can't see us getting one of those for a while,' she said, 'no good, pulled up on the hard track, we'll spell her for the season now.' She left for the bar.

Sandy took a deep swallow, 'That's nice,' he said putting his beer down, wiping his lips, 'the interns?' Tassie told him the story said he'd given his word to them.

'Mate, we're getting a bit old for secrets,' said Sandy.

'For more than secrets, mate!'

'Speak for yourself,' said Sandy. 'Look, we can't have them here being secretive, even as little as this, when they're surrounded by men and women trained to be suspicious. These kids have got the team's trust and you and I know how hard it is to earn it and to keep it.' Sandy leaned across, patted his colleague on the shoulder, 'mate, you did the right thing.

'Mick Darby,' Sandy sat back, 'tomorrow's our first meeting with the Marinya team since I let him know we're in. Question is,' he sipped his beer, 'what do they need to know?'

'If anything?'

'Oh, trying to trick me,' said Sandy. 'They do need to know we're sharing intelligence, or at least information, we may get briefings from him or someone from his team. Can you get that app sorted, Darby's sending through the link tonight. I'll brief the management team first thing in the morning, then Marinya.'

'That's going better you know,' said Tassie.

'Management team? Ah,' he stroked his chin, 'getting more used to it.'

'What about liaison?' said Tassie.

'That'd be me for now. The other districts are twitchy enough as it is, even though they know me, collaboration comes after criminal in their dictionaries.'

'Might be time for them to grow a pair,' said Tassie, 'who gives a fuck if they're twitchy? Their officers are working well with ours, may be out of turn Sandy, but think about delegating liaison to someone who needs to build a stronger network, rural crime?'

'You think,' said Sandy.

'I know I'm out on a limb here but liaison with the districts is not something only you can do or have to do.'

Sandy looked at Tassie who held the gaze, 'OK, thank you, I'll get her on it, ask her, first thing.'

'It was hard to swallow at first,' Tassie said, leaning forward, elbows on the table, 'but the more I think about it. Been talking to a few blokes along the coast about meth labs. They reckon the narcs are lucky, most of their tipoffs come from women who get knocked around by their scumbag boyfriends. Local officers turn up on a domestic violence callout, find a fucking meth lab, scales, chemicals, and broken glass all over the place, blokes in thongs and shorts cooking away, no aircon, maybe a fan. They lock the place up, call the narcs. Job done.'

'We've none of that,' said Sandy.

'We've got good arrests for dealing, possessing, using,' said Tassie, 'and we have no labs, no cooks. Convictions are in the hands of some bastard lawyers who get the trials delayed. And Ankles, on the lawyer's payroll.'

'So, not much to show for it is there,' said Sandy, 'we don't have much time, we need results, or they'll pull the pin on Marinya. We can't find these timebomb labs or we don't have any?'

'My point. Why not? Our meth turds aren't beating up their women, I don't think it's the education program. I've a one-pager on it for the morning.'

'Mate, it's just the kind of thing we're after. Why is it so different here? Only around here, our District? We can set that as a task in the morning. Going to give me a heads-up?'

'There are two options once we rule out the typical poorly run meth lab. Meth's either imported or cooked in registered commercial chemical factories. I don't reckon its imported because the ingredient mix is only available in our District and the neighbouring ones, it doesn't make it to the coast or further inland.'

'So,' said Sandy, 'not economical to import only to the Riverina, you'd expect imported meth to be available Australia wide?'

'Yep, leaves the registered chemical plants, I've a list for the morning, we should talk to them, test the water.'

'Nice one, Tass.'

'Thanks Boss, another?' he stood, held up his empty glass.

'Ah, cheers,' said Sandy when the publican had gone, 'now about these interns,' he took a mouthful, wiped his lips, 'hey, do you want to have tea here, try the new menu?'

'Good idea,' said Tassie, 'don't feel like cooking tonight.'

'Me either,' said Sandy.

Over their meals they talked through the interns and Operation Marinya.

'We get bits, fragments of leads, they dry up, whatever is out there is very disciplined.'

'Your instincts are right though, Sandy. Those nights you spent going through the health, justice, welfare, even school data; we have all the side effects of meth, just not the meth. Frustrating,' said his sergeant, 'mate, what do you want me to do with the interns.'

'I'll pay them as consultants for the six weeks, how about you let them know you've squared it away with me, they did the right thing coming to you.'

Time to go old-school.

Lucas was keen to talk meth business, logistics, weaknesses in their operations, any arrests? Anyone cutting the product, skimming? One, it was good business sense, kept the focus. Secondly, he had to make sure First Water was the front for their meth business, not the main game; 'the prize is money,' Lucas reminded them, 'not water.'

Lucas wanted to know more about police activity. He'd detailed what he'd wanted from them, and now he wanted answers.

'Lucas,' said Harry, 'mate – I've got a bit on right now – especially around Wagga. Not much time for these police reports, mate.'

Mike Nelson shook his head, settled back in his chair, feet apart, flat to the ground.

'Yeah, the Riverina.' Lucas stretched, took a slow drink. He'd chain-smoked through many nights, much the same as Sandy Pelham had, much the same activity.

Lucas had his own police contacts throughout the Riverina and neighbouring districts. Since Pelham had arrived Lucas's sources in the Riverina were fewer, quieter, either they didn't know much or they weren't saying much, he thought it was the former. Ankles promised more but it hadn't come. A lot of people could hear nothing, but a lot of people couldn't pretend to hear nothing. Besides, his informants didn't know each other. He had something though.

Lucas had a question. 'The Riverina. That tattoo shop, got knocked over in Cootamundra?'

'Coota? The Ink Well.'

'Yeah, that's it. I paid the owner the twenty-five grand the cops found and seized. Thing is, the cops reckon they found fifteen, what do you think happened to the ten? Your shop bloke shittin' me?'

'One of the two who turned it over,' said Harry.

'Detective? Senior?'

'Nah –young bloke, detective though.'

'Ten grand, tax free, say six weeks' pay in the hand. Well, I've paid him to work for six weeks, and I've got nothing for it, have I?' said Lucas.

Lucas looked around and then back to Harry, 'a young copper, keen for spare cash, thief, you planning on keeping this prick to yourself? Now, tell me exactly what I've bought for my ten grand.'

'How hard do you want to go with this Lucas?' Harry sat back, relaxed. Not as clever as Lucas but he had the advantage of a couple of conversations about Lucas with Mike. They were worried Lucas was taking dumb risks, involving himself in trivial things, petty squabbles among gang members, and, spending so much time on-line he risked leaving a trace.

'Running a multi-million-dollar business, meth, – and now we're talking about ten grand. One school night at Forest Hill? Seriously?'

'The copper then, how do you know it was him?'

'I've got pictures,' Harry said, putting his phone on the table, 'the cops smashed the camera when they busted in, but old mate had another one they didn't even look for. So, Lucas, the question stays, how far do you want to take this?'

'Two cameras? He had two cameras,' said Lucas reaching for his phone, 'where's the second one?'

'What? The camera, mate, dunno, not obvious if the coppers didn't find it.'

'Find it,' said Lucas, 'I want it, and the footage.'

'Want me to take care of him?'

'No,' said Lucas, and began texting. Finished he looked up, 'how far do I take it?'

'Let me tell you what I have,' said Lucas, 'then we take it from there.'

Harry and Mike were relieved. Neither wanted to work for a boss who backed down. Lucas talked through his findings from looking at crime across the police districts. He knew he didn't have it all, he only knew what his contacts had revealed. He had verified what he could, Riverina guys were getting caught.

'What do you make of it?' Lucas's turn to sit back relaxed.

Harry put his beer down, spoke softly, 'depends on what you want to look for. Am I not paying enough? I don't think my guys are any lazier, we all fish in the same river. I'm making as much as you and Mike. Could be the new guy's very good, Pelham, that's what they reckon. Got some clout, and this Marinya thing. Those lawyers of yours are good, Lucas, got all the trials delayed.'

Lucas, intent, 'so, the cops, I hear they're still interested, going back to the tattoo shops, it's dragging on, so what's changed - it was put to bed nearly a year ago. What are they thinking now? Do you know, any ideas?'

'I don't know. Either no-one knows or no-one's talking,' said Harry crushing his empty can, 'their boss, the new bloke, he's got a gang crime analyst down here, and a cyber analyst, I don't know what for yet.'

'They know there's something different in the Riverina,' Lucas said, 'we know this new boss cop in Wagga is digging around. Our people aren't as well protected as they used to be. They'll soon get the shits about that.'

'I hadn't thought of that,' said Harry. 'Blokes get the shits, talk, get careless, get caught more.'

'Have you heard he's also closing businesses linked to drug arrests? Closed the hairdresser in Marrar because he caught the woman's daughter selling drugs, she worked with her mum part-time, didn't even know her kid was selling, yet alone stashing it in the storeroom. Been closed a week, she's finished.'

'That's not good,' said Harry, 'she one of yours?'

'Yeah, I'm moving her to Coolamon. And yeah, no, it's not good. There's more too, this Pelham's getting the other districts involved about tattoo shops, and he's got different cops going back to the shops your bent detective busted. Anything from him?'

'No, nothing about that. Could be he don't know.'

'Could be,' said Lucas, 'or could be he thinks he's earned ten K, and he doesn't want to talk for nothing.'

'Leave it with me,' said Harry.

'OK,' said Lucas. 'I don't believe the information-sharing will last, cops spend more time looking to catch each other out than looking for criminals. But this new bloke, he's breaking some rules.'

'Reminds me,' said Lucas, 'look after your blokes, especially the ones hanging out with the guys who got caught. Make sure their families get extra, lawyers can only do so much. Harry, they need to be won over every day. Make sure they're not talking.'

Harry grunted, 'I know what to do, mate.'

It was the diver's shout, he gathered the glasses and headed to the bar. 'I could do with a smoke,' he said to the others, 'coming?'

'I can wait,' said Lucas, 'you?' he looked up at Harry.

'Yeah, I can wait, I'll stay here.'

The two men sat, all the time in the world.

'It was a good test,' said Lucas. 'The paint job with the Wiggles' colours.'

'Well, it was hard to resist,' said Harry, 'what with the stories in the papers and spread on-line.' The night the Wiggles' car story appeared in the Advertiser a few of Harry's boys had painted some of the more rural police station and residence doors in purple, green, red, and yellow. A tipoff to the paper got that story in the press.

'A test of how organised we could be,' said Lucas, 'how secretive, how quick we could move. The best part, although not necessary, will be if we can get it blamed on Albury. Wagga and Albury, they're supposed to hate each other. Maybe your bent detective can help with that.'

Mike came back with the beers to find his colleagues now laughing, sharing a joke. He passed the beers around.

'You missed a good laugh,' said Lucas and retold the story about the paint job.

Mike joined in the laughter, 'that was you guys! I heard about that from the cops in Griffith, they were pissed especially about the residences, crossed a line they reckoned.'

'Well,' said Lucas, 'I think it's time to cross a few more.'

'But first, no more phones, only burners, one use only. Use radios too, I have some. Now, same goes for the guys we use as cutouts. Burner phones for them too. Meetings must be only face to face. Find a simple way to arrange to meet. I use missing pet signs stuck to a telegraph pole, time and date hidden in the phone number, place in the pet's name.'

'What's brought this on?' asked Harry.

'Been talking to Chip,' said Lucas. 'Digital forensics in Wagga, seconded to this Operation Marinya, means the cops are probing socials, tugging threads. Some of our dealers and their women are all over socials, the cutouts are not, we must keep it that way and go old-school.'

Captain Cook motherfucker.

Two Aboriginal women sat inside the Land Council offices under a slow fan. The younger leaned across a coffee table and poured tea, milk, offered cake, freshly baked. She faced the window and saw a woman step out of a white Toyota, reach inside for a backpack, her hat and walk to the council door.

'Aunty looks like she's one of us,' she said, getting up to greet their visitor.

'Hello', said the caller, 'I'm Cindi Rios,' she nodded, 'Glenda, Aunty Glenda invited me here.'

Cindi was introduced to Aunty Glenda, offered tea, water, shown the bathroom, and soon engaged in small talk. Cindi had stopped at the edge of the town, used the public toilets, had some water, and refreshed for her meeting, relaxed over tea, enjoyed the cake. Cindi Rios, Chief Scientist Water Security, not that you would know it from looking at her. Her manner, her dress; no clues there as she held no awe for rank. She did take her job seriously.

She wanted to hire a research team from ANSTO, the Australian Nuclear Science Technology Organisation, to monitor groundwater extraction using isotopic methods on country of which the land council was custodian. Cindi was here to consult the elders.

'Are you one of us, Sis?'

The question confused Cindi, she blinked, raised her eyebrows, looked from one to the other.

Glenda laughed and said, 'it's OK, Sis, you don't need to hide it here,' and opened her arms wide, gestured around the room to the Aboriginal flag, signposted photos of Wiradjuri Gardens, NAIDOC posters covering the walls in front of her.

Cindi got it, blushed, rushed her words, 'no, not me, I'm not Aboriginal.'

'Captain Cook motherfucker, eh?'

'No', said Cindi, 'Portuguese, so more like a Vasco Da Gama motherfucker.' All three chuckled, giggled. Some tea was spilt, a friendship begun.

'Could you tell us a little about your family, Sis?'

'My family name, 'Rios', in Portuguese means 'river', so it's no accident I'm here, is it?'

Cindi enjoyed the women's company. Mick had insisted she not push the elders, 'if we can't use their land, we'll find somewhere else, it's up to them, remember.'

She was asked what she wanted with the water. Cindi explained it much like Darby had to the Prime Minister, just like a CT scan using contrast. Glenda got it.

'That dye,' said Glenda.

There was more talking, the women wanted to know if the radioactive isotopes were harmful to anything in the water, or in contact with the water, how long the isotopes remained. Cindi explained the pros and cons, explained half-life, spoke frankly about any risks. The three of them went for a walk around the building, down to a narrow creek bed a kilometre or so away. 'So,' said Glenda, 'show me how it works.'

Cindi used a handful of sandy soil to explain that radioactive salt would be dissolved into the creek, a phone-like device underwater traces the isotopes, captures the signal, her phone was the receiver of laser beams.

'OK,' said Glenda, 'now, the information you get. Where the water goes, where it's from. Where does that information go? Who gets it? What will it be used for?'

'Would you want that information?' asked Cindi.

Glenda laughed, 'just answer my questions, Vasco da Gama.'

Cindi blushed again, apologised, answered the questions. She knew it wasn't a done deal. There was paperwork to follow, a legal agreement, site permissions, but Cindi was confident. Cindi had asked them about water sites they were worried about because she had the equipment to run some tests for them, to check water quality; 'the samples will have to go to the lab to make sure, but I can tell you right away if the water is safe to drink, or not. My kit's in the truck.'

On their walk back to the carpark Cindi told Glenda about the app she used to test water. Take a sample of water, put a test strip in it, scan the strip, and see the results on your phone.

'So,' said Cindi, 'let's test the water, where first?'

'The water tank,' said Glenda, 'it's been there forever.'

"Do you use this water for drinking?' Cindi was horrified, the top of the tank was rust, the downpipe from the building to the tank equally fragile, the tank dented and tagged.

'Nah,' said Glenda 'not this one, it's not connected, there's a plastic one round the back, ten thousand litres. Not that there's much in it now.'

'C'mon Sis, seriously? The rusty tank?'

'Well, I have seen worse,' said Cindi, 'let's do this and we can compare it to the new one around the back. Cindi took a sample of water, dipped the test strip into the sample. The strip changed colour straight away and Cindi used her phone to scan it. She showed the women the results.

'So, we don't drink it?'

'No, we don't drink it,' said Cindi.

She conducted a few more tests. All the water bar the rusty tank was fine.

Another cup of tea with more of the Land Council staff and visitors and Cindi was on her way. She was soon on the phone to Mick saying now was the time to make the water testing app available to all communities in the Riverina. 'Sure,' said Mick, 'nice work. Yep.'

All the water data scanned by the app would be harvested giving Cindi's team Riverina water quality updates, live.

Quite a manoeuvre Sir.

Mike Nelson called repeatedly only to hear; 'the person you are calling...' before he ended the call. Why wasn't she answering? This last time he threw the phone, it bounced off the centre console and out the passenger side window of his ute. He stomped the brakes, swung the wheel to the left, almost managed the U turn, slid on the gravel, overcorrected, corrected, and skidded to a stop near the roadkill he'd glimpsed as the phone went through the window. Crows ignored him. He stopped right beside his phone, front off-side wheel nearly crushing it.

The rushing in his ears slowed, his body stopped shaking; he looked up to see a patrol car stop metres away, facing his ute, the crows looked up. Two officers, one getting out of the car, hitching his belt; the other using the computer to check the registration captured by their rooftop camera.

'Quite a manoeuvre, sir,' said the cop standing a door length from Mike's driver side door, taking no chances.

'The missus. I got a call. Thinks she's early with the baby. Give us an escort to town?'

'Don't see a phone,' said the cop, taking a step closer, peering in, 'not that you'd be using a mobile phone while driving anyway, would you?' He bent down, picked up the mobile, shook dirt, bits of gravel off the case, 'unless you dropped it?'

'Not mine, mate. Look if that's all I'll be away then since you're not going to help.'

'Don't go anywhere,' he said, 'you'd be familiar with the roadside breath test, the drug test. Turn the ignition off, I'll need your licence too, please sir.' For a few seconds Nelson calculated; with the engine running, he'd have to reverse, he felt the cop doing the sums too, taking that small step backwards, his right arm moving, surely to free his weapon.

He turned the ute off, handed over his wallet, cash bulging, license in the window facing up.

The cop refused to take the wallet, 'remove the licence please, sir.'

He handed the licence over.

'Just a moment, sir.'

The two offices conferred, the one who'd taken his licence came back to the ute. 'Your licence has expired, Mike Nelson of...' and he read the address.

'No, I live in Corowa, that's the wrong licence. Mike's a mate of mine, we had to use them,' he pointed to the license, 'to get into the club last night. We must have mixed them up when he signed me in.'

'That's happened to me too,' said the cop, 'but this bloke,' he said tapping the licence on his palm, 'could be your twin.'

'We're always getting mistaken for each other,' said Mike.

Unsure of the driver's name, sure that the licence plates of the Hilux belonged to a Holden ute reported stolen over a month ago, sure the Hilux was unregistered, sure they had the wild U turn on camera, sure the driver's breathalyser results put him well over the limit, pretty sure the phone from the roadside belonged to the driver; the two officers decided to share the arrest and the paperwork this guy would generate and called the incident in.

By the time they were back at the Deniliquin police station, their sergeant had a search warrant for the Hilux. He'd also arranged for a doctor to administer a blood test. Without his phone Nelson could not call his lawyer, and he couldn't now admit the phone found on the roadside was his. He sensed the police knew this, the way they offered him old, tattered phone directories. For the police, the next two hours dragged, for Nelson the hours flashed by. He had two hours to find a lawyer, no way to do that, and time was up.

In the interview room, he sat, silent, for another two hours. Then taken back to his cell.

The officer who had seen the blood test result got a good look at some of Nelson's tattoos. On his break he texted his former boss, living outside Wagga. The text, to Ankles, would then get to Lucas.

The lawyer contacted by Lucas phoned Deniliquin police, asked to talk to 'a young man falsely arrested for drink driving'. The sergeant who took the call said there was no such person at the station and threatened to hang up until the lawyer made himself clear. 'Thank you, sergeant,' said the lawyer, 'not all the details are available to me yet,' he said, 'a young man arrested for drink driving.'

'Yes', said the sergeant, 'I believe I may be of assistance.'

The lawyer told Nelson to give his name, nothing else, and hung up.

Twenty minutes later Sandy Pelham gave the news to his Operation Marinya team. Two officers left to pack for a few days in Deniliquin.

Canberra says NO.

Hardyn Brack sat at the head table, the cardboard numeral one, perfectly straight in its silver sliver. Centre of attention at the annual dinner of the Cotton Federation. His seat faced the stage, not for Brack the courtesy of allowing his guest of honour, the Minister for Agriculture, that privilege. She was seated opposite Brack and had to twist to see the presenter, the performers. She gave up, content to take the hints from her shoulder and neck, satisfied herself by observing the crowd, the fawned and the fawned upon.

After the entrée the candles in the centre of the table displays were lit, wait staff with tapers swift between tables as the lights dimmed. Spotlight on the MC, a retired athlete, descendent of a soldier settler, among the first to grow fruit in the Riverina. A nice touch thought the guest of honour, professional sport and ANZACs, Australia reveres the cheater and the cheated. The Minister didn't have a long speech, guest of the Cotton Federation, she was trophy, cotton candy. She would speak after Brack. Her phone quivered, she read "fun?" a text from the PM, bitch.

As she stood and turned her chair around, watched the crowd clap, cheer and murmur as Hardyn Brack was introduced, he missed the half dozen or so people scuttle for the foyer bar to take a drink outside for a smoke.

Feet planted, no notes, hands still on the lectern, resting, all male, Brack waited.

'I can see that half the people in this room received an invitation different to mine,' he paused, shot the cuffs of his tailored lounge suit, only man in the room not in a tux, 'the ladies were invited to wear cocktail dress.'

Brack welcomed his guest of honour, thanked her, told her they could count on her continued support to further deregulate water trading, announced the Federation's sponsorship of a wetland restoration project, assured her of the votes in the room. Brack's speeches were like spotlights granting light to each piece of the room. First the illuminati, growers who'd produced another record number of bales. Some pieces were geographical, so he'd shine words on the northern Riverina, southern, lower southern; some functional, so words for the banks, the farm machinery suppliers, the gin mills, the scientists with their technological advances. Back to the growers.

'Cotton, more profit per litre of irrigated water than any other crop. We've shown ourselves to be responsible users of water. We want the government off our backs, we want the government to back us, allow us to self-regulate water entitlements and set our own rules and standards. We've earned the right to manage our own land and water.'

Some in the crowd stood to this.

'Thanks to the scientists,' Brack paused, looked to the CSIRO tables, 'with their technological advances and the innovation of our grower communities I can tell you that each producer, each producer here can now feed approximately one hundred and thirty people. Ten years ago, we fed approximately forty-seven people per producer, a two hundred percent increase in ten years,' voices raised, fists pumping, the crowd now on their feet, intoxicated.

Brack's numbers also meant that with every remaining cotton farmer there were fewer neighbours, fewer citizens, fewer voters. Scarce voters but lavish donors, whose money didn't have to be registered.

'You know the metered water in the southern Riverina, breach of civil liberties,' Brack told the Minister as she congratulated him on his speech, 'the sooner water is a national resource the better. Is that in your speech?'

'The better for whom?' she said, and then the chanting started.

'Canberra says NO. Canberra says NO, Canberra says NO.'

Uninvited people rushed the door, filed into the ballroom, spread out across the back of the room, down the sides, now across the front. The Minister, manhandled to the exit, tumbled into the back seat of her car, driven off.

Women in cocktail dresses and men in tuxedos found their voices and shouted at the demonstrators, 'fuck off', and 'get a job,' popular. The MC made his way to the microphone, stopping at tables to hush his own crowd. Earnest demonstrators, shop keepers, teachers, scientists, nurses, mothers, grandmothers, accountants hearing only their own voices quietened, listened, 'you've made your point, the police are here, we have you all on our cameras' said the MC pointing to the top of the stage, 'I'm sure the media await you, outside.'

And that was it, out they filed, ignoring the taunts of half-pissed growers, brokers, bureaucrats, accountants, bankers, scientists.

Servers weaved through tables, replacing empties fixed upside down in wine buckets. Only to reappear with five plates each of the ubiquitous veal or chicken, vegetarian, head waiter confused now by the extent of table hopping.

Table decorations burst into flames. In the confusion candles had been forgotten, allowed to burn right down, igniting the arrangements of dried Australian native flowers, banksia, grevillea, flannel flowers, always up for a fire. The flames were extinguished, glasses of wine mostly. The head waiter gave up, 'just put the plates on the fucking tables,' she indicated the room, 'they can sort their meals out among themselves.'

Brack hunted Liz Evans and his security chief, got them in his sights at the scramble around the doors, and felt pain as his right elbow was gripped. He was spun around to face his bodyguard who whispered, 'not now, not in front of your fans, remember your empathy lessons.'

Brack flinched, paled, he'd been sprung by his bodyguard practising his empathy training exercises in front of his mirror, quotes printed above.

Liz saw him coming and met him at the doors, 'the media are done with the demonstrators, want to do a quick interview,' she said, 'just the few quotes from the end of your speech, no questions.'

'Let me finish by saying when people say they're against profits.' Brack looked around him at the array of cameras and mikes, backed by police holding back the rabble, 'they're really against schools, hospitals and roads, the taxes paid by profitable businesses.'

The questions jumbled out of the journalist pack, random like playthings tipped out of a toddler's toybox, flashes of light, unflickering candles of mobile phones, all pointed at him.

'How much tax did your companies pay last year, Hardyn?'

'Only I heard it was none,' fluffy covered microphone filling his face, 'care to comment?'

'Wetland restoration, funded by the Federation and government, exactly how much from the government?'

'This wetland restoration project, heard of an avocado greenie project, Hardyn?'

'Hardyn, fewer producers with bigger holdings, dollar per litre of water calculations, has the cotton business destroyed the cotton farm?'

'Hardyn, hoarding water until the price goes up? What are your thoughts on that?'

'Delaney Holdings, biggest recipient of government farm subsidies, Hardyn,' another shouted question, 'how many nurses could that employ?'

Super recruiters.

Pelham was on the Charles Sturt campus a few kilometres out of Wagga to meet a police officer who had taken long service leave together with outstanding leave to study fulltime. They'd worked together some years ago, had attracted each other and then his tour of the islands disrupted staying together. Her postgraduate research was targeted policing for crime reduction, and he was interested in that, too.

Sandy got out of his chair as a woman opened the door of the Pulse Café and looked around her. She saw him, they met halfway, she was a head shorter than him, they were both shy and both wore glasses which were dislodged in their embrace. The server took their orders. They soon ate, catching up on former colleagues, crims, replenishing shared networks which had dried up a little in the time since they'd seen each other. They shared little personal stuff, more comfortable talking shop.

The table was cleared, tea left with them, and the woman talked about her research. Pelham was intrigued, a keen student of all things policing he was up to date in some of the topics she covered.

'Maybe you should be doing the talking,' she said, 'you know more than I do.'

They both laughed, she leaned forward, 'here's something though, I have a mate studying at Simon Fraser in Vancouver, RCMP, a Mountie. She is looking at how meth gangs recruit selling networks.'

'Really? Meth gangs different to other drug gangs?'

'The RCMP are interested in this because as soon as a group of youths selling drugs is turned over, another one starts. Here's the thing though, most of the time, a repeat offender is pulled up along with the same co-offenders, group of mainly youths, underage, and now with a record. But some dealers are back working with an entirely new group of sellers.'

She poured tea for them, reached for the milk.

'They realised they may have stumbled across dealers who are exceptional recruiters, rapidly increasing the number of kids selling drugs and therefore the number of users. They targeted them, called them 'super recruiters', because they are generally caught with a group of co-offenders who are younger and who, get this, have no priors. They're the seek dotcom of the meth business.'

'And the dealers, the super recruiters, arrested?'

'Too clever Sandy, arrested for what? They have nothing on them, not carrying, just hanging out with kids who may get a warning, if that.'

Pelham's phone rang, he turned off the sound, it vibrated on the table. 'You'd want to see who it is,' she suggested, getting up, 'all this tea.' She made her way to the bathrooms. Sandy saw that it was his office who'd tried to call and rang back. It was a one-way conversation. 'Be there in twenty,' said Sandy and hung up.

He went up to her as she came from the bathroom, explained he had to go. She had to get to her workshops prep and her books anyway she said. They arranged to meet for dinner, he'd come out to the post-graduate residences and collect her.

Sandy got back to the station and met the team in the room set aside for Operation Marinya, they had news, good news. So, did he and he explained about 'super recruiters', his crime analyst got onto the intel straight away. The good news from the team was the breakthrough in the leads they now believed they had. Mike Nelson in custody, not talking yet, but a matter of time. The team thought that Nelson's guilt was proven by his choice of lawyer. The phone assumed to be Nelson's hadn't been opened yet, again, a matter of time, they needed to get a digital forensics expert on it, and she was in Wollongong for the day.

The follow up of tattoo shop owners who had been interviewed after the police station paint incident had revealed more allegations against the detective who had reported one amount of money, yet the Ink Well owner claimed he'd confiscated more. Photographs and descriptions of the German national known as Lucas were distributed to all stations across the Riverina. They had two witnesses now, scared, but they had given their statements linking Lucas to meth and cash. The possibilities of explosives. There was no news about who had collected the camera and its data from Cootamundra, the tattoo shop had been burgled before it was shut down, the camera and the laptop stolen.

Sandy congratulated them, asked about getting updates out to the Operation Marinya team members not in Wagga and left the station to clear his head, settle down. Marinya had come to life again, a link to Lucas, meth and a query about explosives expertise, officers paired, tasks assigned, paperwork updated. Alone, he sat inside a café and took his first sip of the hot coffee; espresso, double shot. He'd kept the evidence against the detective pocketing money out of his report, figuring it would be a major distraction. He couldn't sit on it for much longer though.

His phone blinked and he ordered another coffee when he saw the WhatsApp message from a former colleague, now at police HQ in Parramatta.

He read that a complaint had been lodged against him by Ankles. He was tempted to ring his mate and see what else he knew, but fuck it, he was on a job and worrying about Ankles having the shits with him was not part of it. 'It'll be either this, or that,' he said, as he rocked one hand from side to side on the table, 'otherwise it'll be something else.'

He texted Mick Darby to fix a time to catch up and sat over another coffee. He'd ask Darby about the bent detective. Sandy wondered how the colourful lawyer knew to call for Nelson at Deniliquin police station.

Trust Cotton.

Cindi Rios sat in a car a hundred metres from the entrance to the Cotton Federation offices.

A text alerted her to Liz's arrival, a peep of long hair, white top, coffee in one hand, bunch of flowers in the other, backpack slung over one shoulder. Give her fifteen minutes, Mick Darby had said, 'she'll have settled into her office, arranged the flowers, opened her laptop, probably binned the coffee, she'll have walked two blocks with it.'

Liz heard the knock at the outer door to the Federation's office which opened to a lobby with a few unmatched chairs separated by two inner doors. One led to the conference room, bathroom, and kitchenette at the back. The other to one long room, Liz's desk and filing cabinets at one end, and farthest from the door Hardyn Brack's workspace, one big, empty, battered desk, sagging chair.

Brack was not expected for a week. Liz breathed herself into a non-negotiable we-don't-need-any-thank-you mode, hesitated mid-stride, what if it was a cotton farmer?

'I'm Cindi Rios,' said the woman at the door, 'you've been looking for me. Well, here I am, so much easier for me to come to you. What would you like to know?'

Cindi noted the dilated pupils, open mouth, shock, from which Liz recovered.

'How did you know where to, how did you find me?'

'I expect you have a lot of questions,' said Cindi, 'sure you want answers out here?' she shrugged as an office door a little way down the corridor closed.

Liz and Cindi settled in the conference room.

'Where would you like to begin?' said Cindi.

'But,' said Liz, sitting with her hands on her knees, head turned to Cindi.

'Let's have no buts,' said Cindi, 'you are Liz Evans, CEO of the Cotton Federation. The chair of the Federation is Hardyn Brack, you work for him. You've searched for me here in your office, from your laptop, at home last night on your phone. You've been up now for most of the last three nights looking for me. You will know that I met your boss in Wagga, and he's asked you to find out about me.'

'No,' said Liz, 'that's not it. Well, it was at first, but it's not now.'

Cindi had followed Mick's instructions, let her know that you know she's been looking for you, give details of where and when, and then listen. She'll need to get some control back, she'll do it by talking. So, Cindi sat, still, attentive.

'Let me ask you this,' said Liz, 'the money for the Cotton Federation education program, the website. How much money, where did it go, who did it go to, when was that?'

Hansard, Senate estimates committee, thought Cindi, day I was sacked, 'you know,' said Cindi, 'I remember almost every detail of that.'

'The three point four million dollars was an electronic transfer, and I'll have to check the account details,' she said pulling out her tablet, 'I kept a few electronic files from that job, never know do you? Do you mind, Liz? Can I charge it please, I've some power, but I don't want it to run out?'

'Three and a half million dollars, fuck. Sorry, a charger? Apple? I've got a spare.'

Liz came back with the charger, plugged it in, apologised for the short cord, and both women moved around the table closer to the device. As Cindi powered up and scrolled, she said, 'Liz, must confess to being a bit confused, the money came here, to the Cotton Federation.'

'That's the thing,' said Liz, 'I can't find any record of it, and I don't remember getting it. I do the books, I'd know if we were that cashed up.'

Cindi turned the screen so they could both see the numbers, 'the BSB, Westpac.'

'Not our bank,' said Liz.

'Account number,' said Cindi, 'let me guess.'

'Not ours.'

'Let me find out whose account this is,' said Cindi.

'You can do that?'

'How about we find out where the money is,' said Cindi, 'it's a lot of money and there's no education program, so eventually, well, people will come to you. I don't want that, do you? Let me call the office.'

Cindi put her phone on the table, and said, 'could you put me on speaker please?'

Darby lobbed the phone to a guy in headphones, 'Cindi, hi, why speaker?'

'I have,' she looked over her reading glasses at Liz, 'someone with me.'

'Liz Evans, CEO Cotton Federation,' said Liz.

'Hi Liz, what do you need?'

Cindi read the account details, transaction details, and they both waited.

'Three point four million dollars, Westpac, Leeton branch, Trust Cotton. I'll need to check out this trust, call you back?'

'No need,' said Liz, 'one of Brack's.'

'OK, I'll get all the details anyway. These trusts need to be set up by an accountant, lawyer. Be useful to know who they are too.'

'Liz,' said Cindi, 'how about another coffee?'

'Let me get a vase for the flowers first. I've been worried sick about this. I'll make some,' she said, 'I don't want to go out.'

'Then we won't,' said Cindi.

Settled again, Cindi asked about the flowers.

'Always like flowers in the office, Brack hates them, so I only get them when I know he'll not be here for a few days.'

'You, oh I don't know,' said Cindi.

'Me neither,' said Liz, 'pathetic, I'm pathetic. Degree, journalist, only bringing flowers into the office when the boss is not around. It's not me, and I'm here,' she sat back in her chair, folded her arms, chin on her chest.

'So,' said Cindi, 'this,' she opened her arms wide to take in the room, 'is you and is not you.'

Liz sat, not moving, one foot on the floor, the other tapping the cross-stretcher, Cindi waited.

'Do you think I'll be off the hook for the money, the three point four million, Cindi?'

Cindi waited.

'Those people you called, that guy found the account, Trust Cotton, not the Cotton Federation?'

'He's going to check out that trust remember. Is there evidence you have that it's Brack's?'

'Evidence? No, I heard him laughing about the name with one of our directors.'

'One of the other Federation directors?'

'Yes. And no,' Liz fell lower in her chair, 'I don't know who they were all in here, I wasn't, just Brack and one of them, they were talking, I could hear the others in the background.'

'Why don't we put this aside for a bit, come back to it later, when my office gets back to us?' said Cindi, Liz nodded, drank some coffee. 'Can I ask why you were searching the web for me?'

'You were right when you said Brack wanted to know more about you.' She tucked strands of hair behind her ear, 'after your meeting in Wagga. He hates meeting people he doesn't have a file on. "Get me her file," he said.'

'And you could do that,' said Cindi.

'Sure. I've lots of contacts in government, and so does Hardyn, way more than me. So, between us, the pollies, the public servants - anyone connected to water, we can get a copy of a file. Costs a fortune but it's worth it.'

'Copy of a file, personnel file?'

'Yep, background check for employment in the Commonwealth, job applications, leave record, performance reviews, when they're done, salary, the lot. Psych assessments if they've had any.'

Cindi's phone rang, she answered it and put it on speaker, 'Trust Cotton, is owned by another trust where the sole beneficiary is Hardyn Brack. Trust Cotton is the name of the education project funded by the government, be one of the reasons no alarms rang. One thousand dollars left in the account, nothing significant there. The day the three point four million was lodged most of the money was transferred to over a dozen accounts, mainly in Vanuatu, can't get anywhere with those. The rest, around one hundred and fifty thousand was withdrawn as cash, last withdrawal, Friday of last week.'

'Who set it up?' said Cindi.

'Law firm in Canberra, different departments and partners handle Brack's litigation, conveyancing, tax, water entitlements portfolio, they do everything for him.'

'Goldens?' said Liz.

'No, Liz. They only do the Cotton Federation work, suburban solicitors, none of Brack's work. That's it.'

Cindi turned her phone off, 'Liz, your boss, Hardyn, takes a few risks.'

'You met him,' said Liz, 'what are your impressions?'

'Gosh,' said Cindi, 'a bad boy, Alpha, one of those your mother warns you against,' she said laughing.

'Well, she'd have been right, charming, charmed the pants off,' she looked away, 'me for a start.' Liz smiled and Cindi wondered if the memories were that good. 'And a few others, had some, ah, quirks. Called me Helen in his sleep, screamed her name.'

'Should have listened to my mum,' said Liz, tears now.

Cindi made no attempt to comfort Liz, sat still, waited, uneasy at Liz's distress, more uneasy with Mick's instructions to ignore her, listened to the bar fridge's low growl. Liz rubbed her eyes, face, looked at her, and shrugged.

'This is all a huge shock,' said Cindy, 'did you ever think, did it cross your mind your boss could get you mixed up in something like this?'

'Something like this? Something like what? I don't even understand it. Three and a half million dollars. Vanuatu?'

'Liz, I've trusted you, let you talk to my office, trusted you with confidential information. Technically, should have you sign a confidentiality agreement.' Cindi stood and pulled a USB from her satchel, 'my bio is on here, more than enough for your boss, most of it is open source. Your computers are networked?'

Liz started to cry again and got up for the bathroom.

'Yes, why?

'If you let me load this for you, then you and your boss will have my resume, background,' said Cindi holding up the USB.

'Would you mind,' sniffed Liz.

Not at all, not at all, Liz copied the USB contents to Liz's computer, her fingers tapped the keyboard, and Darby's office now had administrator access to the Cotton Federation's computers.

Li came back and Cindi put out her hand, 'I'd like us to meet again.'

Liz clutched Cindi's elbow, 'you can't go, I don't know what to do.'

Well, if he didn't.

'You bastards,' she hammered her fists on the door to the police station, stood back and kicked it, resumed the hammering, shouting. Two young officers hurried to open the door, the sergeant motioned them to not, 'better to let her wear herself out,' he said, 'you don't want her kicking and punching in here. She'll only get hurt, and there's the paperwork to think of.'

The shouting and the hammering stopped, replaced by sobbing. The sergeant with two female officers opened the front door to the Deniliquin police station; he saw a young woman, no in fact he knew her; same class as his youngest, just turned seventeen, shivering in shorts and a crop top. Satisfied there was no weapon he nodded to the more senior of the two women.

She sat with the teenager, 'can you tell me what's happened?'

The teenager sniffled, spent, head between her knees, arms around her knees, hands clutching her ankles, heaving, sobbing.

'Nothing,' she said, 'I want to see my boyfriend.'

'Your boyfriend?'

'My father said he was here. Why won't you let me see him?' The sobbing resumed.

The officer, sitting beside the girl, looked to her sergeant. He flicked his head sideways and opened the door, motioned the other officer to wait.

'Why don't we start by getting you inside,' said the officer getting off the ground, 'let's get you out of this cold. Can you tell me your name?'

'Shana. I want to see Mike, Mike Nelson. He's here, isn't he?'

They led Shana to one of the interview rooms. Someone found her a jacket. She wanted water. One of the officers left the room and came back with water, sat in sight of Shana and behind her colleague doing the talking.

The officer handed her a plastic cup, 'now what's this about Mike being in here?'

'My father hates him, said this morning he saw his ute round the back of the station, that he'd probably been arrested. He hasn't has he?'

'Do you know why we'd want to arrest him, Shana?'

'Look, I'm seventeen, I can sleep with anyone I want. You can't arrest him for that,' she said and rolled up her sleeve, began to pick at scabs on her arm, shoulder.

'No, you're right,' said the officer, 'we wouldn't arrest anyone for that. Now can we give you a lift home?'

The girl shuddered.

'Is there a friend's place we could take you to, and you might want to let your parents know where you are then, unless you want them down here,' she waved her hand around the interview room.

'That'd freak Dad out,' she said, the beginning of a smile, 'they think I've gone to a mate's place anyway, so I can go there. We were going to meet there last night.'

'At your mate's place?'

'Yeah, her parents have gone to Henty for a few days, her dad works on the old farm stuff at the museum. Boooring.'

'So, you were going to meet your mate at her place?'

'Yeah, no, me and Mike were going to meet there, he was supposed to call me when he was on his way, but my phone was on silent, so I didn't hear it,' she scratched again, 'when I was asleep.'

'Do you have your phone with you now?'

'Yeah, why?'

'Well, if Mike didn't show up yesterday and he called you, then it might help us to see what time he called you.'

She handed over the phone, 'he doesn't use where's-my-phone app though,' she said.

'No, that's OK,' the officer got up to leave the room, 'I'll be right back and then we can be on our way out of here.'

'Hey, my phone, I need it back, Mike'll call.'

'You can take it with you,' she said, opening the door, 'we'll just take down your details and she'll see you to your friend's place. You told me you are seventeen, that means we'll let your parents know where you are. Rani,' she gestured her colleague, 'can do that from your friend's place.'

She logged Shana's phone as evidence, handed it over and let her sergeant know about the phone and that Rani was giving the girl a lift to her friend's place.

Her sergeant raised his eyebrows, 'Sarge, it's Deni, where's she gunna go?'

They took screen shots of her texts to Nelson, and the record of the calls. The sergeant rang Nelson's number from the landline and the mobile phone found beside Nelson's ute lit up.

Mike Nelson had been arrested the afternoon before and his lawyer had called later in the evening. Nelson had made no phone call and Sandy Pelham wanted to know how the lawyer knew to call for Nelson at the station. The Deniliquin sergeant emailed Sandy a list of his officers' mobile phone numbers. Twenty minutes later Sandy had the name of the officer who had texted a contact listed as 'Ankles', the text read, 'The Diver arrested.'

Sandy called Deniliquin and he and the sergeant had a quick conversation where Sandy let him know he was considering referring the Deniliquin officer who sent the text to Internal Affairs.

'Shit,' said the sergeant, 'would have been last on my list.'

'Perfect, isn't it?' Sandy said, 'they're never the first ones we think of.'

'By the way Sandy, had a young woman in here wanting to see Nelson, claiming to be his girlfriend. She's been driven to a friend's place now. We confirmed the phone found on the road beside his car is his. Nothing else.'

'Thanks,' said Sandy, 'the two blokes from here should be there soon for the interview.'

'He's going nowhere,' said the sergeant, ending the call.

Sandy called his chief of detectives, 'this constable in Deni texted Ankles about Mike Nelson's arrest. Then I reckon Ankles either got hold of the lawyer or contacted someone else who did. We know who Ankles is. The young copper and Ankles for IA? What do you think? Or can we use them now we know the links? Maybe I give them the detective from Coota?'

'You're sure, Sandy?'

'No mate I'm not, not about IA. What I am sure about is none of us need the distraction of chasing down bent coppers.'

'IA won't touch Ankles. He's a citizen now he's retired. So that'd be ICAC. Let's run a background check on the young bloke especially for money, monitor his phone, same as we're doing on the detective at Coota?'

'Yeah,' said Sandy.

'Paperwork for the phone tap,' the detective shrugged, 'some massive paperwork in that, know anyone, fast track the approval?'

'You know what, I do, leave that with me.'

Sandy Pelham met his Chief of Detectives at Wagga airport later that night, last flight from Sydney. Sandy stood near the exit, so they saw each other at much the same time.

'Shit Sandy, no need to come and get me.'

'I wanted to see you as soon as I could. I could have texted but, here I am, hate texting on something like this.'

'What do you make of Mike Nelson?'

Sandy waited the few seconds until they were in his car, although there was no-one around, 'well I think our two young blokes who interviewed him might have revealed something about Nelson,' said Sandy. 'Why is he so confident? Waives his lawyer, although he's talked to him. The lawyer didn't object. Nelson's fingerprints should be with us in the morning. The blokes in Griffith that got him diving in the canals for them confirmed they had his identity as Nelson. Who is he really? It's not adding up, you know what I mean?'

'The young girl who wanted to see him at Deni?'

'Turns out she's met him three times, says he didn't get her the meth. Gave us the arsehole who did though. Also, she reckons he didn't drink when he was with her, that he'd said he doesn't drink anymore. Yet he blew 0.17, well over. And not bothered by it.'

'Sandy, mate, a beer? Romano's? I'll get a cab home; you can walk it from here.'

'Not tonight, thanks, I'll drive you home, no more shop. Promise.'

'Got one question though, Sandy,' said the detectives' chief.

'Ankles?'

'Yeah. Sure about him?'

'No, I'm not,' said Sandy.

'Well, if he didn't, who did he call to phone Nelson's lawyer?'

Lucas had a plan.

Lucas sat smoking at a picnic table in the Paroo-Darling National Park between Cobar and Wilcannia. He was at the peak of a hill, marked as lookout over the Peery lake, twitchers' favourite. There was no lake, no birds, not even falcons, their prey long gone or dead. The picnic table with a bench either side, dry and cracked from the sun, the wood had split where the bolts screwed seat to board, exposing rusted thread. The ground was bare, dust hung in the air above his boots, no trace of last night's dew. He sniffed, smelled nothing, tasted dust. Megadrought took no prisoners.

He'd left coordinates for Harry and Chip. He'd catch up with Harry sooner, Chip a few hours later. Lucas had a plan, had had one almost from the start. He hadn't known what might trigger the plan. Now, he was surprised it had taken so long.

'So, Mike Nelson? Real name you reckon?'

'What's it to you?' said Lucas.

'Just wondering that's all,' said Harry.

'I googled the name, bloke in a TV show way back, a diver.'

'Well, he won't be diving for a while, way pissed, he'll do his licence, twenty percent chance of time, unless he's black, like me,' said Harry, 'then a hundred percent chance.'

'He's pleading guilty,' said Lucas, 'he has no priors, no form. He changed his name by deed poll years ago, there's nothing on him under his former name either. All that man of mystery stuff about a former life, just big noting to pull. An ex-Navy guy, a diver? The lawyer'll tell him PTSD. Make sure the only questions he answers are about the arrest for drinking, anything else is fishing, and the lawyer hates fishing.'

'The business?' Harry asked.

'I'm closing out his patch. Mike is not known to the guys he supplied, all communications on Signal, same as you. And, same as you, cash collected by cut-outs. I know it has cost us a little more over the years. Now, you see why I did it that way. Unless he talks about it, and he won't, there's no risk the meth or the money can be tracked back to Mike.'

'So, why not extend our patches to cover his? Move your territory down and into mine and I run Mike's?'

'No,' said Lucas, 'I'm closing it down, full stop. Nothing gets there again. The labs are so clean it'll only take a few hours to take them apart, bury the glass equipment.'

'That leaves a lot of money on the table.'

'What are you? A fucking banker now? What's it worth to not go to prison?' asked Lucas, 'You already reckon your chances are a hundred percent if you get caught.'

'Lucas, it's a lot of money.'

'Not happening,' said Lucas.

Harry ground out his smoke, kicked dirt over it, lit another, lot of money left on the table. 'Mike's been very busy, done well, there'll be a lot of punters wanting their stuff, hunting for it, it'll get messy.'

'Some of your blokes to the south might be tempted,' said Lucas, 'fuck them, so long as they can't be traced to you, let them go ahead, they'll eat each other anyway. There's bound to be some disputes between some of Mike's guys and yours as their stuff runs out. The only connection to you with Mike is the website, leave it at that. If you go getting involved in a squabble over who sells what, they'll bring you undone.'

'You looking after Mike?'

'No,' said Lucas, 'we both are. Same as we look after us. Mike has places in towns all along the Murray, commercial and apartments. Squirreled away under trusts and companies set up by accountants and lawyers. He knows where the title deeds are.' Lucas reached into his backpack and pulled out a USB, 'same arrangements for you are on this, if you want to see them.' He did.

'So, if it goes pear-shaped, as Mike would say, you get your code to this or your next of kin does. Millions, hidden away. Plus, whatever you've done with cash over the years.' Lucas stretched, lit another smoke, 'if one of us gets caught, we just shut down, like we were never there. If you want out, same plan, you get the code, and your territory is shut.'

'Be useful to have the details now,' said Harry.

'You want them now?' said Lucas.

'Mike got caught, you have his codes so he's sweet. If you get caught, I'm fucked. So, me having that now,' he pointed to the USB, 'is smart.'

Lucas shrugged, 'OK,' he said, 'now is that it? You're happy with this, not coming back to the well again, and again. You can get to your take now, and are you still in?'

'Lucas, just a backup,' said Harry. 'Mate, I'm all in.'

Harry closed the USB, put in his pocket, 'just one thing, what was Mike's real name?'

'Trevor.'

'Trevor? Fuck, no wonder he changed it.'

Harry saw Chip first, pointed out her truck to Lucas. The wind had come up and was behind Chip, looked like she was fleeing a mass of dust. Lucas and Harry tramped over the baked clay to meet her.

The three were camping the night and set up their gear; solar panels for their shared camping fridge, expensive and light camping chairs unloaded, fireplace cleared to bare dirt, not that that took long. Harry set the fire with kindling and logs he emptied out of a hessian sack. Jobs done, beers out and smokes lit, the three of them sat and eased their way into conversation, starting with Mike.

'Mike's devices are encrypted but that only means they'll hire an IT specialist to help them,' said Chip, 'when I find out who they've hired I'll see what I can do.'

'What do you think you could do?' asked Harry.

'Police outsource computer, cyber forensics. Cops still do the investigation part, although that's changing too as more of the forensic police go private. Point is, I'll find out when Mike's gear is cracked, take it from there.'

'Seen this new app?' Lucas and Chip looked over, 'got onto it from the Land Council at Young,' he had his phone in his hand.

'Phone?' said Lucas.

'Burner,' said Harry, 'just this one app, I wanted Chip to look at it.'

'Don't open it mate,' said Chip, 'what's it do?'

'Tests water quality, get a water sample, you dip a test strip into the sample, scan the strip with the app, tells you right away about the water quality,'

'Harry,' said Chip, 'delete it. Here,' she held her hand out, 'I'll get rid of it for you.'

'How come, it's useful this is,' he said, holding out the phone.

'It's a government app, right? They'll be recording your location,' said Chip, 'mate, you don't want that.'

'Should I tell the Land Council. They've been promoting it?'

'No, they'll be fine, useful to test water quality. It's a good app, just not for us. Don't want your location tracked if you could avoid it, do you?'

'Besides,' said Lucas, 'if you tell them one thing, Harry, they'll just do the opposite won't they?'

'What the fuck would you know?' said Harry.

'I do know one thing, your own people don't want you Harry, better off sticking with us. The only blacks who'll talk to you are locked up.' said Lucas.

Harry stood. Lucas leant back, tilted his chair.

'What's this all about?' said Chip.

'Fuck off.'

'Harry don't bother. Hesitation mate never works out. I meant what I said, you're better off with us.'

'I said I was in,' said Harry, and drifted away a few metres, hands in pockets.

Lucas's phone stirred and he wandered away from the others to read the text. Nelson's lawyer. He'd seen Lucas' photo and description on the notice board at Deniliquin police station. One of the officers there had pointed it out to him. 'We get this guy and I'll let you know,' the copper had laughed, 'supposed to be worth a mint. You'll be able to retire,' he'd told the lawyer.

Lucas told Harry and Chip about the message. He walked to his truck, came back with new phones, 'give me your old ones,' he said.

'How the fuck did they get your photo?'

'Mike gave me a few diving lessons late last year, November. One time he had a woman with him, she took photos,' said Lucas, 'I thought we got them all. The copper told the lawyer they got it off Facebook.'

'Got any places for Gino?' Lucas asked Harry.

'Here,' said Harry handing over a piece of paper, 'it's all there.'

'Thanks,' said Lucas. 'Now, the cops have a blurred photo, side-on,' he ran a hand through his hair, 'they'll photoshop it though, get a better description, time for a haircut and a holiday.'

Kickatinalong says NO.

Officers from districts around Wagga had been seconded to Operation Marinya and Sandy wanted to thank their bosses personally, get a feel for the territory his operation covered. He'd deputised the liaison with them, but he knew he'd learn from face to face, plus some time alone to think would be useful. And delegate. He'd found that hard. Couldn't be running the place from his vehicle. He settled into his seat, the pot-holed roads needed all his attention, he only carried one spare.

Later that morning Sandy met his Murrumbidgee Police District counterpart.

'Mate, your two officers I've met on the op, Marinya, they are terrific. I'm in your debt.'

'Yeah, they're good, figured you didn't want my blokes who catch goat thieves.'

'Hillston, easy trip for me,' said Sandy, 'so thanks again, I owe you one.'

'Sandy, I'm an old bush copper, happiest outa the office, especially these fucken days,' he wriggled his back against the bullbar of his truck. 'Bit stiff, just spent two days in a fucken classroom. Leadership,' he rested both hands beside him on the bullbar, 'authentic fucking leadership. Can you believe that?'

'What is it,' said Sandy.

'Well,' he said, 'I think you've a better chance of finding it out here,' he waved his arm at Hillston, 'than in a Wollongong classroom. Anyway, that's enough of me bitching. Thanks for coming up, the only time we get a visitor is infernal affairs, or some pollies and their mates scavenging off the big cotton bloke.'

'The van,' said Sandy, sharing his pack of smokes.

'Short story long,' big drag on his cigarette, 'found near here, now in our shed being taken apart. Got the VIN, the van was owned by a couple who disappeared,' he checked his notebook, gave more details, 'don't worry Sandy, I've a report to email you.'

'And these security blokes you mentioned?'

'Lippy, chemical muscles, my detectives reckon, goes for their boss too. All singing the same hymn, reckon the couple were never cotton pickers. Only we have photos off that website I told you about, and I've got IT searching for more. If it's their van, they were on the property where we're being told they were not. We've not presented them with our material yet. Again, if it's the same couple, they had drones, maps, radios. No trace of any of that of course.

'What do you make of it?'

'Well, there's this other thing. The bloke who owns that property is Hardyn Brack. Who knows what his mother was thinking Any bigwigs come to town here, Brack'll be with them. When you rang about coming up, I took this upstairs, got told the van, two missing backpackers who probably pissed off as their visas expired, all of it is nothing to spend any time on. You've got witnesses, I was told, good men working for a good man, leave it. A day later I got a letter from Brack's lawyers warning me off.'

Another long drag, nearly finished the cigarette, smoke everywhere. 'All pricks, the lotta them, probably shone in that authentic course, so of course mate, I'm sending you everything we've got, taking the van apart forensically. Plus, I've got a consultant onto the pictures downloaded from firstwaterdotcom, you'll have to pay for her though.'

'I'll find the money,' said Sandy, 'Brack, he's well looked after.'

'Brack doesn't like the demonstrations against water irrigation, you know the crowds,' he blew smoke out of the side of his mouth, 'you've had them too, kids, mothers, some young blokes who mainly cause no trouble. Anti-vaxx, anti 5G and anti-Big Water. This Cotton Federation was on my back every day to not issue permits to march. Now it's the left-handed nut growers association, or some such, want me to arrest the whole crowd, letters to the editor, fucking journos lined up outside the station. You get that?'

'We've had the demos, every weekend it's a few towns with the whatever, "Kickatinalong says NO". But I've had no pressure, like you've described. So, the pressure comes when they started up in towns where Brack has property?'

'Yeah, funny that. Gives me a greater incentive to allow the demos, should arrest a few of them just to get them bigger headlines.'

Both men laughed.

'Early thoughts on the couple in the van,' said Sandy.

'Well, they didn't fuck off because of their visa. If they're the owners of the van, the missing couple; Australian citizens, two years ago. The place the burnt-out van was located, interesting, found on burnt ground, but the fire that did the van did not burn the ground on which it was found. Get it?'

'So, they burned the van, then moved it, and burned it again, forensics confirm it?'

'In the email for you. So, let me see if there are dots here to join. I'm warned off, there's a connection to Brack, bullshit from his security people, threat from lawyers, photos of the couple with drones, maps, radios. Have a feeling,' he threw the cigarette away, 'unfashionable these days I know except if they're hurt and you want to go on compo, they were caught up to no good on one of Brack's cotton farms.'

'You wouldn't mind if I had a chat to Brack's employees who reported the van?'

'Only one, a female security guard. Hey, you know what, maybe two of them, she had a bloke with her when we talked to her.'

Sure, I get it now.

Hardyn Brack worked out of the Cotton Federation board room when he was in Wagga. The table held spreadsheets, binders, polystyrene coffee cups, some with cigarette burns, a laptop, and his phone. He read an email, sat back, feet out, hands behind his head, 'hey,' he said, 'what do you know about this?' voice easily carrying through to his CEO.

She moved to his desk, he turned the laptop, she skimmed the email, 'it's a code,' she said, sitting opposite.

'A code? A code for what? It's some bureaucrat in agriculture asking me if I can think of anyone suitable,' he peered over his glasses, 'bullshit, bullshit, cotton, blah blah, water security, ...chairperson. Chairperson, fuck, whatever happened to chairman?'

'Yeah,' she said, 'they want to know if they ask you to chair this that you'd accept.'

'It doesn't say that anywhere,' said Brack.

'They don't come right-out with-it Hardyn, it's here,' she read, '"reaching out to you about whether you would be able to let me know of anyone suited to this important task for me to pass onto the Minister."'

Liz sat and turned the laptop to face Brack. 'Hardyn, they're asking you if you'd accept, then they'd invite you to chair the inquiry, and appoint you. It's just the way they do this stuff. This says they've already decided. They want you to chair it.'

'It mentions a security check.'

'Yeah, references the new Ecological Security Act. So, there'd be a thorough security check, bigger than a clearance for a pass at Parliament House. You wouldn't even know they're doing much of it.'

'Let's find out more about it. Can you do that?'

'Be a coup, chairing this inquiry,' she kept reading, 'almost a Royal Commission this. And you the Chair, running it.'

Brack's phone vibrated, he picked up and read the text, 'OK Lizzie, get some lunch now eh, take your time. Oh, before you go, what's an "avocado greenie"? I got called that at the dinner.'

'Green on the outside, brown, fascist in the middle. Greenie insult.'

'Well fuck em,' said Brack, standing, 'fuck them all,' sweeping the polystyrene off the desk.

'Lizzie!' This was a bit easier to take now she'd met Cindi, I'll give you Lizzie, she smiled as she left the building.

She didn't notice Brack's driver waiting over and down the street.

'What do you have?' said Brack, 'take a seat.'

'Insert this,' he said holding a USB, 'as the bishop said to the actress.'

Brack took it, opened it on his laptop, 'what am I looking at?'

'Lucas. I've printed a few photos, had them cleaned up.'

'Not much to go on. Now what?'

'Don't mention it. We use his website against him,' he took a chair, and sat back, 'firstwaterdotcom doesn't moderate their site, at least not in real time.'

'What does that mean?'

'It means,' he leaned back so the chair creaked on its back legs, 'that I uploaded a photo to their website, and it appeared straight away, so no-one's checking. So, we upload these photos, "have you seen this man" caption onto his own website. See what happens, if anyone puts up any photos, information.'

'Weak.'

'Strategic. Gives him something to stress about, usually prompts a mistake.'

'OK,' said Brack, 'bastards's not worth more time than that.' He upended, shook a paper bag, a phone no bigger than a cigarette packet fell out.

'Got to get all my apps on this,' said Brack, holding up the phone, 'new number too.'

'iPad fail?'

'Sick of the fucking thing. Too big. This is way more powerful. Can see what the water is doing on the farms, can see what the water trades are doing, and now I can follow the robot security patrols. Can set it all from here too.' he held up the phone.

'You won't need to set the water trades. You do know it's all run by bots don't you, you'll never be as fast as them.'

'Bots,' said Brack, 'the modern language.'

'Hardyn, they make search engines what they are. You google cotton, bots search the web for references to cotton, you refine the search, the bots work on that, faster than a million librarians. Same as the trading bots, searches for water at the price we set, faster than a million traders.'

'Sure, I get it now,' Brack grinned.

The face of modern intelligence.

'This is it,' said Mick Darby waving one arm around the room as he opened the door, 'centre of the fight against eco-terrorists.'

'Looks practical enough,' said Sandy.

'Bullshit, it's a reminder from my bosses that I'm not really part of the respectable security service. I reckon most of this stuff came from the old Belconnen tip. You're right though, it's all we need. Come and meet Cindi and we can get started. Coffee?'

Mick, Sandy, and Cindi Rios sat on unmatching chairs with their tablets, notebooks, and coffee around a boardroom table which could seat ten. Scratches scarred the table, rough holes had been drilled into its centre so device chargers could be plugged into power boards taped to the floor. Electronic whiteboards with timelines, photographs, and a map of the Riverina covered in different coloured dots. Sandy had had the water quality app installed on all police mobile phones in the Districts involved in Operation Marinya. While the app showed immediate results for water quality, the data recorded by Cindi's team of scientists also tested the water for illegal drugs and the chemical residual of cooking meth.

'Here,' said Cindi using a laser pointer, 'hotspots, water samples in sewerage systems with higher than usual levels of VOCs, iodine and phosphorus, residues of meth cooking.'

'VOCs?' said Sandy.

'Volatile organic compounds,' said Cindi, 'airborne residue from cooking meth. They're common too in domestic and industrial cleaning compounds so they get into sinks, drains, water systems. We know baseline levels and the hotspots are way over baseline.'

'So, you know where the labs are?'

'Here's a closeup of one of the hotspots,' said Mick as one of the whiteboards changed to show houses, streets, and an industrial park. 'Samples taken from a treatment plant serving close to three thousand households, and these warehouses, factory units,' the laser moved. 'Now, we've also got samples of water from a local creek, and around twenty samples from people testing water quality on their vegie patches.' He circled an area of a thousand hectares, 'a lab in here somewhere, close as we can get.'

'This is really useful,' said Sandy, 'we'll get the data on renters, see what comes up on cameras, get the incidents around there going back.'

They took a break for coffee. Mick showed Sandy around, introduced him to a few of his team. Most made eye contact, all nodded or greeted him, some both. The face of modern intelligence, or rather, the hunched shoulders.

Mick and Sandy stood near Cindi's workstations, above them wall-size screens covered in codes, 'click on a data point,' said Mick, 'and all the water information comes up. Cindi and her team have done a great job with all the indigenous communities throughout the Riverina. For the first time they have incontrovertible evidence of the quality of their water, and they can share it. The state water authorities can't dismiss them now. There are already compensation offers. Everyone pretends to be shocked, but the bastards have known all along. The rush to compensate is more about avoiding a Federal takeover of water than a sign of humanity.'

'You working on the takeover?' said Sandy.

Darby nodded, 'another reason for so many lawyers on my payroll.'

Back in Mick's office Sandy spoke to the information he'd sent, updated him on Operation Marinya, his suspect detective in Cootamundra, the Ink Well tattoo shop and the leaked details of the Deniliquin arrest of Mike Nelson, referrals to Internal Affairs.

'Have the referrals gone to IA yet?' Mick leaned over to Sandy.

'No,' said Sandy, 'I thought I had two, now I have three, reckon there may be more. The last one's a bit complex, he's a retired super. That'll go to ICAC.'

'What have you got on them?'

Sandy opened his tablet, scrolled, and thumbed, 'my notes are here, paperwork for referral, here's what I have.' Sandy talked them through the detail.

'So,' said Mick, 'a guy called Lucas, no family name, photographed with Mike Nelson, suspicious call to your retired super, lawyer turns up for Nelson, cop on camera with money, and a tattoo shop owner, scared of a guy called Lucas. Now, do you know if the tattoo artist showed Lucas your cop on the second camera?'

Sandy looked up from his notes, 'the camera was stolen, no clues, back of the tattoo shop broken in. I'm confident no one knew about the second camera, figure that's why it was stolen, we're still going over the footage we copied.'

'Wait one,' said Mick, and left the room for a few minutes, returning with two of his team. Brief introductions and Sandy went through his notes again.

'Can we talk about the detective in Cootamundra?' said one of Mick's team, 'Sandy, it may be a chance to go on the offensive here, turn the tables on Lucas.'

'Fuck.'

'I'll take that as a yes, to talk about it' said Mick, he nodded to the bloke who suggested it, 'take us through what you're thinking.'

The four men talked it through, the detective not referred to Internal Affairs, informing for Lucas, and, more importantly, informing on Lucas, indemnity, protection, what to say to the Cootamundra officers who suspected the detective, the sergeant at Cootamundra, the shop owner, what did they have on him. And the officer at Deniliquin, informing on the retired superintendent,

Ankles. All through the afternoon, ducking out for more coffee and smoke breaks, they talked it through, sometimes all at once.

'OK,' said Mick, 'minute to midnight. We in this or not? Sandy?'

'Paperwork first,' said Sandy.

'Paperwork, what do you want me to sign. Give it here, I'll fix the paperwork.'

'Not what I mean,' said Sandy, stretching, 'and you know it. I'm up for an approved op, nothing less. My boss signs it off.'

'Sandy, that'll take weeks,' said one of Mick's officers.

'Better get started then,' said Sandy.

'You taking the piss?'

Sandy gathered his notebook, papers, picked up his tablet, pushed his chair back.

'Sandy's right,' said Mick, 'we want it open-ended. Sandy, if we come across any more bent cops, we'd want to be able to enrol them as informants without going all through this again.'

'There's an easier way,' said Sandy, 'but I'd need your help.'

Mick nodded, 'to do what?'

'Phone taps let's see what we learn from that. It'd be done by you though; I'd never get the OK to do that without more evidence. For this op we just want enough to identify Lucas, right now we have nothing to suggest the detective in Cootamundra knows Lucas. Our suspicion is that Lucas knows he stole money and that he'd find that information useful.'

'OK,' said Mick, 'if we don't get enough from that we can also try the informant approach.'

Sandy put his stuff back on the table, leaned back. 'OK, that takes care of Cootamundra. The young bloke at Deniliquin, and his contact with the ex-super from Wagga. Take your counsel on those two, Mick.'

'The ex-super,' said Mick, 'he's lodged a formal complaint against you, witnessed by your local Nats, state and federal.'

Sandy said nothing, immobile.

'You don't seem surprised,' said Darby.

Sandy shrugged.

Mick opened his door, beckoned to Cindi.

They sat down and Cindi thumbed a device, a quarter of the office wall lit up with a cluster of dots joined by straight lines, colours of the rainbow.

'What do you know about small-world theory, Sandy?' she asked.

'The Kevin Bacon thing,' said Sandy, 'no, that's degrees of separation.'

'Yeah, well,' she continued, 'it's more of a fact than a theory.' The laser shone again, 'let me get rid of some of this data, all the calls made and received on this mobile we believe to be one of Lucas's. This set,' the laser moved, 'are calls made and received on the phone contact, Ankles, in the Deniliquin officer's phone. Now, these are the calls on another phone. Let me show the links between three phones, Lucas, Ankles and Brack.' The screen shrank and enlarged, showing a map of calls between the three phones over the last six months.

'Hardyn Brack,' said Cindi.

Mick, 'Lucas and Ankles talk regularly. Ankles and Brack do too, but never Lucas and Brack.'

'Brack's the big cotton operator isn't he,' said Sandy. 'Northern Riverina?'

'We're yet to be across everything this guy owns,' said Cindi gathering the devices, 'or the myriad of company structures he uses to own cotton farms, water, warehouses, cotton gins, all over the Riverina. He also chairs the Cotton Federation.'

'It's getting interesting,' said Mick closing the door behind Cindi. 'Lucas, a meth dealing suspect, angry about water corruption and theft, interested in explosives, and Brack, water thief suspect. And

Ankles, playing one against the other? Maybe on the take of both? We're not sure.'

Sandy started a rough diagram: names, lines, question marks.

'And he bitches about you Sandy. I've got them all under electronic surveillance. They use apps, so we won't get it all. Sandy, I'd let us follow up on Ankles, a counter complaint and investigation, that'd just descend into a squabble between his lawyers and your union. Leave the young copper where he is, Deniliquin, he'll get rounded up along the way. I'll have his phone tapped too.'

'OK,' said Sandy, 'and thanks.'

'How do you feel about the complaint?' said Mick.

'They just follow a process, investigate or not. There's a book of rules about how complaints are handled. They'll just work through the steps.'

'Be interesting when they get Ankles' phone records, bank accounts,' said Darby smiling.

'Wonder why they'd need those?' said Sandy.

'Just one more thing,' said Mick, 'then how about a meal, a drink, and a meal. No walking tonight, Sandy.'

What is it with the one more thing, they must teach them that in their knife and fork course, but said, 'sure.'

'Had some follow up done on explosives experts, ex-military. We like to know where they are. This bloke,' he passed a file, photo over to Sandy, 'is worth a close look.'

'Gino de Bono, why him?'

'We started with those living around the Riverina, thinking the tattoo shop bloke's contacts would likely be there. Four blokes, three doing OK. This bloke, Gino,' he tapped the photo, 'PTSD and out of contact with his treatment team, heavy gambler, guess the rest. We found his bookie, owed half a million by Gino. The bookie sold the debt to a law firm in Sydney two weeks ago. We tap the bookies' accounts, encrypted. Then hours later the accounts were unencrypted, but nearly a million dollars is missing, gone from his accounts. Not transferred. Gone. That's as far as we got.'

'Do you know where he is?' asked Sandy, leaning across the table.

'No,' said Mick, 'Gino's not home, Cookardinia. But his place has been cleaned up, painted, lawns mowed. Cleaning and mowing done by locals paid by a law firm, same one. Thoughts?'

'What do you make of the frozen accounts, encrypted, unencrypted?'

'Typical ransom attack. Guy's been hacked, pay up or you never see your data again. We think the bookie was paid for Gino's debt. To shut him up, whoever he paid it to hacked his accounts, got their money back along with his silence.'

'Thoughts? I'm thinking someone that organised would do something serious with an explosive's expert. If they're behind the fireworks that night near Tallimba...'

'The Ink Well owner, bikie connection, you're thinking OMCG?' said Darby.

'No, he's nowhere near this, way above his head. My guess is Mike Nelson, the ex-Navy diver. He'd have the contacts to track down someone like Gino. If he worked with the hacker, the same databases your blokes used would be open to them. Another thing,' said Sandy, leaning back,' what if the bookie wants the million back? How long do you think Gino'll be around?'

'Enough for one day, please.' said Mick, 'Let's get a few beers at the Civic, and then a meal?'

'Meal'd be good,' said Sandy, 'but I don't need a beer, thanks Mick. I need to get my head around this, today, a lot to take in.'

'I'll pick you up at eight then.'

'I'll be outside, thanks.'

Mick saw Sandy to the lifts, handed him over to one of his officers for an escort out of the building. Cindi turned her head towards Mick, eyebrow raised, 'the line we're running on Brack then, you going to tell him over dinner?'

'Let's see how he goes with the bent coppers.'

Cindi shook her head, 'sometimes Mick, something so simple, you make so complicated.'

'Simple? What's so simple about Sandy?'

'He comes across like, seems like a straight-forward, somewhat old-fashioned country copper.'

'Maybe,' said Mick, 'keep an open mind...'

'Open mind,' said Cindi, 'code for I don't trust him. Why?'

'He's been in Wagga less than a year. Suddenly the drug busts are bigger, rounding up more than the odd user. Discovers an organised gang, turns up some corruption, including suspicions about the guy who ran the District for years before him. Same bloke who has lodged a complaint against Sandy. He welcomed us into his District with open arms, remember. None of his peers in three states wanted us in. And he saw off our blokes about turning those two bent detectives.'

Cindi shrugged, folded her arms, looked up at Darby.

'Well, think about it,' said Mick. 'I mean how fucking naïve is he, take that complaint. "they'll just follow a process." Bullshit they will. He's got no idea, and he should have, or he's a bigger player than he lets on. I don't want us caught up in whatever it is. You think the buck stopped with Ankles? On the take for years and none of his bosses involved. Maybe Sandy's taking all that over.'

'If you're sure he'd walk out on this,' she opened her arms, 'over who signs off on a joint op, just think what he might do if he thinks you don't have his back.'

'Have his back? Pretty sure I didn't say that.'

That would not be the way to treat a mate.

Harry was chained up. Naked chest, hands and ankles cable-tied, gagged, gagging, chains around his knees and chest, wrapped with silver duct tape to a post supporting a shaky veranda.

Lucas leaned against what was left of the shanty wall, an abandoned meth lab, the inside littered with broken glass, empty bottles of bleach, shredded plastic, every surface stained, smelled of cats' piss.

He lit a cigarette, blue smoke hung briefly and scattered. He'd had to call in all his favours and spend up big to smooth over Harry's mess. Lawyers, police, middlemen all worked up over dealers and junkies arrested for fighting and brawling among themselves as Harry had chased down what was left of Mike Nelson's supply. Harry had used some of his own blokes to sell in Mike's former territory, pissing off those in Nelson's crews. They wanted something done about Harry. What pissed them off more though was that when the stock began to ran out Harry diluted the product, dropped the price. Now Lucas had him, not that the three who'd taken Harry knew who Lucas was.

'Oh Harry,' said Lucas, smoking. 'You know, in Germany, your mother would never have let you go. We don't drop our kids, we don't drop our communities, we don't drop our families. That's where you and I are different,' he smiled. 'Fuck me, but you do look like a fucking zebra,' laughing, 'but black with those silver stripes,' he spluttered as he laughed, coughed.

Lucas moved closer to Harry, sniffed his chest, touched a finger to bleeding lips leaking over the gag. Harry's eyes tracked Lucas.

'Never going to happen, Harry, no matter how hard you wish.'

'Harry,' said Lucas, using another cigarette, circling, 'your family doesn't want you. Your community doesn't want you, or rather, they do want you. Want you hunted down for all the damage caused by the drugs you sold their brothers and sisters, their children, their parents. You see Harry, they want you for killing your own people. They're good, reliable buyers. And, Harry,' Lucas came to stop in front of him now, 'I'm going to give you to them,' he traced the chest chain, blew on Harry's nipple, 'gift-wrapped.'

Harry figured there was more to come. Lucas, he had a bit of trouble recognising him, combination of Lucas's new look and Harry's bleeding eyes. This was idle chatter for Lucas, he never did that, he wanted something.

'Just couldn't leave it alone could you, Harry? A chance for easy money. Prick, I trusted you, told you Mike's territory was closed we walk away. But you, too clever for that eh?'

Harry drifted, could barely hear Lucas if it was him, body would have swayed in the wind if he wasn't chained. The man in front of him, behind him could only be Lucas, but seemed shorter, all in black, face shiny, blurred, Lucas didn't ride a bike.

'I'm going to keep you here a few days, Harry, not like this of course,' Lucas frowned at the duct tape, checked the chains, 'that would not be the way to treat a mate. I might have something, might restore you to your people.' He lifted Harry's chin, stood nose to nose with him, 'no more shame, Harry.'

Lucas walked away backwards, stopped, and looked, examined Harry. 'Harry,' he said, 'before I forget, or you forget,' he laughed, 'did you ask the bloke at the Ink Well about explosives experts?'

Harry tried not to but slumped in his chains.

'Doesn't matter really does it, Harry? If I knew to ask the question, you'd figure I already knew the answer.' Lucas turned, walked away, hearing Harry struggle in his chains.

He turned away, walked through poisoned grass to a shed opposite the shack, pulled the balaclava down. 'Keep your eyes on him,' he said to the three young men inside, 'untie the gag to feed him, give him water, a few times a day, the chains come off, the ties stay, someone with him all the time. Give him a dry blanket tonight. Lucas wants him alive and well, first thing in the morning. Untie him before you leave.'

Harry was cold. He thought out his conversation with Lucas' three men, barely out of their teens, if that.

They'd given him a towel to rub himself, handed over some of his own clothes to change into, the ties coming off briefly.

'My clothes?' said Harry.

'Yeah, we went through your stuff, crazy tee shirts bro.' Harry looked up, 'don't worry, we were told not to touch them. We didn't.' Harry shook his head, remembering nothing about these strangers, trying to flex his ankles, looked at his captors. He remembered nothing about how he ended up in chains, confused.

'So, you wanna know?' the youth in Harry's face, 'Taser.'

'Taser?' said Harry.

Like spinning plates.

Sandy took a small whisky, Darby a larger one. They sat and sipped over the menus.

'Been here before, Mick?'

'No,' he said, 'Cindi recommended it, best Portuguese in town she reckons. Hope you like chicken, you'll go hungry if you don't.'

Sandy grinned too, 'I'm happy to let the kitchen decide, unless you want to order.'

'No mate, I'll tell them Cindi sent us, they know her.'

The kitchen obliged, prepared way too much food. Both men waved away the need for doggy bags. Last to leave they lingered over port.

'So, what do you make of the day, Sandy?'

'Like spinning plates, Mick. One observation I'd make though.'

'Yeah,' said Darby, swirling his glass, concentrating.

'It all hangs together, except for one piece,' Sandy reached for his glass, tilted it at Mick, 'wondering if you're holding out on me.'

'Why would I do that?' said Mick.

'Couldn't begin to guess at your motivation, not even sure about my own. But Hardyn Brack, what was the point of that little dog and pony show? That's what you're holding back.'

'Cindi said I should have told you more,' said Darby, 'she was right. We've set a trap for Brack, or we're setting a trap. The prick is so well connected we've not been able to get near him. Been warned off, outside the scope of my operation, agency, et cetera, et cetera, et cetera,' swirling his port in time.

'I was in Hillston last week with the bloke who runs the District around the northern Riverina,' said Sandy. 'Said the same thing. Been warned off looking at Brack's security for the disappearance of a backpacker couple. Pressured to knock back demonstration permits. So, I've held back a little too.'

Darby nodded, raised his glass to Sandy's, 'reckon we take it as square.'

'Cheers,' said Sandy.

'Now Brack,' said Darby. 'Protected. We have to get him away from protection. I've arranged to have him invited to chair an inquiry into water in the Riverina. Once he agrees, he'll be told of a formality.'

'Just one more thing,' said Sandy.

'Yes,' said Mick, 'because the Riverina now comes under national water security Brack'll need a security clearance to sit on the inquiry, far less chair it. No-one can prevent a detailed security check, and it removes him from the usual political and bureaucratic protection. Of course, there's no inquiry and we'll have got our information on Brack.'

'And if he doesn't agree to a security check?'

'He's unlikely to knock back chairing the inquiry with his ego, so, the vetting goes ahead. But if he does, it'd be leaked that he failed his clearance, financial irregularities, and the ATO would want to know why.'

'Why the ATO?'

'Because the one set of facts about Brack we can substantiate is how little tax he pays, how well he benefits from farm subsidies, how many layers of trusts and shell companies he has registered.'

'So why not let the ATO have at him now?'

'Mate, how many more questions,' said Mick finishing his port, 'gentleman's agreement. The ATO want us in this because, a little like you and me, they reckon we've got a better chance together. Besides, they've been warned off, or at least obstructed, too.'

'A lot to take in,' said Sandy, 'water theft, that's what's getting to the people in the central and southern parts of the Riverina. Water stops north of them. How does that rate with you?'

'Top of the list,' said Mick. 'But it's not where we must start. I'll get nowhere exposing him on water, he's so well looked after. I think his allies will fall away on the financial scandals, money laundering we think too, and then we go after the water. It'd take years to get him, make the charges stick on what he's done with water alone. Don't have years,' he said sipping port, 'maybe four weeks.'

'Four weeks, you having a few days off then? A little golf, fishing.'

'You're right,' said Mick leaning back to laugh, 'the two of us and another port, sorted. Tonight.'

'The hurry,' said Sandy, 'what's that about?'

'Well,' said Mick, 'Cindi's team has the projections. Three things really for my simple mind,' he counted on his fingers, 'no end in sight to this megadrought so, no rain expected, no downstream water flow as the water is diverted to irrigation upstream or simply hoarded, what little water there is in the rivers has algae, so little or no oxygen. Four weeks. The fish. The fish'll be dead.'

'The data checks out?'

'That app your people are using, plus the thousands distributed across the Riverina. Water in the north, in the creeks and rivers, seriously low oxygen levels. Every time a water sample is taken Cindi's team does a whole raft of tests, unknown to the person with the app. All data shown by GPS, down to the square metre.' Mick Darby held up four fingers, 'four weeks to get water. No more government buybacks, so I need enough on Brack's financials to seize his water, release it, avoid the fish kill. Four weeks.'

'Those apps, not just sourcing meth in sewage systems, then.'

'Mate,' said Mick, 'isotopes that only belong in aquifers, underground, are turning up in Brack's dams. Bastard's drilling into groundwater. Comes back to custody of evidence. Our technology to store and use these data lags the technology to source the data. I need that NASA licence.'

'Until then?' said Sandy.

'Well, that's why I'm surrounded by lawyers working on the custody of evidence chains as well as the spaghetti of laws. And it's why I need you and your Operation Marinya. I think we must show we're serious about the Riverina in less than four weeks because another fish kill would unite the disparate protest groups across the Riverina, for starters.'

'I thought you were relying on the ecocide laws, to detain and question him.'

'Whoa, hang on,' said Darby. 'We may. Don't forget we've only just now had water included as part of the national security of our ecosystem, first step to national takeover of water. The Riverina is our priority, declared a threat to national security. However, we must have enough evidence to investigate Brack's role in destroying the Riverina.'

'So, water, national security, ecocide, eco-terrorism,' Sandy opened his arms, 'what is all this? Doesn't sound like it's only a job, more like a bit of a mission.'

'Let me ask you this first,' said Mick wondering by how much he'd underestimated Sandy Pelham, 'why are you so naïve to think they'll handle your complaint by following process? That's bullshit, you know it.'

'Of course it's bullshit,' Sandy sipped his port, put it down, 'I could do with a beer. There's no way Ankles got away with whatever he's got away with without bosses, somewhere, knowing, in on it. They'll convince him to withdraw his complaint, or they'll bury it, do a mental health on him, dismiss it. While they're doing that, Complaints will also investigate Ankles, go back over his career, track his associates, anyone he worked with.'

'Seriously?'

'Mick, it's a classic. Hose down Ankles; mate, you're retired, and you don't want this shit. I haven't been officially notified about the complaint yet, and it's already outside the regulated notification period. So, they're already laying the ground for technically dismissing his complaint.'

'Why would they then go over his career?'

'Ankles lodged his complaint, got it signed off by two politicians. Force's dirty laundry exposed to politicians? The Deputy Chief Commissioner who appointed me will take that as an assault on his promotion chances, he's the favourite of two contenders for the next Chief Commissioner but, can't afford any question of his judgement. So, he'll want that complaint to disappear, and he'll hunt down and get rid of anyone who supported Ankles. Remember that Ankles is still connected, the young bloke who replaced him at Wagga,' Mick laughed, 'yeah, the Wiggles, laugh all you want,' said Sandy, 'point is that Ankles got him that job.'

'And I thought we were devious,' said Mick.

'Oh, you are. You knew about the complaint before me, maybe you're part of it. Anyway, I no longer give a fuck what people think, mate. I mean, this complaint, now it's not even about me. Once I thought they were looking after me and they weren't. Then I thought they weren't looking after me and they weren't,' he laughed, 'so why give a fuck, just do the best I can, good enough for me.' Sandy frowned, hunched his shoulders, 'well almost that's enough, I forget sometimes I have a good team around me.'

'Really? How's that going?'

'Well,' said Sandy running his hand over his head, 'what do they say, "a work in progress." Now,' he grinned, 'what are you up to Mick?'

'You sure you don't give a fuck? Is that why you're here?'

'I don't, I'm not interested in where this, all this,' he spread his arms, 'meth, water, cops on the take, where all the shit they're pulling, I don't care where it takes me, or who it takes me to. I want Lucas, Ankles, and I'll work with you on Brack. I don't give a shit about the politics of who may or may not be protecting them. If I end up with a complaint, part of an ICAC investigation, that's what I don't give a fuck about.' Sandy drained his beer, 'and you, Mick, what do you want?'

'This is pretty uncomfortable,' and Mick told Sandy of his stuff-up with chasing surveillance robots in aged care homes for the wealthy in the takedown of a prosperity gospel megachurch.

'We got the bastards,' Mick waved at the owner and held his empty glass to signal two beers, 'but they gutted the Federal Integrity Commission, Ethics Australia. Down to me, I leaked an investigation, nearly got a mate killed. Needed a helping hand,' he sneered.

'A helping hand?'

'Something my old man taught me as a kid, wished he'd never had. Now, I have to unlearn it.'

'Helping hand? You set people up?'

'Only the bad guys.'

'Mick,' Sandy's fist banged the table, 'that's what they all say.'

'Told you. I'm unlearning it.'

'Tell me straight. Is everything we're doing here legit?'

'It is,' said Mick.

'Good enough for me,' said Sandy, 'and now water?'

'I started out in water, plotting a way to get back into Intelligence, I wanted the Chief's job. But now, I'm undecided about that job. I want to see this through.'

'And now?'

'A hypothesis,' he held up one finger, 'Brack, deliberately destroying land, ruining it, stealing water, ecocide.' Another finger, 'Lucas, eco activist turning terrorist, out to destroy Brack, among others.'

Sandy stood, gestured to Mick, raised his glass as Mick stood, 'here's to our mid-life crises,' said Sandy, choking, bent double, laughing, Mick a mirror image, waved the owner and his wife away, 'we're fine, I hope,' gasping, 'really, no thank you.'

And so, it starts.

'Hardyn, there are two sticking points and some formalities,' said Liz.

'You know, I'm getting agnostic on this inquiry Chair deal. And do we have to talk about it now?' Brack looked around the Federation office.

'It won't take long to get through. You'll easily make dinner. It's booked.'

'OK, give me the sticking points, no background, just tell me what they want.' Brack held up his hand, 'look, I know they've not been that direct, but you've worked out what they want, otherwise we wouldn't be sitting here, right? So,' Brack sat back in his chair, opened his arms.

'Release some water, make up for lost environmental flows. They're worried about a fish kill coinciding with announcing your appointment. They figure it'd be dead in the water, along with the fish.' She risked a smirk.

'And so, it starts,' said Brack, tapping the arms of his chair. 'Do you know how much water sells for? Don't suppose they want to buy it?'

'No.'

'Did you even fucking ask? No. And let me guess, the second sticking point is the release of water for cultural reasons, so they can teach their kids how their ancestors caught turtles in the local fucking creeks.'

'Yes,' she said keeping her eyes on the laptop.

'So, let me get this straight. These pricks dangle a prestigious government job and then ask me to buy it. That's it in a sentence, isn't it? OK, what's the formality? Bare my arse in Parliament House?'

'This paperwork,' she said, fishing a file out of her satchel. Brack took it. 'Your agreement to get a security clearance, background check, consent to a psychological assessment, financial records. There's more, it's listed on the second page.'

'OK,' said Brack, 'fuck 'em. I'll sign this shit now, and I won't be giving away any water.' Brack crossed his legs, dumped the paperwork on his knee. 'Got a pen?' Brack signed every page, butted the pages together and handed them back.

'Now, here's what you need to do. We have a list of the scientists and economists opposed to wasting water on environmental and cultural flows, qualifications and papers showing how the water is better used supporting farming. Culture? Bullshit. There's no profit in culture. If there was you wouldn't have to waste taxpayers' money on art galleries and museums. That historian who wrote about the damage to small farmers if they lost their irrigation rights. Wheel her out again, get her talking about how cotton makes more dollars per litre of irrigated water than any other crop.' Brack paced the room. His CEO nodded.

'Good. Get it all cranked up, get 'em on social media, radio, TV. Get 'em attacking that First Water website. We'll take them on the issues they want to avoid.'

'There are some more pages,' she said, 'more questions and referees?'

'Referees? Seriously? They want referees. Give them a few pollies, directors of the Federation, well two of them anyway, you know who to list. Then, how about you. That should do it.'

'That should work, any employees?' said Liz. 'Shows the common touch among serious money and the politicians.'

'Thought you'd do fine for the common touch,' Brack said, turning towards the door, 'OK, Delaney's Security Chief.'

'Tell you what,' said Brack shrugging into his coat, 'fill out the rest and send it off. Spectacles, testicles, wallet, and watch,' he patted himself down.

'You forgot your phone,' she handed it to him.

Brack left, she heard him checking his driver was outside. She locked the office, then texted Mick Darby using an app he'd had installed on her phone, one word, 'vetting,' with the thumbs-up emoji.

The circus is in town.

'This meeting is on the record, in our diaries, the diary for this room. There will be an official record, so, I'd like to suggest we talk through what's on our minds before we start. I want the decisions we take this morning on the record,' the Director of the Complaints Commission continued, 'not the discussions we have as we decide. You know this is how I like to run these more sensitive allegations. Any reason not to this morning?'

Three people sat around the circular table, Sandy's boss, her Deputy Commissioner, and the civilian running the meeting, the Director of the Complaints Commission.

'District Superintendent Sandy Pelham, Wagga District,' the Director read, turning over pages of Pelham's file. 'And the complainant,' she continued, picking up another file, 'Clive Baxter, retired, ex-superintendent, Wagga District.'

'It is,' the Director paused, 'tricky. Retirees must have plenty of time, especially those well-connected. You've seen the complaint, so you know who witnessed it. You may not know that the state member for the Riverina alerted the deputy premier and our Minister to the complaint. And his federal counterpart alerted the Deputy Prime Minister. The circus is in town.'

Sandy's boss picked up the pitcher of water, 'yes?' she gestured the others, and poured three glasses.

'One observation I'd make,' said Sandy's boss, 'they are the only three names on the complaint; the ex-super raised a complaint about Pelham's behaviour, the remaining complaints are reports of conversations he's had with unidentified members of Pelham's staff. He gives no indications the anonymous complainants would be available for interview.'

'Where are you taking us with this?'

'To the anonymous complainants. Pelham's been in Wagga six months. His first two meetings with the union were stormy, all on the record,' she'd chosen the example carefully. 'The relationship with the union now is cooperative, again on the record. It's one indicator he hasn't created an environment not conducive to resolving internal disputes. As you know,' she glanced at the Director, 'cooperative union and management meetings can't be artificially created.'

'My Labor Council days are long gone,' the Director said, 'I do get the point though.' These two continued to circle each other, getting glimpses of common ground, making an occasional note.

The Deputy Commissioner shuffled his papers, drank from his glass, and brushed away its wet imprint with his hand, 'the complaint has been lodged with you, the Complaints Commission. So, your people should decide how to deal with it. My thoughts are the complaint should be investigated. All I want is for the investigation to hasten slowly.'

'Slow? With the pollies in front row seats?' she said.

'Well, I think that's why it's vital to slow it up. The pollies will be worried by something else in a few days. Although our retiree will keep at them. Neutralise him,' he said, 'so he can't hassle them.'

The two women looked at him blankly, 'there's a process for these things. A timeline to stick to,' the Director said. 'I can't.'

'You don't need to,' he said, 'respond to Ankles, let him know the Commission is keen to talk to those he sourced the complaints from, and you'll give them a month to come forward. Wrap it up in compassionate understanding etc, that it's a deviation from a usual approach but the added time to consider the invitation shows the Commission's empathy,' he shrugged, 'whatever the right words are. Just make it so he'd look like an inconsiderate bastard if he rejects the offer on others' behalf.'

'Ankles,' the Director laughed.

'Slip of the tongue, Ma-am.'

'I've no doubt. Why is the timing important?'

The Deputy Commissioner nodded to Sandy's boss who said, 'Pelham and his team need a month,' she said. 'Happy to brief you. Sets a precedent though, a briefing, where operational requirements may be seen to have compromised integrity of a complaint's investigation.'

'Baxter is a civilian now, although he uses his rank. We'd want to check his background, go back a few years, make sure that this complaint,' the Complaints Director tapped the file, 'is not more than the continuation of a long-held grievance. So, I'd need access to information we don't hold.'

'I can guarantee that,' said the Deputy Commissioner, 'you'd want to access Baxter's file?'

'Pelham's?'

'If you want to determine whether they served together, crossed paths, you'd need only one set of records, Baxter's.'

'What's your process,' said Sandy's boss, 'the next steps? When does Superintendent Pelham get to be informed about the complaint? Who informs him?'

'So,' the Complaints Director tucked a stray hair behind her ear, 'if experience is anything to go by, and with NSW Police, it's a certainty, your Superintendent has already been alerted. He'll know a complaint has been lodged, not anything more than that. Has he mentioned it to either of you?' she asked.

'No.'

'With complaints reported anonymously, and in this case second-hand, we would not be informing Pelham until offers to reach out to those who have reported the incidents are exhausted. Those are good enough grounds to delay him official notice. Anonymous reports of misconduct against a senior officer, reported by an ex-superintendent, it's unusual.' The Director sat back, tapped her pen on the table, 'a month,' she said, 'I think that timeline will work. Now, let's move to the decisions and this next part of the meeting will be recorded. Thank you both.'

'Would you mind,' said Sandy's boss, 'before we move on.' She took a thick file from her briefcase and handed it to the Director. 'It might be useful as background to the investigation. The Feds wanted a copy too.'

'The Feds. Are you playing me?'

'Not nearly as much as our complainant.'

'Our complainant,' she said glancing at the file cover, 'Police Service Medal, one of your finest then?'

'No doubt you'll have your own conclusions,' said the Deputy Commissioner. 'Now, if you need more information on Baxter, ask me on the record,' he nodded at her phone, 'I'll give you my guarantee.'

The meeting finished, the Complaints Director gathered her papers, phone and stood to find the Deputy Commissioner in front of the door.

'Could we impose on you further?' he asked, 'use your room for another half hour?' She left them to it.

He sat, rubbed his face, 'we've never been able to get anything on Clive Baxter. Never sure who his associates are. Pelham was in Wagga a few months and he got Baxter out of the shadows. How are you getting on with Pelham?'

'He's a bit of an oyster. Does Pelham know anything of Baxter's record?'

'Coasties,' he smiled, 'always the seafood. Starting today,' he jabbed the table, 'I want updates on Marinya, not just operational reports, I want every development on Baxter. Pelham's got under his skin for some reason, Ankles might get careless. Give Pelham enough to get him interested. I want to know what comes of it.'

I'm gunna free the water.

Harry spent the next hour circling the tumble-down shed and the shack, increasing the radius as he went, avoiding sand. He figured Lucas would walk in, but not from too far away. He'd park just off the track, and come in along the creek sandy bed, or he wouldn't. From the east with his eyes out of the sun; a breeze blew from the east, so Harry lit up and sat on a log beside the track.

He heard Lucas before he saw him, dry wood snapping, saw the top of his body first, slipping on the crumbling bank of the empty creek.

'Over here,' said Harry, moving out of sight.

'Unarmed,' said Lucas, holding his hands high, turning slowly around.

Harry came out and the two men closed the distance between them. 'Let's go back to my truck,' said Lucas, turning and facing the sun.

'That's it,' said Harry.

'You've got those three blokes stirred up,' said Lucas.

'Tell me about restoring me to my people, 'said Harry.

'That,' said Lucas.

'Better be good.'

'I posted a new podcast last night,' said Lucas, 'millions of hits already. Bouncing around the world off all our social media sites. You wouldn't have heard it of course. Know what I said, that so inspired people, millions of people?' Lucas was talking fast, head jerking from Harry to the ground, behind him, back to Harry.

'Harry, this is where you come in. I'm gunna free the water. All that fucking water in Brack's dams and tanks, all stolen. I'm letting it go. Your own people reckon unless there's water flowing in the next week or so, not enough oxygen in the water, fish will die. Then, with so little water, and what there is of it fucked with algae. No live fish.

Biggest mass fish kill coming up. Harry, we must stop that, and we can, we'll free the water.'

Harry stopped, looked at Lucas, took his forearm, 'brown snake.' Metres ahead of them, curled in the sand. Harry walked them backwards, whispered, 'we go around it.'

They were back on the track. Could see Lucas's truck.

'Free the water?' asked Harry.

'Fuck, I wouldn't have seen that,' said Lucas. 'Yeah, free the water to flow downstream. Gotta be done this week, next week at the latest.'

'You're talking a lot of water to get that far; you know how flat it is up there right?'

'Harry, average gradient is less than twenty mils a kilometre. Course I know all that.'

'What do you want from me?'

'Let the communities along the river know that there'll be a flood. Give them time to move. You'll be a hero.'

'No, I'll be a target. Like your three lads wondering why they're all alone in a Maccas' carpark, they'll be missing their mothers.'

'Oh, they're not alone,' said Lucas. 'I didn't think it through, closing. Too caught up with the water, freeing the water. So, I'm not shutting it down, I've got a woman taking over from Mike. Not joining you and Chip, just running things down here. You keep the money you got last week.'

'Lucas,' said Harry, 'where the fuck were you? We've had blokes arrested, fighting among themselves, even some starting to cook their own meth and they got busted. Cops pulling overtime, talking to everyone, got your picture. And you, you just fucked off.'

'I went walking Harry, like you taught me,' he put his hand on Harry's shoulder, 'sorry about the taser. I'm back now, it's nearly over, mate, we get that water free.'

'Who's the woman?'

'She used to run my cooks. I've got someone else doing that now, well,' he checked his watch, 'as of now. I'm down two labs. Must thank you, Harry, all those people on our payroll, they'd be pissed if they were made redundant, with no package.' Lucas giggled.

'And Mike?'

'I haven't told him about the woman yet. No reason not to, or to tell him, just a courtesy,' Lucas said.

'You really don't get mates, do you? Call him,' said Harry, 'and tell him. If he hears from someone else, you know what he's like, he'll come looking.'

Lucas's head darted towards Harry.

'OK, he'll send someone looking,' said Harry.

'If he's such a mate of yours,' said Lucas, 'why did you think he wouldn't come through with a bloke like Gino. The footage from that Ink Well too, you saving that up? Insurance?'

'No, I don't have it, thought you beat me to it, it wasn't there when I went in. As for Mike, well, that was before he came through with Gino.'

'OK,' said Lucas, 'soon as you and I are done here, I'll call him. Well, warning the people about the water, you in?'

'No,' said Harry, 'I'll arrange for them to find out, but it won't be from me. I'll stick with Gino for a bit.'

'You did surprise me,' said Lucas, 'moving on Mike's territory. Didn't take you for being greedy, that interested in money?'

'Free the water,' said Harry, 'and then what?'

'And then what?'

'Exactly,' said Harry, 'fuck all. You'll flood a few hectares, stir up a few pollies and water thieves, give it six months and we're back to where we started. I need the money so I can buy water rights and licences, not just water, and give it to the Land Councils. They'll be able to use it with their communities, that'll give them a chance to change things.'

'And you call me the waterboy,' said Lucas slapping Harry's shoulder.

He won't take me seriously.

The Director of the Complaints Commission briefed her investigators on her meeting with the senior police over the Pelham complaint. She copied them the file she been given on the complainant.

'If we'd had no political interest in this,' she tapped the file in front of her, 'it'd just be dismissed as vexatious. So, how do we go ahead without wasting anyone's time, including ours?'

'Are we that certain?'

'Unsubstantiated gossip, impounding an ex-superintendent's luxury car, signed off by two politicians he's been linked to for years. Complaints raised by a bloke who knows how the system works, and according to this file on him, played the system. No, there's something else going on, not our business, but our next steps?'

'I've studied the file,' said Ashish, 'I'd like to interview him. Go with the month, let him know the officers who gave up their allegations anonymously can come forward to us. Strengthen the case against Pelham.'

'OK,' said a colleague, 'why you? Trip to Wagga?'

'We've all looked at his file. This guy Baxter, it's not just his personnel file, is it? It's a lot more than that, it's also his record, has to have been cover ups by his bosses. Complaints about sexist attacks, belittling of gay officers, threats to transfer those who stood up to him, racist and homophobic comments. None in the last four years that we've determined, but the many complaints about his behaviour dismissed by internal investigations and meanwhile, meanwhile, promoted. This guy,' he said placing his hand on the file, 'is one of the reasons we were set up. Proof positive the force can't investigate their own.'

'All that is in there, Ashish so, what are you getting at?'

'I know,' said Ashish, 'so why this complaint? It's so,' he tapped his fingers on the table, 'it's so feeble. This bloke knows all the ropes, knows where the bodies are, and he mails us this crap.' Ashish looked around at his colleagues, sat back in his chair, puffed his chest, 'I'm gay and black. I'm almost everything he's railed against. He won't take me seriously. I can unsettle him.'

'Let me ask you this,' said Ashish leaning forward, 'if we can separate Clive Baxter from the politicians, and no-one comes forward after a month. Let's say that happens, what would we do then?'

'Well, since the Minister has taken a keen interest, I'd send him a confidential report and leave it for him to decide what to do with a retired citizen making vexatious complaints about one of his senior officers. I'd brief the two officers I met over this too, beforehand.'

There were nods and murmurings of agreement around the table, as one of the investigators spoke up, 'we usually interview in pairs,' she said.

Sound just like my husband.

Ankles left lunch at the Commercial Club in Wagga well before his fellow diners. 'Got to meet some bloke at my place. He's got a name like something you eat, that complaint I told you about.'

He left to a round of 'good luck mate, you'll be right', and when out of earshot, 'bastard, it's his shout too.'

Ashish and his colleague's taxi arrived a little after Ankles. They saw him open his front door, glimpsed the taxi moving away.

They settled down in his lounge room, both leaning back a little to escape the lunch fumes. They took turns to go through the process. Ankles hurried them along, 'you do know that I spent more than forty years doing this, don't you? I do know this stuff. Would have thought a quick look at my file would have been in order before you came. Typical of the force these days, send civilians to do an officer's job. Waste a trip from Sydney.'

'Sound just like my husband,' Ashish said, 'thinks the force is not what it was.'

'There are just a few anomalies we want to see if we clear up,' said Ashish's colleague.

'Husband,' said Ankles, 'but you're a bloke.'

'So's my husband,' said Ashish, setting the complaint on the coffee table in front of him, turning it to the second page.

'I'll have to get my glasses,' said Ankles as he stood and crashed out of the room, 'fucking hell,' they heard him slamming cupboard drawers. He returned with glasses hanging precariously.

'So,' said Ashish, 'we have been in contact with the Member for Wagga's office to arrange to meet him and talk through his version of events.'

'You've done what,' said Ankles, glasses off, hand thumping the coffee table, 'you've not my permission to do that.'

'Oh, we don't need it,' said Ashish, 'when we talked to the Member's office, we all got confused and wondered if you could clear something up for us. The date of the incident with Superintendent Pelham. Is this date correct?' Ashish pointed to the date on the complaint.

'Do I look like the kind of bloke who'd get a date wrong. I'm not the idiot here, boy. Your boss,' said Ankles standing and reaching for his phone.

'I only mention it because on that day,' Ashish checked his notes, 'the day you were troubled by what you allege Superintendent Pelham did, the person whose signature this is, well, he was in Parliament, recorded in Hansard. So, why would he say he'd witnessed the incident between you and Superintendent Pelham.'

'Because', said Ankles, standing, leaning over Ashish, raising his voice, 'he wasn't a witness to that bastard,' the words coming fast, strangled, 'he witnessed my signature.'

'Just a few more questions sir,' said Ashish he patted the seat his partner nearly lost it. 'Please.'

Ankles sat, crossed his legs.

'If he witnessed your signature,' Ashish nodded, 'then why does his signature appear above your signature, it looks like you witnessed his signature. And the same for the federal member, we've got an anomaly there, it does make it more confusing.'

'There's no need to interview the politicians,' he said. 'Not required.'

'Oh, it's required by us, by you in fact, when you named them in your complaint and had them sign it, here,' he tapped the paper, 'and here,' tapping again. 'Both members, their offices are very keen to have this cleared up.'

'No,' said Ankles, 'this can't happen.'

'Your complaint makes allegations about Superintendent Pelham's behaviour and attitude in the station. The allegations are serious, and your complaint acknowledges the officers concerned came to you as they feared for their psychological safety if they raised their concerns with their team leaders, and Superintendent Pelham.'

'Now we get to the point of this,' said Ankles. 'Pelham.'

'Well,' said Ashish, 'just so you can be prepared, we'll want to interview you, Mr Baxter, touch on your career. Given you're retired and you have lodged a complaint on behalf of others about a serving officer, we want to rule out from the very start that your complaint is not sour grapes,' Amish sat straighter in his chair, 'not about prosecuting any issue you and Superintendent Pelham may have had in the past.'

Baxter clenched his fists.

'Not today,' said Ashish, 'our office will be in touch to arrange the time.'

'I know what I'm about to say next is unusual,' said Ashish, 'however the circumstances, the severity of the allegations, the Commission has authorised us,' Ashish turned to his colleague who did not make eye contact, 'to authorise you, as it were, to let the officers who talked to you know that they have a further thirty days to think about their situation at work, maybe take some leave, and decide whether to come forward to the Complaints Commission with their complaints.'

'No,' said Ankles, on his feet again. 'No, that will not happen.'

'Because, as you would be aware,' said Ashish, 'from your service record, anonymous reports are more difficult to investigate, sometimes impossible. We simply want to help these officers,' he tapped the complaint, 'find a way for us to talk with them. Thirty days, we'll leave you to it. Thank you for your time.'

Ashish stood with his colleague, 'we'll see ourselves out,' he said.

'Just fuck off,' a whisper, not a snarl.

It all pointed to a build-up.

Wagga slept noisily. Past midnight and nearly thirty-four degrees. Sandy Pelham walked the streets, had them all to himself. The noise was struggling air conditioning units. He could see water dripping from some of them. Fans he could hear from open windows. He struggled to take a deep breath, wondered if the air was starved of oxygen in the heat. Four weeks, Darby had said, four weeks, until millions of fish killed re-took the front pages of Australian and international newspapers. One of the First Water podcasts talked about fish being sentient beings. He'd had to ring a contact he had with Fisheries to check that one out. He was put through to a scientist who said there were research papers published on how fish felt pain, put a new perspective on the fish at risk.

He fumbled with his phone and put his ear pods in to listen as he walked, the more recent podcasts from First Water. He thought they were well produced, found himself stopping every now and then as Lucas asked himself a question, paused, seemed to pause for a long time before answering. He thought that if Lucas wanted to stimulate listeners, he was doing a good job of it. Sandy had now listened to twelve podcasts, started in his car on the way back from Canberra, a few in his house, and now, walking Wagga. He agreed with the voice analysis Mick Darby had produced yesterday, thought he too could detect the change in Lucas's tone, the increased drama, more inflammatory, and more personal now as Lucas named owners of the biggest water users.

Over the past three weeks the volume of material coming from First Water increased geometrically. Again, one of Darby's experts put that down to the First Water website linking to a dozen or so social media platforms. Every post bounced from one site to the other, every crowdsourced photo or video also bounced from one site to another. Each individual piece joined with every other piece, creating a flood. First Water had a regular column in newspapers local to the Riverina communities. Readership of struggling papers like the Leader and the Eastern Riverina Chronicle soared in weeks, boosting advertisers.

It all pointed to a build-up. Rolling demonstrations across the Riverina were bigger, noisier, went for longer, exhausted Sandy's resources and yet were not getting more violent. Wagga says NO, Coleambally says NO, Culcairn says NO, Albury says NO, and on they went, linking every demonstration, building community from tens of disparate and desperate towns.

Sandy found himself back in his own street, shook his head, checked his watch, and figured he'd make a few hours' sleep until he got to the station.

Sandy took coffee in his office, read outstanding reports, actioned a few, signed others, redirected them. He refilled his coffee machine and cleared the desk and the conference table which took four if everyone knew each other well. Tassie, and his Chief of Detectives would be in soon. Together they'd draft the agenda for today's Operation Marinya meeting. He made a quick call to the IT guys to make sure everything was set up for remote officers to dial in.

The three men settled in around the table, armed with coffee and talked through who would be coming in, who would dial in, the easy details first for a few minutes.

'Canberra, how'd that go?' said Tassie, 'Mick Darby buy you dinner again?'

Sandy laughed, 'a gentleman never tells.'

'The agenda,' said his detectives' chief, 'I don't want to rush you, but I do want to rush you. Sandy, how much time do you need? Breakthrough or background?'

'Definitely background,' said Sandy, 'I need an hour mate, and they'll have questions. After lunch though, it's all background, and I'll have slides by then, being done up now.'

'OK, an hour, includes time for questions? And are you sure you want them after lunch, they'll be asleep.'

'An hour tops. They won't want to miss one word,' he grinned.

'OK, then I'll move the liaison update to before lunch, she'll he happy with that.'

'Good,' said Sandy, 'she's won the other districts over. Doing a good job. Update on Koen Barrett?'

'It's run out of puff, his phone was a burner he'd used for the two days before his overdose, and the number he called – a burner too. That's it, nothing.'

'OK,' said Sandy, 'close it will you, thanks for following it through.'

They discussed the other items, sorted the breakthroughs in order of impact on the op, and split up. Tassie to sort the logistics, parking for visiting officers, protocols to handle general inquiries, device, and phone charging stations.

Sandy walked the offices, getting himself back into the station after a few days away. He ended up back in the conference rooms, checked the whiteboards. Men and women started to file in, a few animated, many quiet. Marinya was taking its toll. He didn't think he'd help them by saying they had four weeks.

Sandy headed over to catch up with the forensic technician from Wollongong. He was stopped by the head of Rural Crime, 'can I have a word please Sandy, private?'

Sandy nodded, led the way to his office and she shut the door, 'have you heard the rumours about an expected fish kill? The guys up north are worried about the talk.'

'Talk,' said Sandy, 'they have anything behind the talk?'

'You knew, didn't you?'

He had no answer.

'You fucking knew, and you weren't going to let on, were you? Did you see the people in that room back there,' she flung a hand over her shoulder, 'they're exhausted. They're sticking with this, but you must tell them what's going on!'

Sandy slumped on the corner of his desk, knuckled his forehead, 'of course you're right. Do you have anything other than the rumours, which they should know about anyway?'

'I'm expecting an email anytime. I've reached out to the CSIRO, they've got researchers on country, and they promised to get back to me for the briefing. And, my mob is certain, unless there's water in four weeks, another huge fish kill.'

'OK,' said Sandy, 'let me call Cindi Rios, see if she knows anything. Take a seat, if she has something better, she talks to you.' Sandy opened his door and took out his phone, 'I'll let Tassie know we may be a few minutes.' How fucking stupid.

Coffee, tea, and pastries appeared and so did the rest of the team, video screens lit up as remote officers joined.

Sandy got up and the room quietened. He gave it another thirty seconds, welcomed them, and said they'd have to wait for him to say more until after lunch. The 'nos' faded and he told them, that as usual, the breakthroughs were first on the agenda, followed by the background, handed over the room and took his seat.

The name Trevor Thurlough appeared on screen, and a few seconds later the face of the man known to all as Mike Nelson. The Marinya team's forensic accountant stood.

'Trevor Thurlough changed his name to Mike Nelson in New Zealand, twenty years ago, he's now aged thirty-eight. You know much more about him. Financially, Trevor lives on a Navy pension and reports income from occasional consulting, diving work for the police. We were asked to examine his finances. We got nowhere with the name Nelson.' A diagram, list, dense, appeared on screen, some of her colleagues leaned in to make out the names, others didn't bother, 'thought we were starting with breakthroughs,' came from the back.

'Complex isn't it, like everything to do with this case. Here's the thing, here are names of accountants and lawyers, alongside names of three financially related entities. The names of the entities are partial anagrams of Trevor Thurlough, combined with a word salad of, like, property trust, holding company, investment trust.'

She put her hands out to slow a rush of questions, 'thank you,' she smiled, 'I've never felt so popular.'

An officer at the back of the room stood, 'I'm sorry I doubted you,' he said, 'I was the one with the crack about breakthrough. I wonder if I could ask the first question.'

'Watch him love, he's married.'

'Do you know how much money we're talking, and how it gets to Nelson?'

'All of these entities were set up less than two years ago, their combined value is a little over six million, money appears in these accounts quarterly, moved through the entities. Two of them,' the screen changed again, 'Trouver Holdings and Ergot Properties, own commercial properties valued at another million dollars. These are rented out and the rental agreements are signed by Nelson's lawyer. The rental income goes to a blind trust, the sole beneficiary is Mike Nelson. The trustee is his lawyer.'

'Do you know where the money in these trusts comes from?'

'They were set up with seed funds from four, at last count, international entities. Money has been paid every quarter, for the last two years, various five figure amounts. Again, names, always an anagram, or partial anagram of Von Lucas, with a sprinkling of financial terms. The Vulcan Trust for example. We are yet to prove the ownership of the international entities.'

Sandy called a break and asked the accountant about anagrams. How did she know to look there?

'Psychological profile,' she said, 'anagrams appeal to clever fraudsters with big egos, male and female. Anagrams are a clever way to disguise your real name, naming things after you is an ego trip, hiding your name in plain sight is another ego thing. It's all about something you said about Mike Nelson's name. He's a smartarse who thinks he's cleverer than us. It's thanks to you really, sir.'

'I can see you mean that,' said Sandy. 'But you and your team must take the credit,' he shook her hand, 'great work.'

He made his way to the officer from Hillston. This was the first time she'd come to the meetings in person.

'Superintendent,' said the officer, 'my boss sends his regards.'

'Yeah, thanks,' said Sandy, 'we had a good chat. Great to have you here.'

'My boss said I should get down here, spend a day, more, that's why there's only one of us, meet the others face-to-face, socialise a bit - even if it's only a night. Build a network, not something we have to do around Hillston,' she laughed.

'Good idea, stick with these officers,' Sandy nodded to a group of detectives stationed at Wagga. 'Your boss told me the burnt camper van is causing you a few headaches.'

The officer looked down, put her hands in her pockets, 'not even square one,' he said. 'My boss said to expect you to raise it with me, might have a few ideas, sir.'

'It's Sandy, and I do. Let me introduce you to the Chief of Detectives here. He'd like to learn what you know. If you're up for it, he could second a detective to work with you, bounce ideas off. You see, the van and the couple feature on the First Water website. This guy Lucas who runs the website, he wants to know if anyone knows anything. Now why would he be so interested? Were they working for him? Selling meth to Brack's seasonal workers? Brings it all under Operation Marinya.'

Sandy stood before the Operation Marinya team, no strangers in the room now. Sandy's plan was to keep the analytical teams, forensic accounting, cyber, water quality based on the data from Cindi, social network analysis by the two interns, and to focus the remaining officers on a couple of initiatives guided by the analytical team's information. This meant he was keeping small teams of detectives focused on only a couple of the matters of interest to Marinya, he realised they had their day jobs back in their local stations too. After backgrounding them on his trips to Canberra and his meetings with his peers in the other districts and commands of the Riverina, Sandy explained the challenge.

'Sit back,' he said lowering his hands, 'your body's telling you to slow down after lunch. I know mine is,' he patted his stomach, 'so slow down. Let me take you through the key pieces of Operation Marinya. Let it wash over you. Four weeks, maybe fewer. You know that we'll be managing the fallout of any fish kill, to do that I'll have to suspend this operation. So, four weeks, it's what we have, give and take a day or so, we can do that. We will make a lot happen in four weeks.'

Sandy talked as he walked around the room, along each side, sometimes in between the chairs nested around tables, pleased to see no-one on phones or devices, a few fidgeted. He talked soft enough so that his voice landed just on the walls of the room.

'What do you make of all this,' he said, 'where we have three factors coming together? They're connected, why?' Sandy opened his hands, 'why are they connected?' he asked. He felt the anticipation, tension.

'Let's take them one by one. First. Secrecy. Let me start there. From encrypted apps to burner phones, money hidden to avoid tax and fund crime, laundered, proceeds of meth. Two. Cyber expertise. Same players on the activist, eco activist website, First Water, and their firehose of a social media campaign about the corruption of water and water management in the Riverina for the benefit of the cotton industry. Three. Weapons. Same players, linked to explosives, recently recruited an unstable explosives expert, ex-military.'

Sandy slapped his hands together, 'tell me, why are these three criminal activities linked, secrecy, eco-activist hacking, and weapons? Talk it over among yourselves, answers in three minutes, nothing ruled out. We'll get a list of what you've come up with and then evaluate. No judging as we go along.'

'What do you think, Boss,' said Tassie watching as the officers huddled in groups of two, three, talking, gesticulating, writing; 'get any good out of this, change how the operation runs?'

'We might,' said Sandy, tucking his shirt in more neatly, 'we might, but for certain what it does do is two things. One, it builds everyone's stake in the op as they all have their say, secondly it lets everyone know the big picture so they can see where their part fits. You might spend your day in front of a computer chasing money. But, if you know it's linked to the other three crime sets, thirty minutes of this,' he waved an arm at the room, 'and you're part of bigger day, you're in.'

When was the last avalanche?

Gino leaned against the wall of the swimming pool, arms over the side, chin resting on the tiled edge, water ripples picking up hints of the faint moon. Harry watched him and two of his team in the water, the two young men trod water, soundless, leaving no trace, it was as though the water didn't even know these two were there. The water knew Gino was there.

The other members of the team Lucas had given Gino appeared behind Harry, took off backpacks. One of the women took out a black tarp, spread it on the deck surrounding the pool, paint faded, boards splintered, loose nails popped. All three emptied their packs of canisters, boxes, electronic detonators, wires and arranged the contents on the tarp. No rush, no hurry, they placed their stuff on the tarp once, didn't need to move it again. Everything in its place thought Harry, he could hear his mother. The pool was kidney shaped, three metres at the deep end, down to a metre at the shallow end where it was fed by a four-metre-high waterfall.

Gino's plan was to blow the waterfall and the bottom of the deep end of the pool.

'Down there,' said Gino to Harry, 'ten metres behind you, the ground falls away to a small dam. The dam wall is high and acts like a terrace. A small charge there too in case the wall holds. We should get the water across the road we drove up, to the creek on the other side, and then it's gone. These guys'll set the charges, check them, set them off remotely, read about it in the morning,' he grinned.

'What's next,' said Harry, 'another pool? I've got three more to choose from.'

'Nah,' said Gino, 'if this works, we're all set.'

'Set,' said Harry.

'The guy Brack, Lucas reckons had the couple killed in Queensland, we're going to blow his dams first. Payback. That's what this underwater caper's all about.'

'Deeper that a swimming pool but,' said Harry.

'Yeah, but we don't need to go that deep. The lower you go in a dam the stronger it gets. Blow the lip of a full dam and let the water do the work. The water spills over the wall and tumbles, just like a swimmer, but it tumbles against the wall, churning, eating away where it's weakened by the blast. His dams cascade. He's rearranged the landscape so water flows to his irrigation centres, computer-controlled gates, and sluices, very smart. But also very vulnerable, get that cascade out of control, there'll be water everywhere.'

'Fuck,' said Harry, 'pretty big payback.'

'You know I like Lucas, got his priorities right, said a person's life is worth more than all the water in Sydney Harbour, reckon that's right.'

Harry nodded. 'Where do you get this stuff from?'

'Really?'

'Curious,' said Harry, 'look mate, if's a biggie,' he shrugged.

'Snowy Mountains. Avalanche control,' Gino grinned.

'When was the last avalanche?' said Harry

You're putting a lot of weight in anagrams Sandy.

Sandy and his management team talked over the priorities, finding Gino de Bono, finding Lucas, and Harry, working on the money laundering suspected of the law firm and the accountants handling the money funnelled to Mike Nelson. Sandy wondered if one of the interns tracing the social networks wouldn't be better used with forensic accounting.

'What do you have in mind?' said his detectives' chief.

Sandy sat back, steepled his fingers, 'well, we suspect Lucas has a couple of others he needs to look after, this Harry for one, and a couple of my officers on his payroll. So, what if we had the finance people look for other anagrams of Lucas among the entities and intermediaries these people set up or have dealings with. I'm not sure I've got my head around it to be frank.'

'You're putting a lot of weight on anagrams, Sandy.'

'I am, aren't I?' he sat back, crossed and uncrossed his arms, 'but, you know,' he opened one hand, splayed the fingers, 'there's smartarse Mike Nelson, plays with his former name; Lucas, clever bloke, best meth in the country - I know,' he cut his detectives' chief off, 'assuming he organises the cooks, also plays with the letters of his name. The organisations funding the companies named for Nelson, Von Lucas, 'von' is German for 'from', such an ego. So, Lucas attracts one smartarse, maybe no others, but tell me this,' said Sandy, 'would he change the way he names companies? Four years he's hidden this shit. I'm thinking he figures he's so clever with that arrangement, and it's been a good arrangement, he'd want to stick with it.'

'OK Sandy, have the intern. We do need him back though working with my detectives. I was going to give him Hardyn Brack to investigate, social media, profile, and his network. Most of the content of the First Water website, the pictures, videos of water stored, suspected illegal dams, diverted water is on land owned or managed by Brack. Then there's the missing couple, there's a lot of angst about that on some of the subreddits, memes and gifs of Brack's security contractors. A bit more and I'll be back for a warrant.'

'Let's see what two days...no, I have no idea about time on this shit. Let's ask him. Better still, the forensic accountant? Let's bring her into this.'

'What names do you have?' the accountant asked, flipping open a tablet, keying in her password, scrolling to a blank page, 'I can set it up for your intern, he can do it tonight if he wants. We set it up, let it run, set an alert on our phones when there's a result. He doesn't need to sit there all night.'

'Of course,' said Sandy, 'of course I knew,' he paused, 'nothing about that,' he laughed, and the accountant tapped her tablet, 'names?'

'We have two more. Totally secure this?' said Sandy.

'Your suspects will never know,' she said.

'Gino de Bono,' Sandy said. 'It'd be very recent, this last two weeks. We're interested in a bloke called Harry, not much to go on and we'll get more. And Clive Baxter.'

'OK,' she said, 'We can do more on Lucas too, you see we stopped when we uncovered the links to the Thurlough companies, but he may have kickstarted others.'

'Nice work,' said Sandy.

'Very clever,' said the Chief of Detectives, 'very clever.'

'I can talk to your intern right away. Start when he's ready.'

'Thanks,' said Sandy as she left them.

'Baxter?' said the Chief of Detectives, crowding into Sandy, breathing into his ear, 'Ankles?'

'Yeah. He got a call from a young copper at Deniliquin, called a number whose owner we can't find, that same number called the lawyer who turned up for Nelson, same lawyer whose signature is on many of those word game companies. You reckon Ankles waited until he turned seventy to do Lucas a favour?'

A kindergarten hacker's dream.

Perched on uncomfortable chairs were Hardyn Brack's suited bodyguard and his security chief. On speakerphone his Sydney-based specialist IT and cybercrime consultants. Behind his desk, on his ergonomic, leather chair sat Brack, red-faced, veins in his neck standing out against his white tee shirt.

The four were listening to Brack rant about a collapsed dam wall. Brack had had a series of levees built, disguised as raised roads, to trap flood plain water. When it rained on Brack's land none of the runoff got through to rivers and creeks that he didn't control. A network of levees trapped the water, and were sloped so as one vast, shallow dam threatened to overflow, gates were triggered, and the spillage cascaded, leading to underground water storage, or ponds.

Two days earlier, as water was pumped from the top dam down, the gates didn't open. Water spilled over the top of the dams as they filled, damaging the levees. The water gurgled and hurried as the distance over which it ran grew. Gravity helped and by the time it reached the fourth levee the build-up of water hammered the levee wall, breaking it. Water danced and burbled like busloads of teenagers released from school. The land welcomed the prodigal water, gulped it down.

'OK,' said Brack, 'go through this one more time, I've got some fucking dummies in this room who need to hear this.'

'The take-away is that part of your water management system failed. You have two main interconnected networks, Hardyn. Your corporate network; office stuff, remote controlled smart home devices. That network is vulnerable, inadequate security. What I call your cotton network, your farm and water management network is highly protected. So, your water management, storage, irrigation, fertilisation regimes, your remote-controlled ground and water sensors, all of it highly protected. Your problem is that that your corporate network is interconnected with your cotton network.'

'Hacked! You fucking guaranteed me I couldn't be hacked.'

'You were not hacked. Your internet went down, exposing your network.'

'Why?'

'We've got you back up and running. We then investigated your system, your drivers were outdated. We had alerted you to have them automatically updated. They failed and now we've set you up, it won't happen again.'

'Let me get back,' said Brack and slammed the speaker phone to end the call. The consultant shrugged, there was more for Brack, but if he didn't want to know. He could be hacked through his office at the Cotton Federation which connected to his home office, and his new mobile with all the apps he'd installed was a kindergarten hacker's dream.

'You,' Brack pointed to his security chief, 'fuck off, you're sacked.'

'You saw my report, you ignored it. You get what you pay for. You don't pay enough to hire security guards to deal with your computer system. A guard has to go to special menus, open different windows to see what is going on. They get lost navigating that. As your security chief,' he consulted his phone, 'I emailed you about this...'

'Security chief my arse. You didn't stop photos going up on firstwaterdotcom, you lost it over the two backpackers, and now this. Leave an address and your stuff will be sent on. Put your phone, keys, whatever on the table,' Brack pointed. 'Now,' he stood, fists clenched, 'empty your pockets and fuck off.'

The security chief stood, emptied his pockets, one at a time, found cigarettes in one, lit one, ignored Brack's scream about smoking in his house and walked out of the room, backwards, alert to an attack from either of the men in the room.

'Insolent and incompetent,' Brack sat down.

'He's sacked, but you know what to do,' he said to his bodyguard. 'Exit interview? Hear it's a thing.'

Brack stood and opened a window, 'interview? I think he's done enough talking, don't you?'

Have you come to do my washing?

Sandy's call wasn't answered. His operator repeated it, again. Third call was answered. The operator requested status of their equipment and was assured it was all it should be.

'Confirm you understand the protocol is immediate response,' his operator pressed the men in the van a few houses up from Mike Nelson's house.

'Confirm,' came the reply. The operator pressed a few keys, turned to Sandy, 'I wouldn't worry, sir,' he said, 'equipment checks out. Probably one of the guys farted, it happens, hard to talk and not breathe at the same time.'

'They can fart all they like when it's done,' said Sandy, reaching to answer his phone.

'OK,' said Mick Darby, 'the Feds served the warrant on the lawyers, confiscated their phones, laptops, tablets and are now dismantling the computers. They'll have other phones, so we can expect Nelson's phone is about to ring, hope we have the right one tracked so he'll know his accounts are frozen.'

'Either the lawyer or Lucas will call with the bad news, thanks, Mick,' said Sandy.

'Fuck,' said Mike Nelson, ending the lawyer's call. He thumbed his phone and reached Lucas.

'You've heard the news?'

'Text.'

'Fuck that, Lucas, you need to sort this. I don't have the time. Fuck.' He was talking to no-one, threw the phone at the kitchen splashback, and heard the knocking at the door. He grabbed keys, picked up the phone, left the kitchen and stepped into the laundry, where he saw armed police out the window.

He opened the back door, hands in the air, 'if you've come to do my washing, you're a day fucking late.'

'Mike Nelson, previously known as Trevor Thurlough, I am arresting you...' The officer saw Nelson flinch at the reference to Thurlough, and continued the spiel, she did it by the book as her colleague handcuffed him.

'We're coming inside,' she said, 'is there anyone in the house with you?'

'You'd be welcome,' said Nelson.

'I'd take that as a no, wouldn't you sergeant,' she turned to the officer beside her.

'Especially,' said the sergeant looking at his watch, 'as school's in.'

Nelson lunged, shouting, and met two hands on his shoulders, chest, he was pushed back, turned around and met by another officer in his kitchen. The four of them left through the front door. Two more officers armed with evidence bags and a trolley stood aside to let them pass, and Nelson was bundled into the back of an unmarked car. He was on his way to Wagga.

Not for me.

Chip didn't get it. She'd found two ways to get to Brack's water management system and control it. Satellite connection to Brack's smartphone, access Brack's office, and then through to the remote water control system all manageable through the Cotton Federation network. But Brack paid a lot to a specialist IT crowd, surely, they were better than this. Chip wondered if there was a trap. Get closer to getting in and find masked men at my door? So, she farmed out the tasks to a couple of young hackers she mentored. Each one got a little further than the other. No masked men or women anywhere. She logged them out and set to work. Lucas had given clear instructions.

'It's about remote-controlled gates and pumps,' said Lucas, 'they will all be wrecked downstream of where Gino's explosives go to work. So, the gates, think of them as like a lock, and the pumps upstream of where Gino goes to work, they need to be opened. When Gino blows the dam walls there's already momentum building from the water you'll have released. See the timing problem.'

'Yeah,' said Chip, 'Gino's stuff goes off remotely?'

'Yeah, the swimming pool test was perfect,' he laughed.

'OK,' said Chip, 'what's next?'

'Bring up the Brack water system,' Lucas hunched over Chip's shoulder.

'Here, let me get you a chair.'

'No, this is fine.'

'Not for me,' and Chip pulled a chair over for Lucas, moved hers a little.

They studied the configuration, matching it to satellite maps of the farms, made notes, sketches.

'Lucas, what do you want from this?'

'From what, the network?'

'No, why Brack?'

'Brack. He did my people in the white van, they were there picking cotton and going out into the night to feed the website. He's also got the most water, all those pictures on the website.'

'OK.'

'He's a clever bastard,' said Lucas as he pointed to different parts of the map. 'These are separate properties,' he pointed them out, 'all different titles and as far as I could find out different owners. But, and here's the thing, the one water management system.'

'Really?'

'Yeah. I think Brack owns everything here,' he drew a circle on the map with his finger, 'water unites it. Hack his system, you now control all this water, and I want it freed up and, in the rivers, and creeks. Why Brack? He's stolen so much water, he's so well known, we'll show he's vulnerable and they'll all be worried. You up for that, Chip?'

'Yeah,' said Chip, 'I am.'

'Why are you up for it?', Lucas sat back, hands joined behind his head.

Chip picked up the map and pinned it to the wall, she turned back to Lucas, 'I said I was.'

'Guess that'll do,' said Lucas.

'The timing?' she pointed to the map, 'what's first?'

'It's got to go at the same time. The highest dams, tanks, artificial lakes. All of it. That way they'll not be able to get to the pumps and the gates lower down and work them manually. The land for kilometres around is so flat we need the momentum only volume can give us.'

'We know the capacity of at least some of these?' she pointed to dams.

'Roughly,' said Lucas, 'I'll get Gino to get you his calculations too, compare them with yours. Latest photos coming in on the website show they're all full. Even in this drought, Brack's into the aquifers.'

'OK, Gino will contact me? How?'

'You're right,' Lucas wrote on a slip of paper and gave it to Chip, 'you'll find him here. What have you found from your forensic mates, the cops, and phones?'

'They think they can link you with Clive Baxter, and to Brack.'

'Never been in contact with Brack, but Baxter has? Is that it?

'Yeah, Baxter links you and,' she tapped the map, 'this guy.'

'Leave you to it,' he patted Chip on the shoulder and left.

Chip planned to be out of the country within hours of the water breaking. Knew she'd be leaving a signature, Brack's system, firstwater website, Gino's gambling debt, her digital laboratory contact.

The stables need a clean-out.

'No.'

'Is it the money?' said Brack.

'No.'

'OK, what is it? I don't have time for this,' said Brack standing, 'and neither do you while I'm paying you.'

Brack's bodyguard sat, hands resting in his lap, 'I've enough to do, so I'm not adding security chief,' he crossed his legs, 'to my position description. Get your mate Ankles up here to do it, suits retired cops, get him used to the place, doing the rosters, keeping an eye on the team, making sure the vehicles are clean, and then get him to recruit his replacement.'

'There's a bit more to it than that,' said Brack sitting.

'Yeah, oh I forgot, beating men and women to death, burning camper vans, moving them around, starting grass fires, abusing, harassing, and screwing the cotton workers, attracting the cops. Let's see, that about cover it. Ankles'll be fucking perfect.'

Brack stared, looked around the room, shrivelled in his chair as his bodyguard stood and spoke, 'get him to straighten out that pack of arseholes, daily drug tests, uniform inspections. This chair job committee thing, there'll be people we usually keep out coming in and wanting to go all over this place, all your places. Ankles wants to make sure the idiots are courteous, mannered, clean shaven in uniforms that fit.'

'Anything else?' said Brack.

'No.'

Brack thumbed his phone, 'fuck, his number's not in here, where's my old one?'

He took the old phone out of a desk drawer, thumbed it, grunted, and the call was answered in Wagga, one of Mick Darby's eavesdroppers logged the call.

'Clive, it's me,' said Brack.

'Hardyn.'

'I've a lot on, so I'll be quick,' said Brack. 'My security chief, well I don't have one and I want you up here for the next few months. Take over his duties. He was getting a bit slack, so bring your broom, the stables need a clean out. When they're cleaned out, recruit someone to take over, and you can retire in even more luxury.'

'Stables? You into horses now?'

'No,' said Brack, gripping his phone with both hands, 'never mind. No horses, can you be here tomorrow?'

'Tomorrow, mate, bit sudden.'

'Yeah, I know, this has caught me out big time, too. Clive, I need a bloke up here yesterday I can trust. Take over my security team. They've been allowed to fall into some bad habits, I need them straightened out and earning their pay, strong rosters, daily drug tests, uniform inspections, that kind of thing.'

'Important, this?'

Brack saw no choice, 'very, otherwise I wouldn't call.' They don't call him Ankles for nothing he thought.

'Sounds like a big job. I'll come for a week, check it all out. Then, if it's as bad as you say, I've had my eye on a young bloke, get him up there with me, and in a few months, you'll have a new security chief, and a reformed team, all trained up.'

'See you tomorrow then,' said Brack.

'That plane of yours available?' said Ankles.

'If only,' said Brack, 'not this time. Advance going into your account as soon as we're done talking. Good enough?'

'Good enough. See you tomorrow.' Brack thumbed his phone again.

'OK,' said Brack, 'he'll be here tomorrow.'

'Keen, was he?'

'Greedy, too greedy.'

'Well, let's get him up here, settle him in, there'll be time then for a quiet chat, I'll look after him.'

Maybe the answer's in the water.

Mick Darby and a few of his team sat around a conference table, facing a screen filled with Sandy Pelham's face.

'Hey Sandy,' said Mick, 'mate, you might try moving back a little, turn off your desk light, better still leave it on and put it behind your screen, get the light in front of you and behind the camera.'

'You'd think I'd be used to this setup by now. We staying with the agenda, or do you have a change?'

'Hardyn Brack first,' said Mick. 'I've got transcripts of recorded conversations to send you. The important one is Brack's water management system had an event twenty-three hours ago. Brack's PR people are putting it out as a malfunction, quoting an engineer's report of no structural damage.'

'Did water leave Brack's properties?' said Sandy.

'No, why is that important?'

'Wonder if the runoff made it into any creeks, has bought us any more time to prevent the fish kill. Internet down or his water management system was compromised, and now it's fixed. And it could be nothing. It's confusing.'

'Cindi here, Sandy, it got a little more confusing. Land Councils up and down the Murray and the Darling have been alerting their communities to expect flood waters. So, the science says we're three weeks away from a massive fish kill, and the word is there'll be floods.'

'What?' said Sandy.

'Yeah,' said Cindi. 'Had calls from some of the women I met on country, they're sceptical, but taking it seriously.'

'How far north is the talk?'

'I've heard about nothing north of Hillston.'

'Mick,' said Sandy, 'Brack's security clearance, have you identified all his properties yet?'

'Only the ones easy to find, we're yet to get at the ownership of the trusts and shelf companies linked to his other properties yet. Why?'

'One more question,' said Sandy, 'what about his water rights, entitlements? There'll be records.'

'No, he got exemption. The bloke who authorised it retired early,' said Mick.

'Be good to have it before I see him, no pressure,' Sandy laughed. 'Look, it's hardly a reliable tip but some of the local irrigators say Brack owns the water entitlements in that triangle formed by Hillston, Lake Cargelligo, almost to Griffith. The word is that the properties covered by that water are all owned by Brack, no matter what the land records say. Mick, the firstwaterdotcom site, do you think that might have data to confirm it?'

Mick looked around the room, saw some nods, 'you can see the interest in that, Sandy. Cindi, you've got that. You're thinking someone else may want Brack's head?'

'He'd be keeping secrets for a reason.'

The call continued, talking through only items where the status had changed since their last call. They hadn't found Lucas, Harry, Gino. And Nelson's lawyers were stalling, saying nothing.

'This Temora swimming pool incident,' said Darby searching through papers in front of him, 'do you want to tell us more about that?'

'Not much to tell yet, local dentist and his family came home after flying to Adelaide for the week, buzzed his property before he landed, noticed the empty swimming pool. Now, he didn't report it as it shouldn't have been full.'

'Not full, why not?'

'Temora's on level five water restrictions, need approval to top up a swimming pool, he didn't have it. His neighbour noticed water on his own property, cows going through a fence to get at it. The pool had collapsed; the owner's thinking is the waterfall collapsed, broke a pump, and the pool sides fell in, so dry the ground that it made the pool unstable. I've a team there now getting the pool dug out.'

'So, Sandy, why did you send us the report?'

'A pool collapses, while the owner's away, you know how rare that is, Mick? Maybe it's something,' said Sandy, 'maybe it's nothing. The other thing about it is this,' Sandy leaned into the camera on his laptop as he pecked at the keyboard, 'footage of the protest at using water on a swimming pool for two people.' The screen froze for a few seconds, then brought the protest to life, angry men and women, student climate strikers, Temora says NO signs and a few personal signs, 'no drilling', 'illegal extraction'.

'Temora,' said Sandy, 'quiet town, something like this, you'd get a few letters to the editor in the local rag, couple of shitty phone calls to the dentist's receptionist, cancellations. But not now, I've had to pull people off the pool site, just in case.'

'Thanks, Sandy,' said Mick, 'what do you hope to learn from digging it out?'

'I've a forensics explosives investigator on the way there, she says she'll be able to detect explosives from the debris, another reason why it's taking so long. Can't just let a bobcat rip and tear.'

'Maybe Gino?'

'Let's see what she finds.'

'Maybe the answer is in the water,' said one of Cindi's nerds, 'thinking out loud here.'

'Go on,' said Mick.

'We figure Brack's water management system is remotely controlled, fully automated, sensors, the lot. Remote, wireless, satellite and Bluetooth communications systems, he combines the lot, you'd only do that for extensive land holdings. If we identify the water, dams, pipes, storage, lakes, the irrigation channels controlled by the system, then we know what water Brack has, with or without entitlements.'

'Brilliant,' said Cindi, 'trading of water in the Riverina is run by brokers, so secretive, we've not yet been able to get their records. So, water ownership is shrouded. But data on the remote-controlled management of water, that'd kickstart the conversation. Nice work,' she ruffled the officer's hair.

'OK,' said Mick, 'that's for your team, Cindi. Before we move on, Sandy, what information do you need about Brack's water?'

'The configuration management system.'

'Which in English,' said Darby, 'would be?'

'Think of it as a whiteboard plastered with different coloured post-it notes,' said Cindi, 'the position of each post-it on the board follows a code. The notes represent sensors, software, servers, controllers, computers, lines joining the post-its show connectivity.'

'Do we have this configuration management system?' said Mick.

'We can put it together,' said Cindi.

'Thanks,' said Darby, 'the couple from the burnt-out van, Sandy?'

'Nothing yet, I have one of my officers in Hillston. She and one of the locals,' Sandy looked away from the camera, 'they'll arrest the security guards tomorrow, drive them here. I'm hoping to cut through their bullshit when they realise their protection's gone.'

'Mike Nelson,' said Mick, 'last on the agenda, Sandy.'

'He'll be in Wagga in an hour. A local lawyer's already been here, don't know if he'll be taking her though, she's not the calibre he's used to. Nothing on the number he used to call Lucas. There've been some violent assaults on dealers, some users caught up in some of the violence around Swan Hill, Deni, Albury in the weeks since Nelson's arrest. Brothel windows smashed, arson in a wrecking yard, tyres still burning. Consistent with what we know of turf warnings, bit of muscle flexing. Thing is, we've not had this kind of stuff for years. Informants are not giving us much. They will be when it settles, they'll figure out who to inform on.'

'OK,' said Mick, 'what do your people make of it?'

'They want to find out from their informants, turf wars over meth, not had one, so the most common theory is a new player, no evidence of that though. If it's connected it could be that Lucas, if it's him, is losing control. The discipline is weakening, we also picked up a load of illicit tobacco, two warehouses of counterfeit clothes.'

'I don't get it,' said Mick, 'the significance.'

'Illegal tobacco, counterfeit goods, and violence go together. Usually in high-density, low-income areas, where there's a market for cheap stuff and the violence keeps everyone in line. Thing is that what's been missing, or at much reduced incidence, here for a few years. Now, it's up, why? What's changed?'

'We'll get what you need to you on Brack's system right away. Thanks for your time, mate.'

'Good talking as always. Now you're not about to do a Columbo on me again are you?'

'Don't know,' said Mick, 'you may have heard already. Ankles is to be Brack's new security chief. Starts tomorrow,' he ended the Zoom call.

Let's just leave it all behind us.

'Trevor Thurlough,' said Sandy.

'Let me stop you right there,' said Thurlough's lawyer, 'my client's name is Mike Nelson. I insist you refer to him using his legal name.'

The interview did not get any better. Sandy had a bunch of folders in front of him, almost twenty centimetres high.

Sandy opened the top one, removed a single sheet of paper. Photograph of a Toyota ute, registration details, VIN, ownership records, he pushed it across to Nelson, 'would you confirm your ownership of this vehicle please?'

Nelson pushed it back, one finger.

Sandy produced photographs, mobile phone records, downloaded GPS tracks, list of vehicle registration plates, video footage, sound recordings, lists of company names, financial records, invoices for vintage motorcycle spare parts, property records.

During the breaks Sandy sought advice from senior colleagues and Operation Marinya's allocated psychologist. He used most of their suggestions. Still using the one finger Nelson pushed documents back, kept pushing so the pile in front of Sandy threatened to spill. He restored them, arranged neat batches, tapped them on the desk to straighten the edges. He wondered if Nelson noticed, the lawyer certainly did, he could feel her eyes on him, assessing him. Would it distract them though, get them off guard? Or let them know something they could use on Sandy?

'I can see,' said Sandy, pushing all his paperwork to one side, 'this is difficult for you to talk about. I had to try and make sense of all this information, all this,' he smoothed the papers beside him, 'all this different, some conflicting information. Now, let's just leave it all behind us.'

'I hope you'll be leaving it behind with me,' Nelson's lawyer said, but stopped talking as Nelson put his hand on her forearm.

'So,' said Sandy, 'you'll allow me,' he sank in his chair, 'to leave it all behind us and see what we're going to do about it all? Do you have any suggestions, ideas about where we might go to from here?' The lawyer leaned in, sat back when Nelson again touched her on the forearm.

'How would you feel,' said Sandy, 'if you could not see any of these people again,' he tapped the piles of paper, 'not spend any of this money,' tap, 'not ride these bikes,' tap, 'not live in these properties,' tap, 'not go out with these women,' tap, 'not drive these cars.'

I've had more rapport with a statue. Sandy sat back in his chair, gathered the papers, shuffled them together, tapped the mound on the table to straighten it, the paper resisted order, so Sandy arranged and rearranged, he looked at Nelson, 'we'll just go ahead anyway without your participation. We have a process, we'll make decisions about you, on your behalf, decisions without your input.'

Sandy stood up, aligning paper on the table corner, felt their eyes on his obsession, opened the top file and held out an envelope, 'you might want to read this.'

'What decisions?' said Nelson ripping the envelope, reading the single sheet headed "assets forfeiture order"'.

'Those decisions,' said Sandy, seeing Nelson stumble as he tried to stand, mouth open.

The officer inside the door moved towards Nelson, who sat down, his choked questions kept coming. The lawyer began to talk, this time, no check from Nelson.

'My client,' said the lawyer, 'has the right...'

Sandy checked his watch, leaned over the recording device, 'interview terminated at 1540 hours,' and switched off the machine.

Mick Darby had listened to the key parts of the interview record and called Sandy.

'How did you feel doing that? Silent type, isn't he, keeps his mouth shut?'

'Probably useful skill, underwater.'

People around their offices looked up, looked at each other, shrugged, bosses laughing, someone's in the shit.

'Stop it,' said Darby, tissue to his eyes.

'Right until the very end, good job you got that assets order through so quick. Catch you tomorrow.'

More of a FIFO.

'Tassie, you got anything on tonight?'

'Apart from the usual you mean.'

'I'll take it then you can spare me an hour or so. How about you come round to mine around seven thirty,' said Sandy, 'steaks, salad, few beers, a nice red. Just want to think out loud, away from all this,' he waved at the offices through his door.

'But...,' said Tassie.

'Of course,' said Sandy getting up, 'look mate, we won't be on our own, you know. You know we get together whenever she's at the uni, which is not often enough. She's been seconded to the uni so moving in then, and consulting all over the country, looking forward to it. Its not a problem, not a problem she'll be there and not a problem that everyone knows.'

Sandy opened his door at seven thirty, welcomed Tassie, took him inside, introduced him to his partner.

'I'm more of a FIFO than permanent part-time,' she said, laughing, arm through Sandy's. He reached for her hand, she no longer imposed chaos on his order, and accepted he walked for much of most nights.

'I won't even pretend to understand that' said Sandy, 'come through, mate, too hot to eat outside so we're in here.'

Tassie looked through the sliding doors.

Sandy nodded, 'yeah, barbie, otherwise the stove'll heat the place up. I'll put them on in,' he talked to Siri on his watch, 'eight minutes.'

They took their beers outside and when the timer sounded Sandy put three steaks on the hotplate, 'rare, medium rare, not well done?'

'What's your rare like?'

'Rare. It'll come running if you call it.'

'Rare then, thanks mate.'

Sandy set his timer again, turned the meat when it rang, set it again, took the temperature of the steaks, turned the gas off, 'a few minutes to rest,' he said.

By nine o'clock the three of them had settled in lounge chairs, red wines, and port.

She sat snuggled up beside Sandy, 'happy if I stay?'

'Sure,' said Sandy, hand out to Tassie.

'Hoping you do,' said Tassie. 'You put us onto the super-recruiter. Nelson sits at the top of one bunch of them.'

Sandy, 'for us, the prize is meth throughout the Riverina. Operation Marinya. That's where Mike Nelson is important, why we need to find Lucas, Harry. I think those three, they're the ones we want, they're so well quarantined from everyone else we get hold of, dealers, users. There's something we're not getting though don't you think?' He passed cheese around.

'Last six weeks, we've had more pub fights, assaults, presentations at hospital with serious injuries, and everyone we've picked up has prior, no civilians. Shoplifting, young, old, men, women, how long since we've had so much shoplifting? Add the tobacco, counterfeit goods.

Tassie sat back, 'the guys say it's yet to peak, breaks and enters are up, homes and non-dwellings, stolen cars, mainly four by fours.'

'Stealing from cars, what about that?' she said.

Sandy and Tassie spoke at once, 'no.'

'Refills?' said Sandy.

'Have you guys taken any meth labs, seized meth?' she said.

'Yes, two very different labs,' said Tassie, 'just in the last month, before that, nothing, well no labs anyway.'

'Two labs?'

'One was an easy catch,' said Sandy, 'put all their rubbish - Coleman camp fuel, starter-fluid spray cans, drain cleaner, empty cold-medicine packages, plastic tubing, glass jars, funnels, scales, coffee filters, needles, syringes, empty bleach bottles, broken glass in the Otto bins, including the green one, so the Council tipped us off.'

'So, not our smartest.'

'No,' said Sandy, 'the guys we're after, take Mike Nelson, he'd go nowhere near these clowns. So, Tassie's spot on, we've busted a lab, we would have anyway.'

'Now, the other one. We had to track it down, we got intel from Cindi Rios, chemicals, and meth residue in water treatment plants. They narrowed the areas down for us. As they got more water and sewage samples, we could pinpoint where the labs were, in one case to it being one of five small properties. Then with rental records, building specs, surveillance, we rolled them up.'

'Never heard anything like it,' she said, 'no media stories.'

'Not so far,' said Sandy, 'not before the courts yet, keeping it quiet, we're not finished.'

'So, you busted this one through technology, not dickheads, what other differences were there?'

'Tassie's across the details.'

'It was spotless, ventilated, cooks all women, protective gear, masked up, an example to us all. We watched them, saw their rubbish collected, again blokes in protective gear, as thorough as professional forensic cleaners.'

'Fascinating,' she said, getting up to pour more port, 'arrests?'

'That's where it gets tricky,' said Tassie, 'the lab also ran legitimately; chemical testing, small scale chemical manufacture, supplying nail salons, tanning studios. Victorian firies, Fire Rescue, sent fire debris for chemical analysis to them, raved about their work.'

'Arrests?'

'All women, quiet, no fuss, cooperative, polite, well-drilled. Expensive lawyers, no boyfriends screaming, bailed. They've even lodged a business interruption insurance claim, got that on our back. Mountains of paperwork, orders, despatches, invoices, import records to fossick. We found no meth, just the makings, materials, and most of the chemicals.'

'Tipped off?'

'Tassie and I,' said Sandy, 'we think not, we think we got there at the end of a batch. We're following up all vehicles logged in and out, the women under surveillance, going through their houses, nothing so far.'

'We have a few, Sandy's boss in Wollongong included, who reckon they were tipped off. Doesn't add up. Why come to work if you were tipped off? Their information must have been in time to clean the places out, but nothing destroyed, nothing dismantled, makes little sense. No, we reckon they'd completed cooking a batch. The women claim they were just processing routine orders.'

'Clever, they expect to get away with it,' she leaned forward, 'they know, they know they'll get away with it.'

'If you connect the dots, it's this guy Lucas.' Sandy opened his tablet, scrolled, and flicked, 'check this photo,' he said to Tassie, 'I've sent it for release.'

'I extended the search for scientists who'd been sacked in the last three years to post-graduate students. This guy from South Australia, undergraduate and postgraduate science, dropped out of a PhD in environmental science, Lucas. False surname. Tassie, does it fit, could it fit?'

'You know, the question I ask is, is there a reasonable explanation for it not fitting? If it's not Lucas, Nelson, Harry,' said Tassie, 'if they're completely unrelated, then is the lab legit?'

'The question I ask,' she said to Sandy, 'is why are we here,' she gestured to Tassie, 'two of us listen to you think out loud.'

'I don't like to do it at the office,' he said, 'some are yet to get used to me, still got officers too keen to impress, too quick to take everything I say as gospel. Delegating for me, well, let's just say it's a steep learning curve, which means for them trust and confidence is a work in progress, for some of them still anyway. No, not you two. Plus, you don't shoot me down just for the sake of it either.'

'Wouldn't count on that,' she said, blowing a kiss.

At the front door, 'thanks for the feed,' said Tassie.

'Anytime, and thanks, got it in my head now I think, got a better handle on it, I'll walk you to the end of the street.'

'How much have you got from Mick Darby's tap on that bent detective in Coota?'

'Nothing, not a whisper. He's had a few of those bullshit texts about an unclaimed parcel, ever get them.'

'Fuckers.'

'Yeah, well the texts are a bit weird, Darby's nerds reckon those texts are a contact, and so he must call back on another phone.'

'Too clever,' said Tassie, lighting a cigarette.

'Yeah, so I'll run it past the team about reporting him to Internal Affairs. He's been useless for us, and now as we learn more, we don't know who contacts him, and who he talks to.

'And Darby?'

'Happy. His people think if the Coota guy's in with someone that clever, he's unlikely to turn easily, and neither of us have the manpower.'

'You're not doing everything yourself,' said Tassie breathing smoke, 'not keeping stuff to yourself, your managers notice the change, they're talking about it, they like it.'

'Thanks mate, it's giving me more time, I got, still get, a bit lost in the weeds.'

'See you in the morning,' said Tassie, 'and thanks again for tea, mate. No, you won't be in tomorrow, will you?'

'Off to talk to Brack. Mick Darby thought it'd be useful for me to take him through the security vetting process. I agree, want to get a handle on him, be gone a few days.'

'Still surprised Darby wants you to interview Brack,' said Tassie.

'Typical Mick, hands be glued to his chest,' said Sandy, 'other than Mick, there aren't many choices, it's not only Ankles that Brack has on his payroll. Plus, I want to meet him, get a feel for the guy. Be interested to find out if he knows Lucas also has Ankles in his pocket.'

Tassie laughed. 'Be the end of Ankles.'

'Yep.'

'Enjoy yourself then, mate.'

Tassie turned left and Sandy right to go around his block. He could walk Wagga with his eyes shut he thought, as he twisted in his ear buds, chose his podcast, walked the next block, and the next. He lit another smoke at number thirty-seven, smiled that their air-conditioning was fixed.

Moral character.

'They've been coy about this, what is the role, do you know?' Hardyn Brack was talking with his back to Sandy, waving him to a seat, the other side of the desk.

Sandy stood.

'I know the vetting process, security check, financial check, it's extensive, biggest one I've been a part of, so the role is very important. Future of the Riverina they're calling it. They've completed quite a background, detailed profile,' Sandy riffled through a file of blank paper, 'so I also know they are very keen.'

'You keep saying "they",' said Brack, reaching for the file in Sandy's hand.

'Sure,' said Sandy, 'it'll be yours to keep when the vetting is complete. As to who is behind this, I only know I was asked by Water Intelligence and Security.'

So far, the interview with Brack had gone mostly along the lines Sandy and Mick Darby had predicted. Brack was used to controlling interactions, he asked the questions, he decided when a conversation was over, he decided what was to be talked about, he decided what next. Sandy and Mick figured Brack would be difficult to shift, couldn't expect him to be the opposite of what they knew of him. Sandy's task was to get Brack to compile his own on-line assessment, rather than the one sent in his name done by Liz, on her laptop. They had data on Brack's business, had their assumptions, information, now they wanted Brack's story, as told by Brack.

Brack got up and walked past Sandy, opened the door, stood aside. Sandy stood, not quite to his regulation full height and stepped forward to shake hands with two metres of conceit.

'Clive Baxter, my Chief of Security,' said Brack. 'I've heard you've met.'

'Well, well,' said Ankles, 'look who's here, hoped you parked your car legally. Yellow tie suits you Pelham.'

'Clive,' said Sandy, 'always a pleasure. I wasn't expecting to meet you here,' he turned to Brack, 'there's another Chief of Security listed as one of your referees on the background you provided.'

'Forget him.' said Brack, 'No longer with us. Baxter's not here as a referee, he's the witness to this conversation.'

'In that case,' said Sandy, 'he should have a copy of this too.' Sandy opened his satchel and took out a few sheets of paper, handed one each to Brack and Baxter, 'it's a list of the areas we want to go over today, not covered in the paperwork you've submitted.'

'Long list,' said Baxter, 'sure it's all relevant, Pelham? Looking to sticky-beak into how the other half lives, eh?'

Brack studied the list, 'you know what Clive. Don't think you'll be needed here at all.'

'I don't think you'll have the time for all of this.' Baxter waved the paper at Brack.

'Thanks Clive. That'll be all, oh,' he called him back from the door, 'leave the paperwork behind, would you? Thank you.'

'Now,' said Brack, 'I'm taking these as conversation starters?'

'In no particular order,' said Sandy, 'I'll take some notes, if you don't mind, and let's cover as much as you've time for.'

'Cover them all,' said Brack. 'Got to love the excitement of a new hire,' he smiled, gestured to the door, 'like a new puppy, you hope it doesn't piss on the carpet.'

'He's hardly new,' risked Sandy.

'You two know each other?'

'I followed him into Wagga, I know of him, met a few times socially. I inherited most of his staff, good officers.'

'Yeah, I hear you've been pissing on carpets in Wagga, worse than that. The new pup in town,' Brack barked, hands up like paws. 'They still use his nickname?'

'I've never encouraged disrespect of officers,' said Sandy.

'Ah,' said Brack leaning back, hands on his armrests, 'conservative?'

'There's nothing on here about your politics,' said Sandy picking up his copy. 'Can I clear up one thing, though? Is Clive now a referee?'

'Shit no.' said Brack, 'I've only known him a week.'

Sandy made a note, only interested in material to be used in later interviews with Brack.

'Let's move to digital footprint,' said Sandy. 'I don't know who makes up these names, but this one made sense when I understood it to mean anything you've touched on-line.'

'Could have fooled me,' said Brack.

'Apparently, they're not that interested in porn. Be more interested if you hadn't accessed any.'

Brack's cheekbones warmed.

'Of interest,' said Sandy, 'is stuff like this. You signed your signature, digital signature, to your on-line assessment. Thing is that assessment was completed on Liz Evan's laptop in the Federation offices while you were not in that office.'

'What, I'm supposed to do that myself? Sit at a fucking computer for hours. She knows everything about me needed for that stuff. I had a look and cleared it with her.'

'They really want you for this job. They never give a candidate a second go at a security assessment. You're the exception, they told me. Hardyn, the politics of water in the Riverina, I'm sure you're across it. You run, what a thousand square kilometres of the Riverina?'

Brack didn't deny that.

'The Minister wants you to chair this enquiry, wants you involved up front in helping finalise the terms of reference. It's been made clear to me also what she doesn't want. She doesn't want to know of any reason to not appoint you.'

Brack was hearing Sandy as he saw himself in an armoured Commonwealth car, parked at the reserved lift under Parliament House, ushered into the Minister's office, all while his broker traded water ahead of anyone else.

'So,' said Sandy, holding up a printout, 'this would blow it. Wrong,' he put the papers on the desk, 'wrong digital footprint.'

'Sandy,' said Brack, 'ten years of my life, overseas visits, relationships, financials, now this digital shit, where does it all end? I'll just dictate it, sign an affidavit.'

'Twenty years,' said Sandy, 'not ten, twenty.'

'I was in the States then, Sandy, fuck I was only a student. How the, how is that relevant?'

'Twenty years and not ten. Back then you were in Texas on a Rotary scholarship, won a Monsanto scholarship and married, then divorced a US citizen, who now works for a Texan senator. Same senator headed the scholarship fund which awarded you the grant. That Texan senator spent four days here, in your home, two years ago on a tour of the Riverina. That visit was not listed in this material,' he slapped the printout. 'Because it's not listed, the Minister's rivals would assume you've something to hide, sniff conflict of interest. Future of the Riverina,' Sandy shrugged, 'apply to join the public consultations, you'll be in the queue just like everyone else.'

Brack picked up the list, 'details of partners, relationships, overseas relatives,' he read, 'let me jump to financial details, real estate holdings, investment accounts, major assets. Twenty years. On-line plus supporting documentation, in here at my computer. Is that it?'

'Almost,' said Sandy, 'you complete this, submit the details, all the other checks will be done.'

'Other checks, what checks?'

'Police records check, ATO, passport check on overseas travels, referees' check, including referees not submitted by you.' Sandy wanted to say enough to stress Brack but not frighten him off.

'Referees, what do they ask them? Is that what you'll do?'

'No. Referees are asked to talk about things like your relationships, political views, use of alcohol, a mix of personal and professional.'

'And then.'

'All that material is used to develop an overall picture of what they call, moral character. Your integrity.'

'Integrity. Hmmm. Speaking of integrity, all those checks you mentioned, and I'm guessing that's not the full list, I'd need to give my permission?'

'Oh, you do,' said Sandy, 'you need to agree they be done, and you have.' He picked up the printout, 'and they've started.'

Brack sat back in his chair, even for a bloke his size it seemed to swallow him.

Sandy gave it enough time to cause Brack a little more discomfort, 'look, the thing is, a security check comes down to one thing, one thing,' said Sandy. 'Is there anything in your last twenty years that might improperly influence your job as Chair. She'll want to be dead sure there's nothing.'

'Improperly influence, that from Jane Austen?' Brack sniffed.

'You tell me,' said Sandy leaning back, his job done, not disclosing in a vetting process that you hosted a Texan senator whose family holdings include the biggest cotton conglomerate in the US, major competitor of Australia in the international cotton market, gave you a scholarship, what was that, pride or prejudice?'

'Ah fuck,' said Mick Darby, his colleagues heard him over their headphones, 'Sandy, you've gone too far.'

'The process is personal.' Sandy stood, gathered his papers, tracked by Hardyn, 'it's sensitive, it's part of the paperwork used to decide your clearance, it's the clearance that's public, not that paperwork.'

'Sensitive? Private?' Brack's hands on the edge of the armrests, feet back on the ground, flat, back not yet straight.

'Hardyn,' said Sandy, sitting down, hands open, elbows at his sides, a shrug of the shoulders, 'this is how you're coming across to me. Every time I mention this,' he put a hand on the clearance paperwork, 'you push back, find an excuse not to do it. So, are you not up for this job? You trying to tell me that because that's the impression I'm sensing. Now, I don't want to go away with that impression of you, report that impression, if it's not correct.'

Brack reached behind him, opened a bar fridge, and took out a bottle of water, sparkling. It slipped, before it hit the table he grabbed it, opened it. Water fizzed over the desk, over Brack, 'fuck,' he stood, wiped himself down.

'You know we could log this as the preliminary record,' Sandy held up Liz's attempt at the online assessment, 'you wouldn't need to repeat the information filed here.'

'It'd be accurate, everything that girl does is accurate,' said Brack.

'Accurate and incomplete,' said Sandy putting it in the desk, 'great start.'

Brack looked at the printout, gathered the loose sheets so they faced him.

'What do you think you might do?'

'Get a proper chair, this one's just for show, gives me a crook back when I use my computer. Looks like I'll be here for a while, twenty years of records, fuck.' Brack ran a hand through his hair.

Body language, so revealing, isn't it?

'Didn't expect to see that bastard Pelham again. Not up here,' he stood and pointed at the lake dominating everywhere he looked, 'not on my second day.'

'Let's make sure it's not your last, Clive,' said Brack's bodyguard.

'What the fuck are you talking about?' said Baxter, heart rate doubling, 'I don't even know your fucking name.'

'That's OK old son,' he said, 'I know yours and if you're a good senior citizen, boosting his pension with money he won't report, I may even tell you. Now, just take a seat, here will do nicely,' he pushed Baxter into the chair he'd just left, 'that's it, comfortable? Herdyn has asked me to induct you properly, on-boarding I believe it's called now, into the culture of Delaney Holdings.'

The tall thin man sat opposite Baxter, started talking. Baxter had to lean even closer to hear. The man would follow every piece of information, each instruction with 'you got that, understood?' and jab his knee with knuckle of his index finger. So hard Baxter's knee jerked.

'I'll take that as a "yes" shall I? Body language is so revealing isn't it?' Another jab to the patella, another knee jerk reflex.

Clive Baxter needed a piss after an hour, and this tall, thin bloke dressed in black was not letting him go, a spot darkened the front of his khaki jeans, he could feel more dribbles.

'You see, play nicely, I'll get you a uniform, black, then when you piss yourself, it won't show.' Another jab. 'Will it?'

Playing nicely Baxter learned was a job for six weeks until the rollout of robot security patrols was done. Tasked with firing the existing security crews to a schedule he had thrust at him, train up two crews of casuals from a labour hire company in case they were needed, stay away from Brack, all at half the pay Brack had promised.

'Don't worry, you'll know if he wants to talk to you, so be ready. Understood?' Baxter winced, but the jab didn't come.

Later that night, dressed in his black uniform, pants too loose, shirt too tight. Baxter took his smokes, refilled his flask, and left his donga, limping. He coughed, tasted tobacco, spat, took a sip from his flask, rinsed his mouth, another sip, swallowed this time. The clear night, close stars, moon on the lake, lost on him. He contacted Lucas.

Fill the swamp, not drain it.

Lucas, Harry, Chip and Gino finalised the attacks on Brack's water. They had maps of the Brack controlled water and land, which Chip overlaid with transparencies of the web-based water management system.

'It's got to be simple,' said Harry. 'Gino's explosives break levee walls, dam walls, canals, locks, and weirs. When these barriers are breached the water will rise, overflow. Chip's task is to open gates and keep them open so that water flows freely. The sensors monitoring water levels need to be disabled. We want the water to flow southwest. Lucas, that's where you want it?'

'Yes,' said Lucas, scratching at his chin with both hands, shifting from foot to foot, 'I want the water south to the Lachlan River. If we get enough water freed up it might even reach Griffith here,' he pointed,' and Booligal here,' he traced the map, 'it'll spread out, slow down, but it should get grass in the paddocks, keep the fish alive. Everyone's gunna fucking love it.'

'How much water do you need?' asked Gino.

'All he's got,' said Lucas. 'All of it. Fill the swamp, not drain it,' Lucas jumping, hands in the air, 'fill the swamp, fill the swamp, don't drain it, fill it.'

'OK, OK mate.' said Chip, 'what if I open these,' she pointed to symbols on the map, 'if they're compromised, everything dependent on them, bores, pumps, water lines, regulators, channel outlets, is compromised.'

'You can do that from your laptop?' asked Gino.

'Agritech,' said Chip, 'geographic information systems, GPS, on-site remote sensing, automatic controls, miniaturised computer components, mobile computers,' she drew breath, 'yeah, Gino, from a laptop.'

213

'Gino, where are you and your team on this?' Harry pointed to the map.

'Mark up these coordinates,' said Gino holding a sharpie to Harry, 'OK and join them up too.'

'The water here,' he pointed to the northern end of the boundary, 'is held back by levees, connected to each other by underground pipes activated by pumps, for example, here and here. Roads connecting each site sit on top of the levee. You can see from these satellite pics, the water is stored in huge rectangular, artificial lakes on what were the flood plains. It's a grid, so, we blow the weakest points, where four lakes intersect. Here,' he marked a red cross, 'here, here, and here. We lay strips of explosive at the intersections, and above the pipes which interconnect.'

'The pipes, how much time to get down to them, what four, five metres deep,' said Chip.

'Ah,' said Gino tapping the side of his nose. 'At the intersections there are valves so that any of the four pipes can be opened or shut. One failed a few years back and they took days to find and fix the problem. Now they have IPs, inspection points at every intersection. They sit proud of the roads, like an old-fashioned silent cop, little metal cap, comes off with a handy hook, three hundred mils shaft right down to the valve. Just drop a stick down.'

'Drop a stick down,' said Lucas, 'drop a stick, fill the swamp, fill the swamp,' taking little jumps, arms out by his sides.

'Lucas,' said Harry holding him around the shoulders, 'how long since you had a feed. Come on, take this,' a can of Jack and coke, 'I'll cook these up,' he held up a couple of MRE packs, vegetable curry, 'won't take long mate.'

Quite right, me, I love a day off.

Brack's security guards worked ten days on, four days off. Housed around his properties, they didn't leave until the end of their ten days. Some didn't leave then, exercise, gym work, video games, porn, satisfied with making the most of a temporary home.

The two guards the detectives sought were among those keen to get away at the end of their roster. Unknown to their boss and their colleagues these two were an item.

Sandy's team knew they were a couple, knew they liked to hurt people, each other.

'Stop their vehicle as soon as its off Brack's land, here, along the flat,' Sandy's finger traced the road. 'Normal random breath and drugs test, there'll be an unmarked stopped already, backup, and pull over the vehicle behind them, more backup. They're murder suspects, and they're sure they've gotten away with it, cocky and dangerous.'

They were driven to Wagga separately. Everything in their ute confiscated, data on their phones downloaded, copied.

Sandy and Pip, the Hillston detective, took coffees and sat in Sandy's office with Marinya team leaders and refined their approach to the interviews.

'Let's see if we can get them to talk to us without a phone call, without lawyers,' said Sandy. 'You've talked to these two before Pip.'

'I got nothing after their lawyer turned up last time, and even then, I only had their names. Then my boss told me we'd have to find another way, pressure from upstairs. So, I guess this is the other way.'

'Let's interview the woman first,' said Sandy.

The three of them settled into one of the Wagga station's interview rooms, all sitting easily, nothing to fear here, used to it. The security guard looked about her, took in the two and a half by three metre room, industrial lino, small triangles of pet dust in each corner, walls faded and scuffed, a table between her and the detectives. Sandy and Pip introduced themselves and informed Brack's employee of the charges, cautioned her, read her rights, she didn't want a lawyer.

'I thought you'd want to talk to us together,' she said.

'We'd like to follow up, routine stuff where we're hoping you can help us out,' said Pip.

'Follow up what?' said the woman.

'We met in Hillston,' said Pip, 'you were interviewed about a missing couple, last seen around the properties of Hardyn Brack.'

'That's it, this is over,' she slammed her hands on the desk, leant forward, 'phone call each, I remember you now.'

'Always nice to be remembered,' said Pip, 'thing is you have three and a half days left of your four day lay-off, your lawyer's not local. We'll hold you until she gets here, you won't have any time left for the art galleries, museums, and wineries. This is an invitation to talk to us, clear up a few details, loose ends. Shouldn't take long.'

'So, why did you caution me? I want to call our boss,' she said.

'Hmmm.'

'"Hmmm," what is that?'

'Look, security guard, casual, not permanent,' Sandy with hands in front of him, one on top of the other on the table, 'I get it, you need to get on well with your boss, stay in his good books, so you can get a leave pass together, get the rosters that suit your relationship. That how it works.'

'Look, I need to call him, let him know where we are, I'm entitled to a call. He's an ex-cop, he'll have you two.'

'Your new boss?'

'I never said he was new.'

'Clive Baxter, ex-cop, used to be my boss in Wagga when I started out.' Pip leaned into the guard, brushed hair from her forehead, lowered her voice, 'taught me a lot, Clive did. This missing couple is very much BMT for Clive, but he doesn't want anything to come back and bite him now it's his watch.'

Pip picked up a piece of paper, turned it over to show the guard a photo of Clive Baxter in his black Delaney Holdings uniform, 'c'mon mate, how do you think we knew when you were leaving Hillston?'

'BMT, what is that, a secret cop code?'

'No. "Before My Time". What that means in your profession,' she gestured at the guard, 'and ours,' hand on heart, 'is that no one wants to get surprised by yesterday's crap. I bet he asked you if there's anything that's gone on that he needs to know about. Never forgotten the day he asked me that.'

'Look, we're not team leaders, we're grunts. You've talked to Baxter then? Been there?' she pointed to the photo.

'Let's have that talk,' said Sandy, 'you can always call him or your lawyer, if you feel you need to. Let's give you some time to think it over. Coffee, tea? Can I get you anything?'

'No, I'm good,' she looked up, 'thanks.'

'You're doing a good interview in there Pip,' said Sandy. 'Just enough to get her off guard and not enough to close her down.'

'She's not said anything useful, has she?'

'Pip, she's talking, she'll find that hard to stop, even allows my interruption.'

'Rapport, establishing rapport,' said Pip.

'You know,' said Sandy raising his cup to take a sip of water to find the cup empty, he crushed it, 'I'm not sure what establishing rapport means. I am sure that getting suspects talking in these rooms,' he gestured down the hallway, 'about anything to begin with, them talking way more than us, that's what you're doing. She's staying with you, she's looking at you and she doesn't want a lawyer.'

'I'll take her through the photos,' said Sandy, 'watch her and jump in if you think I miss an opportunity. Then you take her through the complete picture.'

The interview room's aircon kept the room comfortable, Sandy and Pip came back in, shut the door, and sat.

'Interview recommenced at 1013 hours,' said Pip and announced those present.

'Just for the record,' she said, 'for your benefit if it's needed later. You'll want to be able to let Baxter know exactly what happened, right?'

'What was he like to work for?' she said.

'He's never been my boss,' said Sandy. 'Thanks for sitting down with us. We're interested in going over the details of you and your partner finding the van. I'll take a few notes now and then, if that's OK, helps me think.'

'You need help, do you?'

'Ouch. So, you saw the van?'

'Yes.'

'Can I show you a photograph,' Sandy put two photographs down and slid them across the table, adjusted them so they fit together, 'this is the van?'

'Yes,' she looked down at the photos.

'Got a few more photos here,' he put another three down, butted them together side by side, 'can you confirm this is your vehicle, your private vehicle at the fire scene. And this,' turning over one of the photos, 'can you tell me who this is beside your vehicle?'

'Well, it's my ute, and that's me obviously.'

'OK, thanks for that, taking our time here. I'm interested in, I want you to tell the truth as you know it. Tell me about how you discovered the van.'

She kept talking, needing few prompts, Pip made a few notes, she'd do the next part of the interview. After twenty minutes they took a break. The officer at the door brought in water.

The two detectives walked out.

'A few holes in her story, aren't there?'

'Yes,' said Sandy, 'notice how she gives more detail than we could possibly want on some responses, and at times skates over the detail, you can follow that up. Let's go back in.'

'A few comments you made,' Pip looked up from her notebook, 'want to make sure I got them down right. We've talked to other employees, your colleagues. The complete picture,' she shrugged, 'who gets to look at that? We do have some information. It's a little different from that you presented. Let's see if we can make sense of it.'

'I've told you all I know.'

'You're saying you didn't see the smoke until you drove off the levee road, through the trees, then you saw the smoke,' showing her the map of the route she'd taken, 'that would be here, right?'

'Yeah, about there.'

'Now, I've driven that road with two of your colleagues, it's about twenty metres high. Then you took the side track down off the levee at the corner, here,' pointing, 'now you're level with the ground the trees are on. Come through the trees and see the smoke, thing is the trees are not twenty metres high, ten at most. Your colleagues are saying they could see the smoke from here,' Pip moved her finger, 'right back here where the road starts, kilometres away.'

Pip kept her eyes on the map, finger tracing the bank, back and forth. The security guard tracked the movement.

'How do you explain that?'

'Maybe they saw it when the fire started. Time I got there the flames were nearly out, grass burning, the van was out. That's why I couldn't see it.'

'That might be why you didn't see the flames. It doesn't explain why you didn't see the smoke.'

The security guard sighed, leaned back in her chair, then shook upright.

'Did you smell the smoke?'

'No, always too hot to have the windows open.'

'Only, you said you waved to the guys in the vehicle behind you, put your blinkers on...'

'Like I said, to warn them. Mobile reception bad out there, non-existent at that time.'

'And yet, your window was not down.'

'I must of put it down to wave then, mustn't I?'

'These are your mobile phone records for the days before and after the incident.'

'How'd you get hold of them?' she shrank from the table.

'Told you, used to work for Baxter. Never forgets a colleague.' Pip smiled. 'You say your phone wouldn't work, yet here, you on the phone to your mate next door,' she gestured to the wall, 'five minutes here, and again at the fire ground, and fifteen minutes later. So, either the phone was getting reception, or it wasn't. Which is it?'

Chin out, arms folded, the guard glared at Pip.

'The crew in the vehicle behind you didn't see you wave out the window. They say they didn't see you at all. They weren't on that road at all that day,' Pip said.

'The smoke,' said the security guard, 'you said they saw the smoke.'

'I did say that', Pip turned the pages of her notebook, 'so did they. But they were not right behind you, not on there at all.'

Pip put down the map, the phone records, the photographs of the van, the statement the guard had signed, witnessed by her lawyer, one by one on top of each other. 'Every document, an inconsistency. Every other person I've talked to, tells me a detail inconsistent with your story. Is it that they are all lying. Is that what you're saying?'

'We're taking a break in the interview', said Pip, gave the time and turned the recording device off, 'a short break. This officer,' gesturing to the woman at the door, 'will escort you to the bathroom. Can I get you tea, water?'

'Water.'

'What do you want to do next?' said Pip.

'She knows we have a lot of evidence, where she was, who was with her. You press on with the photographic evidence,' said Sandy, 'showing her with a couple near the van. Get her to confirm they are the missing people.'

The aircon struggled a bit with the noon sun, stalling, kicking back in every now and then. A different officer brought the security guard back, stood with her back to the door.

'Will this take long?'

'Oh, you're doing fine. Still OK to keep talking to us? We've a few more photos, details, if you could help us out with?'

Pip unfolded a map, spread it out on the table, handed over a Sharpie, 'so much ground to cover on your shifts,' she said.

'We don't cover all this on one shift,' she said, 'what's this for?'

'We have photos of the van, we believe it's the one you found, here,' she pointed, 'here and here.'

The security guard pointed to a location on the map, 'that's not part of Delaney Holdings.'

'Yet you patrol it.'

'Look, Delaney Holdings, the logo,' she pointed to the chest pocket of her shirt, 'our uniform. We're employed by Delaney Holdings, and all of this, these parts here, is the holdings,' she drew a rough circle with her finger. 'It's huge. Some of those places where you said there were photos of the van, that's not part of Delaney's.'

'So, why do you patrol it. You work for Delaney Holdings and this land here,' Pip drew a rough shape with her finger, 'is not part of it?'

'We guess it belongs to Brack, other farms, other names. The robots are programmed to cover there too.'

Pip sat back, 'that's important, we wanted to check the boundaries,' she turned to Sandy, 'might have to widen the search.'

'Do you mind using this sharpie,' said Sandy, 'could you draw the boundaries of Delaney Holdings on the map, and where you patrol outside Delaney Holdings, we can then get started straight away. Have you worked across the whole place?'

The security guard took the pen, started drawing, 'oh yeah, I had a squad until someone made up some complaints against me, supervised the crew installing the reflective landmarks for the LGVs all along this line here.'

'LGVs?' said Sandy.

'You really should get out more – the quad robots, laser guided vehicles, it's that hard, is it?' She handed back the pen, pushed the map away, 'good as I can get it, don't want it coloured in, do you?'

'Thanks, this is very helpful,' folded the map and gave it to the officer at the door. Photographs of the map, their first insight into the extent of Brack's land would soon be with the Marinya team leads and Mick Darby.

Pip opened a fat folder and took out a bundle of photographs, sat back and opened her notebook.

'You're not local, are you?' the guard said to Sandy, 'that's why you didn't have the map,' she sat back, chin out, 'for all you knew it could have been upside down.'

Pip put three photos on the table, 'you've already identified yourself and your private vehicle,' she said. Used a pencil to point to three people in the first photo, 'can you identify this woman?'

'What is this, you pervs. Where'd these come from?'

'Social media.'

The woman was topless, sitting on an esky, smoking, 'well that's me again isn't it. Suppose you want to check? See if they really are my tatts.' She opened her shirt, worn unbuttoned over a white t shirt.

'And this couple?' Again, the woman was topless, the guy as well, both leaning on the security guard's ute.

'Cotton workers. It's our day off right, nothing to do with anyone what we do in our spare time.'

'Quite right, me, I love a day off. Who took the photo?'

'He's next door,' she jerked her thumb at the wall behind her.

'And this one?' Pip put the photo down, she pushed it back, Pip pushed it forward.

She sobbed, 'it wasn't supposed to happen.'

The guard picked up the photo of the four of them, the two security and the missing couple, naked for a selfie, held it in two hands and rested it back on the table. She sniffed, reached for the tissues.

'You've seen our stuff, so you know we're into rough sex, pain, and pleasure and all that. In a place like where we work, there's not much available, and you can generally figure people's interests out quickly. So, the four of us clicked. Skinny dipping in the dams, canals, one thing led to another, four of us in the cot. Then there was a fuck up, we were nearly caught in the canals by one of those fucking robots, so we went back to their van.'

The two police officers held their breath.

She kept talking, the van didn't really hold four, they kept bumping into each other, trying to dry and get dressed, then she fell against a cupboard, shaking the door open, map pinned to the back of the door, bags of equipment tumbling to the floor.

'These were the people our boss and Brack had warned us about. We were all looking for them. They had drones, cameras, video cameras, maps.'

'Warned about?'

'Yeah, there's this website firstwaterdotcom, posting all this shit about cotton and water. Brack wanted it stopped and we were told to confiscate cameras, maps, report it to our boss. He was paranoid people'd find out how much water he's got, where he gets it from. And all this time we'd been fucking them, they were fucking with us. I, we, trusted them,' she sobbed now.

'What happened next?' a whisper from Sandy.

'I lashed out, she screamed, it just went pear-shaped is all, her partner was too pissed to do anything, it was over. I rang our boss.' The guard blew her nose, put the tissue up her shirt sleeve.

'Your boss,' said Sandy.

'Bloke before Baxter, he came, and we loaded all their gear, cameras, maps, and drones into his truck. The guy was out of it, so our boss gave him a hit. She was unconscious, she'd hit her head. He injected her too, she fitted for a bit, would have looked like ODs. The three of us buried the bodies and fired the van. Couple of days later, early, I towed the wreck to where I reported the van fire, just lit the grass.'

'That's a lot of activity. How come no one noticed you?'

'We're all GPS monitored, vehicles too, so our boss knows where everyone is all the time. Plus, with your shift you get assigned your patrol, checkpoints. And it's geo-fenced, go outside your boundary and alarms go off, miss a checkpoint same thing. So, all he had to do was fix the rosters, change the robot patrols, so no-one came near me.'

'Robots, robot patrol, did you mention them earlier too, nearly being caught by robots?

'Yeah, robots, some of the blokes give them names, they're not pets or kids, they're fucking robots. We call them the clowns.'

'What do they do?' asked Sandy.

'Our jobs, replacing us, that's what they do. We're losing a crew each week. By the end of the month, security there, all over here,' she circled an area on the map again, 'will be twenty-four-seven robotic, cameras, sound cannons, solar powered, batteries for night. All run by Wi-Fi and a laptop. Delaney Holdings'll be a human free zone. One of the fields, cotton, was picked by a robot, beginning of the end of cotton workers.' She slumped in her chair, chin down again, arms loosely down her sides.

'That was the end of it...,' said Sandy.

'Except for the nightmares,' she sniffled, 'no, not the end of it. The boss told Brack of course. Brack wanted to see us. He had his driver there too, creepy guy, wanted to know all about it. We made up a story about catching them at it, they put up a struggle. We expected the sack and worse, but Brack gave us a ten grand bonus, cash, just pulled it out of a drawer in his desk. Said accidents do happen, they shouldn't have been trespassing anyway, and when the cops came, he'd have lawyers for us.'

'Which he did,' said Pip.

'Yeah, he did,' she slumped in her chair.

'Your boss?' said Sandy.

'Dunno. He got the sack, you know that. No-one's seen him since or heard from him. Someone said all his gear, personal stuff was burned and buried under a new levee wall. That's why Baxter replaced him. Lotta gossip in this place, though.'

Sandy and Pip stood, gathered their paperwork, Pip suspended the recording, 'it's been a long time sitting down, thank you, would you like a short walk? Be only inside, but it's a walk.'

'I'd love a smoke,' she said.

Mr Backhand Dah

Lucas began the podcast with his favourite piece of music by Schubert, faded it to praise the Cotton Federation for pointing out how many litres of water it took to produce one almond. 'Kraut bastard has some sense,' said Brack, 'but I hate that music.'

'I invited CEO Delaney Holdings, biggest cotton grower in the southern hemisphere, biggest user of water in the southern hemisphere to come on and talk about cotton, he declined. But relax, I have a stand in. We recorded this interview earlier.'

High pitched and nasal, a voice to wish you weren't hearing it. Hardyn Brack, his bodyguard, and Liz Evans seated around the table in the Cotton Federation boardroom, all muscles contracted as they listened to the podcast. The voice belonged to the character Mr Backhand Dah, Hardyn Brack's stand-in.

'Mr Backhand Dah,' said Lucas. 'Congratulations on the almond piece, lots of hits, migrated from the mainstream to social platforms, forty bucks an almond.'

'Should be outlawed,' whined the stand-in.

'How much water to produce the cotton for a t shirt, say a medium, men's, retailing for nine bucks at a chain store.'

'That's a very complex question, Lucas, not sure we have the time for me to fully respond to that. Let me say this though, Australian cotton growers are the most efficient users of water in the world,' said the stand-in.

'Five hundred litres, nice figure?'

'There's the weight of the T shirt, grown with irrigated water, bore water, organic, or non-organic, so the fertilisers impact water use...'

'Even eight hundred litres, I'm hearing more bullshit. I figure I'm warmer. Even at eight hundred litres, at three bucks a bottle, your own test with almonds, which makes it two thousand and four hundred dollars in water to produce the cotton for a nine-dollar t shirt.' Lucas's voice rising, 'we haven't even made the fucking t shirt yet, the cotton's yet to be baled, driven off to the mills, that's more money. Haven't paid the people to make the t shirt yet,' he paused, 'not that there's any costs there, right?'

'But, but, but, but, but, but, but, but, but...' Here the voice had been speeded up, so it sounded like 'bubbabubbabubbabub,' a shriek now.

'You know what, 'said Lucas, 'the real figure. Number of litres of water to make the cotton for one t shirt, medium, buy it at Kmart for nine bucks. I'll tell you in my next podcast...'

Listeners heard Lucas laugh, giggle, 'bubbabubbabubba.'

'Turn the fucking thing off,' said Brack, sounding a bit like his stand-in, 'I'll sue.'

'He's not done yet,' said Liz. Subscribers were with Liz, familiar with one of Lucas' techniques, knew the punchline was coming.

'Twenty-seven hundred litres of water to grow the cotton for one t shirt. The currency is three dollars a litre, bottle of water at your local servo. A quick calculation,' Lucas tapping, 'carry the two. Fuck. Eight thousand, one hundred dollars of water in a nine-dollar cotton t shirt.'

'Mr Backhand Dah,' said Lucas, 'Mr Backhand Dah, just how do you explain that? It's like the cotton industry or at least the southern hemisphere's biggest cotton grower, has discovered how to reverse alchemy, reduce the value of water by a thousand percent.'

'bubbububbububbub.'

'Here's some music you won't have heard for a long time, be back in five,' said Lucas, playing sounds of rippling creeks, water lapping the edges of sandy river beaches, waterfalls.

The music stopped. Lucas's headache hadn't, 'meanwhile Mr Backhand Dah. Now, of course he'll argue on tomorrow's radio that three dollars a litre water doesn't hold up.'

'And he's right. You pay the three dollars a litre. Here's how, Delaney Holdings steals water, pumps it up from deep aquifers, stops any water leaving their empire, hoards it for carryover, sells it to the government when prices are high, buys it back when prices are low. So, you run out of water, hasn't rained in ten years, so you pay three dollars a litre for a drink because the free water you should have is not there.'

'No buts, we're counting.' Lucas' voice strained, just audible. Unlike what he was hearing, can you do more than blog?

Sandy Pelham listened to Lucas' podcast. He could hear the pressure in Lucas' voice, the short gasps of breath between, in the middle of, at the beginning of sentences. Lucas' podcasts were not usually like this. Pelham reached for his phone.

'Did you catch that?' said Mick Darby, also out of breath. 'That's the threat right there. Lucas and Brack, you were right. And the anagram too, Mr Backhand Dah. We got anywhere with more money hidden in anagrams yet. Loves his word games.'

'Do you know where he is?' asked Sandy.

'No, not yet' said Mick, 'but we know where he's going. Also, Liz Evans just let us know Brack wants Lucas killed, got his bodyguard organising it. No pressure.'

Sandy continued home, pissed on his lemon tree, and went in to lie down, set his timer for an hour, nothing to be gained by adding to the adrenaline in the office.

Your boss knows mate, should have told you.

Two vans, eight seaters, darkened windows, slowed and pulled up at the Delaney Holdings boom gate. The security guard closed the half door to his booth, stepped out scrolling his tablet. He squatted and held it to the first van's license plate, leaned on both knees to stand, sighed, walked to the back of the van, checked that plate, photographed the plate of the covered trailer, came right around to the front of the van, nodded, and signalled the driver to open his window.

'Names,' he said looking from the tablet to the driver. 'No blackfellas in there are there?'

Harry felt Gino's hand on his shoulder, 'mate, I'm just the driver, your rookies are in there,' he gestured to the rows of seats behind him.

'Yeah well, the boss don't like 'em, not allowed on the property. Say your names,' said the guard peering over Harry's shoulder.

Satisfied, the guard moved to the second van, repeated the performance with his tablet, motioned the driver to open his window.

Harry heard him struggle with some of the names, 'say again, say again,' he heard the guard. Job done, the guard came back to Harry's window, told him that he was to park to the side of the road when he was through the gate.

Harry pulled in, waved to the driver of the second van which continued along the road. He got out of the van, pulled out a smoke.

'Don't smoke or get out of your vehicle,' said the guard.

'Mate,' said Harry holding out his cigarette.

'Back in the vehicle, the chief security officer of Delaney Holdings,' puffed the guard, 'will be here soon. Call him "Sir", if they,' he indicated the back of the van, 'want to keep this gig. He likes things his own way.'

'What about those other blokes?' said Harry.

'They're going back to school first, day on their arses, lectures all day. The crew you've driven in are doing practical security patrolling, they'll be back in school later this week.'

'Well, when do I come back and get them?'

'You don't. You're to stay here too. Part of the exercise I was told.'

'Shit, I'll need to call my boss,' said Harry.

'Your boss knows mate, should of told you,' he said, and walked back to his booth, out of the morning sun.

'All good,' said Gino from the back of the van.

'Yeah,' said Harry, 'here he comes now,' as Clive Baxter parked his ute alongside Harry's, driver to driver.

'On time,' said Baxter. 'Good, follow me and we'll go over the maps.'

Harry, Gino, and his team stood around the bonnet of Baxter's ute, following his finger as he traced red lines over the southwest corner of Brack's land, 'here's where Lucas wanted me to lift security. It's done, sensors disabled, robot patrols rerouted, no manned patrols, some are in the classroom with that other team, the real casuals they are here,' he pointed to the north and the west on the map, 'or here. Nowhere near you,' he said to Harry. 'We've met before.'

'How long are the patrols for this area,' Harry pointed to where they were going, 'disabled?'

'Twenty-four hours, well, another twenty-two hours now.'

'Nearly enough,' said Harry, although they'd be out in ten hours, they'd rehearsed so many times.

'That's all I can give you,' said Baxter. 'Lucas told me you were professionals, done surveys before.'

'Twenty-two hours? You work a thirty-six-hour week for your crews, three twelve-hour shifts, so you can give me thirty-six hours. It'll raise fewer questions than a roster change. The robots, you can disable them a little longer, program them away from here.'

'Thirty-four hours.' said Baxter.

Harry stopped the van at the first intersection point, unloaded two motorbikes and unhitched the trailer, pulling it to the side of the road. Two of Gino's crew loaded saddle bags, climbed the bikes in pairs, heavy backpacks on the passengers, roared off. Harry drove Gino and his offsider to where they would set explosives in the levee banks along the most western part of Brack's land, left them to it.

He walked west, puffs of dust rising, settling into his rhythm, waist bending slightly with each stride, shoulders, legs in step. The rocky ground, flat and brown in all directions. He stopped after three ks, took a sip from his water bottle. The stunted remains of a tree over two hundred metres away stood up straight and waved at him.

'You fucking idiot,' laughed Harry, and ran to hug the tree.

Lucas led him to his camp, a sandy depression in what soon would be a creek bed, boiled water and they settled down for a smoke and black tea.

They sat and chatted. Lucas talked about the weeks he tramped out around here, 'I was out this way when you moved on Mike's blokes. Mate, I saw jetties three metres off the ground, used to be water here, now dust, sand, rocks.'

Harry caught him up on how they got in, meeting with Ankles.

'Mate, it's getting Gino and his crew out, going to be cutting it fine, real fine. I wouldn't want to lose them.'

'What's the problem?'

'The remote detonation. Brack's place is bigger than we thought, Gino hasn't said anything, but he'll be too close to the explosives when he detonates, be lucky to get away.'

'He'll be fine,' said Lucas, 'he's not said anything because he won't set it off. I will,' he opened the top of a canvas holdall, 'wireless and remote mate, waterproof, best Pakistan can make.'

'So, Gino gets away?'

'Well, the detonation won't kill him.'

'OK, where will you be?'

Lucas pointed west, 'way out there, got a bike three clicks away.'

'Tell me,' said Harry, 'time to reach the bike, where to from there. Who's going to meet you?'

'Relax, Harry,' said Lucas, 'it all fits together. You've taken your money, cleaned out those accounts, haven't you? The properties should be OK.'

'Yeah, soon as you warned me about Mike's.'

'Can't believe the bastards cracked the anagrams. What did you use?'

'Family names of a Koori women's cricket team, way back, beat the poms.'

'They'll never think of looking for that.'

'I figured. So, mate, a beer in Wagga, somewhere classy, Turvey Tavern?'

'My shout,' said Lucas, standing up with Harry, shaking hands.

Yes Minister.

For the first time Mick Darby was happy with Ministerial interference. Lucas's podcast and blog caused a dozen phone calls from federal and state Ministers, chiefs of staff, bureaucrats all saying Brack and Delaney Holdings had to be protected, 'that's the job of Water Intelligence and Security.'

'Brack and his coterie will be most impressed by your response to the call to protects his assets,' said Darby's Minister, 'should I know how you managed it?'

'Good intelligence and good police work, Minister.'

'Nice to be loved,' she pointed to the list of calls to her office insisting Brack be protected. 'Now the podcast, the professional analysis?'

'The speaker is Lucas, second name unknown. The podcast is being examined now, compared to earlier ones. I have a graph here.' Darby opened his leather folder, 'of the thought form of the podcast.'

'What? Maths, graphs, and acronyms, not what I need,' she waved it away with a folder wrapped in white tape, 'I don't need this either, legal opinions are just that. This exercise will be the first test of the ecocide legislation, don't want to lose it, no matter how long it takes. Take me through what you have on Brack. Complex but, I must get my head around it.'

'Overview first, then detail if you want it. We have, that is my department has, we have Brack for wanton destruction of land and water; land destroyed includes middens, scarred trees, rock art, I have a list of artefacts compiled by the land councils.'

She shook her head, 'maybe later, and water?'

'Water; poisoned water, diverted streams and creeks, illegal floodplain harvesting, illegal fracking, wetlands now dry, illegal bores into aquifers, Brack's hoarding of water will result in a fish kill in seven days, unless the NSW government can finalise their buyback.'

'OK,' she leaned back in her chair, 'Mick, we know he's broken multiple laws, what I don't get easily is how it's ecocide?'

'We could take him to court every year for fifty years and still not prosecute him for all his crimes. Then you add corruption of public officials, so ICAC, criminal charges, two counts for accessory to murder, and tax evasion so the ATO.'

'Mick...'

'Hang on, hear me out. What connects all these, and the other charges is Brack's motive. Why? His motivation is to destroy, poison the land or starve it of water, hoard water and stop environmental and cultural flow. The land he's flooded, most of it was arable now ruined. He makes no money out of most of his land, trades small amounts of water to buy more land, which he then destroys, twelve bulldozers, side by side, drivers in shifts, twenty-four hours a day. Ecocide,' Mick sat down, 'destruction for its own sake.'

'You have him on all of this?'

'And more,' said Mick. 'We do need a confession for his motivation though.'

'Confident of a confession?'

Mick Darby nodded.

'Let's leave that for now,' she said and put her glasses on. 'The sound bite,' she read, '"stealing, hoarding water, cornering the water market to the extent that it threatens the survival of the Riverina is a catastrophic risk to Australia's water security, and so classified as an act of domestic terrorism." That's all I should say?'

'Yes.'

'Now, the tax evasion, money laundering, corruption allegations?'

'Crown advice is we have jurisdiction. We have at him first. There'll be a point where all investigations are parallel.'

'The Superintendent from Wagga, Pelham, you, and he seem a good team. Do you need him here?'

'No, thank you. Sandy, Sandy Pelham, has his hands full in Wagga. His people are chasing down Lucas. My team,' he handed her a one pager, 'we're coordinating security of Brack's assets and the computer management system he uses to control those assets. We're going to find more evidence of water entitlements, water storage and properties he has yet to admit are his, assets hidden through shell companies. When we find those assets, I'll need forfeiture orders.'

'Yes,' she said, 'I received your application this morning,' she reached into a drawer under her desk, 'here it is, signed, so do be careful what you write in here.'

'Yes, Minister.'

'Better I hadn't heard that. Now another document for you. NASA license. That it? Is there anything else you want from me, Mick?'

'Minister, I'll let you know,' said Darby shaking the Minister's hand.

Be nice to know.

Sandy and his management team met for two hours. They trawled the Operation Marinya data, planned the meeting for the next day, reviewed rosters, recalled officers from leave. The head of Rural Crime also briefed the commanders of the other districts covered by Operation Marinya.

Tassie was checking the paperwork coming out of the interview with the two security guards from Delaney Holdings. Marinya couldn't go near Brack without warrants, search warrants, and seize orders for vehicles, radios, robots, computer logs, the radio network.

'Some big decisions here, Sandy, we need all this,' he waved the paperwork, printouts. 'Thing is our warrants for the search, orders for IT and communications asset seizure, warrants to arrest Brack, this bodyguard and the ex-security chief, effectively compromises Brack's security, exposes him to anything Lucas might be planning.'

'C'mon Tassie, he has Ankles,' said the detectives' chief.

'Oh well, an early night all round then,' setting them laughing.

'So,' said Sandy, 'do we have any people to spare, and where would we put them?' He walked to the enlarged map of Brack's land, 'where would we start with security?'

'Mick, spare me five minutes, we've an Operation Marinya investigation closing in on Brack tomorrow.'

'Sure, 'said Darby mouthing five minutes to Cindi and his other officers as he left the room, 'by the way, my Minister wants to meet you when this is done.'

'Hmmm, got a complication,' Sandy explained the security guards' interview.

'What are you going to do?' asked Darby.

'Got a forensics team ready to drive up, recalled the forensics lead from leave, she's on her way back, they'll bring the bodies out as soon as they give us the go ahead, might take a few days.'

'OK, Brack, his security chief and his bodyguard?'

'I'd like to talk to them, after we retrieve the bodies, if they're there.'

'OK, by then I'll have Brack, under arrest. Might take a while for you to get to interview him. The other two, I can detain. Keep them at Brack's place?'

'OK, let's do that,' agreed Sandy. 'The one I must get to first is his security chief, ex, the bloke he sacked. I don't know where he is yet.'

'Righto,' said Darby, 'what time you going in?'

'Driving to get there by dawn. We have the coordinates where we expect to find the two bodies.'

'Do you need the locals on this, Hillston?'

'No,' said Sandy, 'the boss at Hillston has all the details and he knows his unit may be compromised, so he doesn't want anything to fuck this up. He's staying close to the officers we figure are on Ankles' payroll. Why?'

'I'll be using them and more, securing the properties, some are already positioned. I've got great cover, under orders to protect Brack's properties from an expected terrorist attack.'

'Be nice to know,' said Sandy.

'Mate, it's lots of pieces, moving very fast, talks between my Minister and her state counterparts during the night.'

'OK,' said Sandy, 'so, Brack's bodyguard is still there?'

'Yep, hasn't left, doesn't look like leaving. He'll organise the hit on Lucas. Brack will want him close by.'

'How do you know where he is,' said Sandy, 'not Liz sending regular messages surely?'

'No, I just got off the phone with Brack. He's furious, reckons Lucas is a threat to democracy, western civilization. I told Brack we were taking over security of his properties, to expect us in the morning, to have password access codes ready for us, people at our disposal. Interestingly, he doesn't have many security staff, gone for robot security patrols, which is good for us. Asked me if "this whole thing" will threaten his appointment to chair the enquiry. He's got no idea.'

'OK, Mick,' said Sandy, 'I've got to go and let my guys know Brack's security's covered. Tomorrow mate.'

Send in the robots.

At five minutes to five Sandy Pelham watered his roses on the front porch with water saved from his shower, pissed on his lemon tree, and was called out by his neighbour, 'it's good for them,' Sandy replied, 'enhances the flavour,' and went back inside, reappearing at five.

In the cool of the morning, he figured a leisurely fifty-minute walk along the river to the station, he'd shower there again, change into his uniform, and open the Marinya team conference at seven.

He heard them before he saw them, then he was caught up. As he crossed the highway at the lights a posse of mothers and prams ahead of him, some chanting, and some counting.

'Wagga is counting, one, two....'

The counting stopped at ten, started again, toddlers joining in, some lost before ten, school children, already in uniforms tempted to go to eleven, twelve, quickly brought into line. Must have been up for hours, kids ready for school at this time, serious.

The crowd grew outside the Riverina Water offices, 'Wagga is counting, one, two....'

He rang his duty staff, 'this demonstration, Riverina Water....'

'They're everywhere boss, out front of council offices in Albury, Corowa, Forbes, and Hillston. Noisy, peaceful.'

'I'm at Hammond Street now. Send an unmarked, no lights, no bells. See if you can get me a name of an organiser. Get the message out I only want a watching brief in our district.'

Sandy cut the call, thumbed a contact, 'Mick, Lucas' podcast has inspired early morning protests about water,' he said. Listened, 'what, outside Brack's?'

'Yeah, he's ropable. Reckons our protection is crap. Makes it tough for anyone to get out though, so that's some help. I've split my teams here, leaving some at the gate to deal with the crowd. It doesn't change our plan, slows it a bit, or the plan for your team. Heard from them yet?'

'They're on track, their ETA is six am, in thirty minutes. When they find something, I'll get them to contact you. No sense having to come through me, now. I might have my hands full here.'

'Be in touch mate.'

'They either can't or won't arrest this mob at my gates,' said Brack, throwing his phone onto his desk, pacing his office. 'Reckon they're peaceful, not on my property, so it's legit. And there's another mob in town outside the council, police protecting the Hillston council chambers, waste of time that is.' He stopped and challenged Baxter, both tall men almost nose to nose, until they caught each other's morning breath.

'Well, ex-superintendent Baxter, decorated, extensive career,' Brack said backing away, 'what would you recommend I do,' he turned to his driver and back to Baxter, 'recommend we do.'

'Well, you've sacked almost all your security, so send in the robots,' said Baxter, 'they're ready for patrol. Use the sound cannons, you can do that from here, the remote's on your laptop, that'll get rid of the hippies.' Baxter stepped back from Brack and the bodyguard.

Sandy's EA put her head around the door, 'Mick Darby calling from Hillston,' she said.

'I need the Marinya team.'

Sandy took the call in the conference room, 'putting you on speaker,' he said, 'wait one,' as officers took their seats.

'Mick.'

'Sandy, haven't heard from your forensic team yet, anything to report?'

'Not yet,' said Sandy, 'how'd your end go?'

'We're OK,' said Mick, 'waiting for everyone to get here, took longer to get through the boom gates than I wanted. We've trucks on the way to move documents, computers, they're just threading their way through about a hundred people now, strung out along the road to the gate, haven't attempted to cross, peaceful.'

'The fuck was that?' Mick said, barely heard over thunder, 'call you back.'

Take a seat, read it.

'One grave, three bodies, no weapons. Not much blood. Two killed here, bashed. One killed somewhere else, shot.' The policewoman reported to her boss by phone. 'Uh, dumped here, recently.'

'OK, make ready to move.' Sandy said. 'There've been explosions around lakes and dams northeast of you. Chopper is four minutes away. Load the bodies and collect whatever you can. Leave the trucks. Until the chopper confirms different, you only have time to retrieve those bodies before water reaches you.'

'Water out here? How much?'

'Around ten square kilometres of it and about a metre deep,' he said, 'all of it moving southwest from breached levees, dams and lakes, which puts it coming for you...' But she'd already hung up.

Cindi was patched through to Mick and Sandy, 'NASA satellite feeds. Got a map handy, I'll give you coordinates, we're tracking the water flow, now it's to the west and north of Brack's house and the road to Hillston. That won't last and the flow is steadily increasing, volatile though, you have two hours before you need to be flying out. Shit, the feed's down. That's all I've got.'

Sandy rang his team in the chopper watching water fingering the burial site.

'Sandy, we've got as much as we could get, we photographed and mapped the scene, collected soil samples, no insects, no pollen, we can tell they used a bobcat to get down to two metres. Got the two bodies, the couple. The third body, male, got samples of the soil above and below him, should help us identify where he was killed, not here, he didn't bleed here.'

'The third body,' said Sandy, 'wasn't expecting that. ID?'

'No,' said the policewoman struggling with the noise and her headset, 'wearing a Delaney Holdings black uniform though.'

'Thank you,' said Sandy, 'and the team. Now, I've arranged for you to be flown to the Forensics lab in Canberra. It's run by the Feds, they're expecting you and your access is approved, there's a lab there dedicated to you, and the bodies.'

Hardyn Brack saw the police outside his front doors before he heard the knocking and his doorbell, then Mick Darby's face in the monitor.

When he opened the door, he was served a search warrant, 'what the fuck is this?' Brack crumbled the paperwork, walked to his office. 'The Minister promised protection, you're too fucking late, I knew you couldn't be relied on. That fucking German has destroyed my farms. You were supposed to protect me, these idiots,' he gestured to his bodyguard and Baxter, 'useless.' Brack pulled his phone from his back pocket.

'Thank you, sir,' said the police officer and took the phone.

Brack lunged at her and found himself on a chair, arms pinned behind him. Mick Darby smoothed the crumbled warrant, held it out to Brack, nodded to the officer.

'Take a seat, read it,' said Darby as he waved his team in, 'start with his office. You have all the passwords and codes, empty the safe.'

Mick Darby had Hardyn Brack, his bodyguard and Ankles handcuffed and bundled into separate vehicles, officers with them.

'Don't ignore any invitation to hit any one of them, forcible restraint,' said Darby, and turned to supervise loading the trucks.

He took Sandy's call, 'Mick, I've got one chopper in the air, better I put you through, you can get it first-hand.'

Darby listened, ran inside, and traced an area on the map covering one wall of Brack's office. He called some of his team over, phone on speaker, they got most of the report.

'OK,' said Darby, 'we have the time to do this properly. Get it all Brack's stuff photographed, labelled and loaded. We're out of here.'

He had Brack's staff assembled and let them know about the suspected sabotage, told them to leave, that one of his team would lead them safely to the boom gate, get them through. He held up his phone, 'we have your phone numbers, next of kin from your employee records, and we'll be in touch over the next few days about returning here to collect anything you'll have left behind, help sort things out.'

Darby got a report from the boom gate. The chanting crowd was dispersing, this time counting to zero from ten, fear and dark humour, boom.

'Cindi, Sandy's got reports of fires, flash fires, separate from the explosions,' said Mick.

'Yeah, we've got that downloaded too. We're back online with reports from the NASA live analysis. It's methane gas exploding.'

'Methane?'

'Yeah, methane gas, Brack's been fracking, drilling coal seam gas wells, illegally.'

'We're into Brack's water management system, the passwords Brack gave you were correct. The system's destroyed, nothing is responding, no pumps, no valves, no sensors, nothing.'

'Can you call Sandy for me please, bring him up to speed. I'll have to brief the Minister.' said Mick.

Chip was in Chang Mai, on the biggest bed she'd ever seen, under a mosquito net. Harry was walking back to his camp, long legs winning over stunted grass and occasional rock. Gino had disappeared.

A Joseph's coat of fish.

Lucas was swimming. In the channel, floating, drifting with the current, slow, the fall of the land so marginal. His alarm let him know the system was down. Kilometres of pipe, dozens of pumps, gates, water meters, automated sewage and chemical waste treatment plant, computerised maintenance and management systems, all destroyed.

Lucas rolled onto his back, saw pipes fill with water, gates open, valves stick, pumps stop, no alarms to summon a manual override. And fish, a Joseph's coat of fish wriggling, darting, spreading, bunching, chasing, slow, fast, shimmering. He detonated the explosives.

Lucas had shown what you could do with the Murray-Darling He'd done more than blog.

Vast lakes, private and illegal, fifteen or more kilometres square, up to four metres deep were draining, the lakes they fed overflowing, water that had backed up was spilling up to caress the walls, reaching, curious, nibbling at the tops and over levee banks, readying to surge.

Levee walls crumbled. Water from ruptured levees moved at first not much quicker than Lucas drifting in the channel, bursts of gas bubbling around him. Wrinkles of water from different dams, lakes, and ruptured tanks sped now over roads and fields joining in ripples of high fives. Retracing ancient watercourses to the Murray-Darling, a riverine ancestry dotcom.

The water slowed even more as the bore feeding Lucas's channel collapsed. A piece of shrapnel landed fifty metres ahead of him.

Methane gas ignited, the water flashed, burned. Sucked all the oxygen. Lucas didn't burn, he suffocated, how fish die, no oxygen.

The channel water level dropped. Lucas' body bobbed, bumped against the smooth concrete of the walls, drifted again, turned around, came to rest and restless still, carried on. Until the level rose, fortified by Sydney Harbour amounts of water, breaching levees, rushing pipes, assaulting dam walls and lakesides, ambushing levee roads. Lucas's body led the water, a forced march across barren cotton fields, flooding channels, mugging electric fences, filling natural water courses and creeks, limb-snatching gums, then to be cast aside, combat over, as the water liquified desert. His body jammed a narrow channel, water tore his clothes as it circled, jostled and teased him out of its way leaving him pressed up under a rock which collapsed other rocks, stones, tree roots, crushing, burying his body.

Make sure it's only the perception you change Mick.

The Minister dismissed her chief of staff, took one of the armchairs clustered around a coffee table opposite Mick Darby.

'Thinks I've made some mistakes,' she flicked her right hand towards the closed door, 'tell me I haven't, Mick?'

'Not as long as you've someone to take the hit,' said Mick.

'Oh,' she said, 'there's no need to worry about that.'

'Now that's out of the way,' said Mick.

'OK, that much water in the Riverina, the Minister for Agriculture is flying over it, instagramming her way west from Canberra,' she held up her phone, 'of course I'm following breathlessly.'

Darby thumbed his tablet, half the Minister's wall glowed, 'this is live, the coordinates along the bottom of the screen show us where we're looking at on this map,' another screen.

'Huge volumes of water, yet to get an estimate in megalitres, and moving. The land is so flat, fall measured in mils per kilometre. Because it's not heavy rain, the ground is soaking the water up, like the first coat of paint on an old paling fence.'

OK,' said the Minister, 'water security. I take it the flooding, I can call it that, isn't damaging water storages south of here,' she used a laser pointer. 'The legal ones, town supply?'

'The engineering advice is no, the water moving so slowly, and getting slower should leave these storages intact and full.'

'So, some of the water is captured?'

'Yes, some. What's not captured will boost the cultural flow and the environmental flow.'

'The fish kill. Averted?'

'Yes,' said Darby, 'with a week to spare.'

'Right, good news so far then. Water security, depends on the structural safety of the storages, doesn't it?'

'We've explosives experts all over the storages now,' said Mick, 'all nil returns so far, and they've covered seventy five percent of the public storages, channels, canals, dams and underground. We've got engineers and hydrology experts checking public water utilities, treatment plants, bores, sewerage systems. We'll start on privately owned storages when we get to ninety percent of the public sector, we'll be able to spare some experts then.'

'Why? How's that going down?'

'Not well. The lobbyists are earning their money and lawyers don't want property owners incriminated by the data revealed by structural safety checks. Proof positive they're illegally storing water or storing illegally gotten water.'

'And why the ninety percent threshold?'

'Public reassurance. Our intel still shows civil unrest. The demonstrations have stopped, we know of no more planned, still some comments and photos, videos being posted to firstwaterdotcom, but the site is no longer administered, no blogs and no podcasts from Lucas. But there're still high levels of chatter on social media; anti-government, water hoarding, trading, carryover, secret owners, along with 5G, anti-vaxx, climate strikers. People believe government is only there to protect agribusiness interests in the Riverina. We must change their perception. The ninety per cent threshold is one way.'

'Make sure it's only the perception you change, Mick,' the Minister turned back to her desk, 'no minister will want to own that ninety percent threshold. Better it comes from you. National security includes private security, not the other way round, and don't quote me.'

'I'm doing the same with cybersecurity threats, all public installations first....'

'Before we come to that, physical infrastructure, especially the dams, weirs, and pipelines, make the threshold one hundred percent of the public storages. I want them all checked, remediated if necessary before we spend one cent on the private sector. Water stored privately; dams, artificial lakes, tanks and underground tanks, the owners can hire a civil engineer to check their private storages. Plus, they're insured, they shouldn't get a free kick from us, don't even go near them.' she said.

'Hundred percent,' said Darby.

'Yeah, I want a chance to get at the insurers.'

Darby knew insurers had kept up steady opposition to the ecocide proposals and had donated heavily to ultraconservative, free market independents.

'Of course,' he said, 'the teams could do with the respite. Cybersecurity, same arrangement?'

'Yes, they can hire their own consultants, another insurance fest.' She studied the maps on her wall.

'Found anything yet?'

'No,' said Darby, 'other than so many of the facilities are exposed to cyber breaches. Generally, have ignored government cyber security advice.'

'Storages are the responsibilities of the States?'

'Yes,' said Darby, 'try not to enjoy that too much.'

'I've had Treasury and Finance in here too this morning. They've estimates of how much money was wiped off the water market with the release. Water trades in the Basin are over a billion dollars a year and the Riverina's a big part of that. The early estimate, usually inflated, is they've lost half of that. That's a lot of Porsches. Brokers, traders, hedge funds managers, and superannuation companies, lobbyists, are on the phones, reminding all of their donation records. Farmers, generally unhappy, some had just bought water at record prices and now can't give it away, other cancelling their orders as they capture the run-off.'

'The same bastards who got exemption from ASIC,' said Darby. 'Well, again, maybe something else to enjoy, may be just what we need to clean up water trading.'

'By clean it up you mean bring water under regulation. ASIC for a start.'

'Yes,' said Darby. They'd talked before about the links between financial stability and ecocide, terrorism threats more generally, 'be a good start.'

'There's been talk of a code of conduct for water brokers and traders,' she smiled.

'Don't tell me,' he said, 'supported by self-monitoring and a half hour voluntary education program.'

She nodded.

Darby continued, 'not good enough, I'll finalise a paper for tomorrow, bringing water trading under ASIC.'

'Of course.' she said. 'After your briefing yesterday, I alerted the Prime Minister to a cyber-attack on Australia's biggest cotton producer, and that as some of the infrastructure collapsed, fires broke out, igniting methane gas leaking from illegal coal gas seam wells. He's called a national Cabinet meeting, invited the States.'

'Perfect,' said Darby, 'let's keep any mention of the explosives out of the collapse of Brack's water storage. We're certain of the explosive's expert, we have the name, just time until we pick him up. Even when we do get him, the story we need to background journos is about a cyber-attack, not a bomb, it'll be too much, create panic.'

'Yes,' she said, 'people are used to them, come to expect them, explosives not so much. Now,' leaned towards Darby, 'who is behind it all, you have a name?'

'A false one. So, no.'

'Lead? Anything?'

'No,' said Darby.

'Not even an optimistic "not yet,"' she said.

Darby shook his head. 'Explosives? Do we know of any caches missing,' said Darby, 'your colleague?'

'Defence,' she said, 'I wouldn't have thought we'd find out. Their last audit showed they were unable to fully account for what they had, far less what they should have had and didn't. No, you're on your own with this one.'

'Soon as the water subsides, we'll have a forensic team in there. Once we're certain there are no unexploded devices we'll be able to retrieve any wreckage, examine it for explosive debris.'

'And if you find enough in the wreckage to source the material?'

'Until we get there, speculative, Minister.'

Bells rang summoning the Minister to the House, she picked up her device, 'thanks Mick, it'll have to wait.'

Hardyn Brack, where to start.

Superintendent Sandy Pelham's walk started with a smile as he saw buds on his lemon tree, a reward for his daily piss. Just on four am his walk took him up past the Base Hospital where he shared a sneaky, and regular cigarette with some ambos and nurses. Up and over the railway line, around the construction site that was once the southern campus of Charles Sturt University, through Turvey Park and up Willan's Hill where the cigarette he'd finished, and the others he'd had last night reminded him to take his time.

He stood, studied the city sprawled below him, many lights, and much darkness. How the fuck do people sleep, a few taxis, many trucks, he knew the bakers were already at their ovens, in the industrial parks business owners were at their machines, setting up, printing, grinding, fixing, making, yet to understand they only had jobs in their own businesses, could only make them work by putting in eighteen-hour days. He remembered the chamber of commerce burghers had attacked him for removing patrols during the day, rostering them at night instead.

'We've lost a visible police presence,' they'd wailed, quoting some internet fleapit.

'Precisely,' he'd said, 'police will be visible at night when you're gone from here and your businesses with their cheap locks, and your stickers lying that you have cameras, are exposed.'

The move was unpopular with some of his officers too, until the arrest rates improved, and the crime rates dropped.

Too cold now to stand still he set off down the hills, remembering to bend his knees, sun beginning to light the sky to his right. He was to convene the last Operation Marinya team conference this morning and he began to organise his thoughts, murder on his mind.

The two security guards in custody awaiting trial, charged with the manslaughter of the backpacker, cotton-picking couple. Brack's bodyguard charged with the murder of the security chief whom Brack had sacked. Clive Baxter in hospital. What happened there he wondered. Pelham wanted Brack charged with conspiracy to murder, wanted twenty-five years, knew he was unlikely to get it. Darby was stalling, wanted Brack for ecocide, destroying thousands of hectares, ecosystems, polluting water. Sandy pushed him and Darby's response was that his Minister would decide.

Next, update on the crowds demonstrating, there'd been a few spontaneous celebrations, but no-one knew what was going on. There was no leadership from firstwaterdotcom.

He figured he'd get the Internal Affairs reports out of the way then. The Complaints Commissioner had called him late last night to let him know that Clive Baxter had made a complaint against him, had withdrawn it, but that Baxter'd be charged with making a vexatious complaint, or would be after he was out of hospital. She'd let slip that material from the Baxter case was being prepared for ICAC. Investigations into the other officers he'd referred were complete and discipline recommendations were before the Commissioner.

Meth manufacture, and supply, the original Marinya mission, born of insomnia. He had charts and maps prepared by Cindi and her team, data from the water quality testing app. Data showing a monthly downward trend, little evidence of meth use and manufacture in the Riverina. The analysts reported the super recruiters no longer active on social media. Users and suppliers were still on-line, but searching for meth, not arranging meets. He knew that would change as others found the market, but it appeared the labs he was convinced existed were closed; the gang gone.

Gino de Bono, nothing.

He was along the river now, with early morning joggers, runners, and cyclists for company.

Mike Nelson, had, other than for a brief outburst kept quiet and continued to serve out his drink driving conviction, while the investigation into his finances progressed. His lawyers were appealing the asset freeze. Lucas had vanished. Along with Harry. Hardyn Brack, where to start.

The café owner welcomed Sandy with a cheery 'bonjour' and led him past empty tables, chairs upended still on most of them and tucked him into the back corner.

'Saturday paper?' he called.

Surprised by the paper and surprised he'd had to have been introduced to it by the Frenchman, Sandy thought of it as the only useful rag in the country. Shit, someone had completed both crosswords. He put the paper aside, might have to buy his own.

Ham and cheese croissant and two coffees later, Sandy slumped in his chair, head resting on the wall, content to hang out in the café, let the snatches of talk, the unfinished sentences, the gossip of other customers wash over him. Literally this morning, water flowing from the north the shared conversation currency. People out in public, it's what they did when they felt safe. Busy pubs, clubs, restaurants, cafes, walking trails, all settling for Sandy. Places where people from all walks of life, mingled in places with others with whom generally they neither work nor are related.

Sandy sat, sipping coffee, remembered the parable about policing being like dipping your foot in a bucket of water, unmissed once you removed your foot. He looked around. He didn't believe he was indispensable, but he didn't believe the bucket of water bullshit anymore.

Leaving the café to 'bonjour, merci' Sandy walked to the station, showered, changed, and outlined his Marinya presentation on his tablet.

'Come on in, Tassie, take a seat mate, just give me a few more minutes.' He locked down, 'train of thought.'

Tassie sat, crossed his legs, happy to wait.

'Done,' he closed the device.

'Got a breakthrough,' said Tassie.

'Always a great conversation starter,' said Sandy leaning back

A call from the managing partner of the law firm suspected of setting up money laundering schemes for Mike Nelson, and Lucas, Tassie explained. He repeated some of the elaborate details, the Anagram case, it was called informally.

'And now, what have you got?'

'Sandy, the firm is dropping the action and proposing a way ahead.'

'And so, this damascene conversion. What pushed her?'

'Who, not what. Her daughter. Her daughter is on meth or has been using and is now on life support. She broke down when she accepted that her work, her profits, enabled those who contributed to her daughter's condition. She, they, knew all along the money was dirty, but.'

'Fuck,' said Sandy leaning across the desk, 'can't get any closer to home, can you?'

'So, here we are,' said Tassie, 'reinstating the freeze. They'll hear it today, there'll be a limited liability claim by the law firm in exchange for their cooperation. The crown prosecutor thinks the lawyers will throw the accountants, real estate agents under the bus. Apparently, that's what limited liability means to lawyers.'

'Right,' said Sandy, 'agenda, the murder case first, then internal affairs, then you, Tassie. You know the Victorians will want to extradite Nelson, he's a Victorian resident, Shepparton. The lawyers are Melbourne based.'

'Yeah,' Tassie shrugged. 'And then, what's next?'

'Sitrep on Brack. Meth report, gangs report. Won't take long, there's not much going on,' a grin from Tassie, 'then, the no-shows, Lucas, Harry, Gino.'

'I'll take it from there, Sandy, wrapping up, closing files, cleaning mobile phones and devices of references to the op. You'll want to write the commanders who seconded officers to us?'

Let me know where to send flowers.

'Tassie, you have to help me.'

'Clive, I don't have to do anything.'

'For fuck's sake, no need to be such a prick.'

'I'm hanging up, Clive.'

'Tassie,' a scream and a sharp, shallow breath, 'no don't. Give me a chance to explain, OK? Then make up your mind.'

'I can do that, what's on your mind?' said Tassie.

'A bandage,' said Baxter, 'thanks to that bastard Brack and his mate.'

Tassie laughed, put his phone in his other hand and wrote a note, waved it at a junior officer. 'OK, I'm listening, you still in hospital?'

'Until the morning.'

'What happened?' said Tassie.

'Look, I need some help if I'm gunna talk. I don't want to see the Feds, and they've been around last night and this morning. I'l talk to you, no one else, Tassie.'

'You need help to get out of hospital?'

'I need immunity, and then I'll talk to you.'

Tassie looked up, put the phone on speaker as Sandy came into the room.

'Clive, do you have your discharge papers?'

'I'm waiting to be cleared by the quack, tomorrow morning. I'll be out. So, what is it, you want to solve this case or not?'

'Well Clive, that's the thing, we're on top of things down here. Speedy recovery. Let me know where to send flowers.'

Sandy shook his head.

'Flowers,' sharp, shallow breaths again, 'so, smartarse, you've got enough to nail Brack have you?'

'Clive, Brack's a Federal case, you'll need to talk to the Feds about anything you may know.'

'Not the Feds. No-one until immunity.'

'Clive, you know it doesn't work like that, but since it's you, give me an hour and I'll call you back. Let me check your number.' Tassie read the incoming number, repeated it, hung up, turned to Sandy.

'Did you get enough of that?'

'Yeah,' said Sandy, 'mate, well done, what do you think? You know him well.'

'I don't think I know him at all. He deserved his name, and he was a bully, but bent, that bent, never thought.'

'Let me call Darby.' said Sandy, 'We get Darby to phone Baxter, scare him. Then have the locals pick him up from hospital and we'll bring him here, see what he has to say for himself.'

'The locals need a good reason, Sandy.'

'Accessory after the fact, murder of the security guy he replaced, that should do it.'

'But...,' said Tassie.

'I know,' Sandy shrugged, 'it'll get him here though.'

'Sandy,' said Mick, 'tell me you've good news.'

'All lawyered up, are they?'

'Brack, his bodyguard, yeah. Gino, we've nothing, haven't found him yet.'

'Liz Evans, thought she'd be a goldmine.'

'She is,' said Mick, 'got her busy all day, half the nights, verifying the information we have about Brack. We have some anomalies to chase up, pressure on the agency to not write that off that three and a half million they gave him, so we'll get a result there.'

'Trust Cotton?'

'Arrogant, eh? He'll have made a simple mistake. Takes time to find it that's all.'

And my immunity?

Clive Baxter sat upright, feet planted, hands in his lap, odd tufts of longer hairs ruined his designer stubble, shallow breathing irregular, he tugged at the bandage across his forehead and winced. He watched Sandy Pelham all the way into the room, looked him up and down as he sat.

'I'll talk to Tassie,' said Baxter.

'He's out there quelling a riot,' said Sandy.

'Boys want to buy me a beer.'

'Something like that.' Sandy reached into his pocket held up a bottle of pills, 'your painkillers, apparently the blokes who picked you up forgot to give them to you.'

Baxter took the pills, 'best young blokes can do these days, refuse prescribed pills? In my day...'

'This is your day,' said Sandy, holding out a bottle of water, 'your first day in a long time where it's after nine o'clock in the morning and you're yet to have a drink.'

'What?'

'We've been all over your house, your donga on Brack's property. We've had time to have a good look, down to your bathroom cabinet, toothbrush, toothbrush cup,' Sandy paused, 'you pass out on your couch at night, and you clean your teeth in the morning with whisky.'

Sandy turned over a sheet of paper, a photograph, a very young Clive Baxter on graduation, smile challenging his future. 'Was this what you saw for yourself?'

Baxter's face, grey in the strip lights, heightened by the ugly beard, eyes watering. Sandy thought it could be due to the pain, broken ribs, a collapsed lung, bruising to the back, lack of alcohol and painkillers; or to the shame, maybe both.

'Your injuries,' said Sandy, 'pressing charges?'

Baxter shook his head.

'Let me take you through what we have, and let's take it from there. I'll do the talking, know that's hard for you right now. What we have'll be on the screen behind you, here, let me move the chair.' Sandy moved the table, chair, now Baxter could lean forward on the table in front of the screen. Sandy scrolled a tablet, 'these are in no particular order, video footage, audio recordings, documents, phone records, bank statements, sworn statements, that kind of thing.'

Baxter held up the empty pill bottle, 'any more of these?'

'One every four hours,' said Sandy, 'it's not gone four hours.'

Sandy scrolled, the images changed. Baxter slumped, eyes strained.

'Now, this one,' the monitor split into four showing photos of Baxter talking to people in a van, 'this one's interesting. That's you, isn't it?'

'Yes,' said Baxter.

'Not sure about anyone else in the van, except this bloke,' close-up of the passenger in the second row of seats, 'that's Gino. Gino de Bono. National search out for him, whereabouts unknown.'

'Don't know him,' said Baxter.

'Traces of explosives found in the damaged levee walls match explosives stolen from Adelong, where explosives are stored just in case of avalanches in the Snowy.'

'I need something,' said Baxter, sweating, breath rasping.

'Take some water. Listen a minute, I'm nearly done with the intro.'

'Can hardly breathe.'

'There was one group of casual security guards due that day, you changed the records to make it two, told the guard at the gate you'd arranged a practical exercise for this group,' he zoomed in on the van with Gino. Baxter squinted at the screen.

'The people in the van set the charges that were detonated two days later. You reprogrammed the security robot patrol. You let these terrorists in, you led the investigation into the explosives stolen from Adelong. Charge of terrorism, that's what you're facing.'

Sandy picked up the photo of the young Baxter, thrust it in front of his face, wondered if Baxter smelled this bad in the photo. 'Was that what you were thinking, back then? When I grow up, I want to win the Police Medal and be a terrorist, and then be stripped of it, die undecorated, unmourned.'

Baxter groaned, closed his eyes.

Sandy took loose pills out of his pocket, 'my mistake,' he said handing over two, 'it was vitamins in that bottle. Here's what you need. We'll get you some breakfast, coffee, then we'll chat some more.'

Sandy left the room, instructed the officer outside, 'stay right with him, don't hesitate to hit that panic button. I don't care how many false alarms, OK?

Sandy was back with Clive Baxter, a new Clive, breathing evenly, not so much as colour in the cheeks but the grey was gone.

'Now where were we?' said Baxter.

'Well, you were in deep shit, 'said Sandy, 'last time I looked, so,' he pushed the files in front of him to one side leaving just his device, 'we can come back to all that, tell me about your beating.'

'And my immunity?' some of the aggression back.

'Clive,' said Sandy, hands open on the table, 'this shifting away from the goal of the interview now. I'd like to think there was something I could do to get your attention. I hope so.'

Even Sandy thought he was waiting too long to say anything, but he figured a lot was going on for Baxter.

'Brack and his driver, bodyguard, broker actually, even though he's been struck off.'

'So, what happened?'

Baxter talked to Sandy about his onboarding, about his contact with Lucas.

'How did you get in touch with Lucas?'

'Burner phone sent a code, then we used Slack, untraceable, encrypted, arranged the call,' said Ankles, chin up, eye to eye with Sandy.

'And then?'

'I was feeling pretty good after talking to Lucas, knew they'd get theirs's. The crowd at the gates, demonstrators, security detail around Brack, figured they wouldn't hold them. Brack asked me what I'd do. So, I said, send in the robots. Remember it clear as, I was thinking of that song, send in the clowns, but they were already there,' Baxter laughed, a smoker's laugh, flinched, clutched at his chest.

Sandy laughed, 'good call, get a laugh, bet that felt good? Clive you all right?'

Baxter stopped coughing, 'yeah, I'm OK. Felt fine for about ten seconds. I'd been feeling like shit ever since the bastard kept hitting on my knee. Funny thing though is that the security staff still around, one of them saw me limping, asked if I'd had my onboarding session. They'd been hostile until then, and now they opened up, he'd done it to all of them, so some of them decided to find out more about him. He's a struck off share trader, they reckon Brack paid his fine, I, well you know, their gossip's like here, it's all adrenaline, boredom, gossip. Except for them, there's not so much adrenaline.'

Sandy took some water, 'and so after your crack about the robots?'

'You know what, it wasn't just a smartase comment. The robots, they're like quad bikes they are, electric, two have sound cannons. Brack got them from the States. They would have worked on that crowd at the front gate, deafening noise, not deadly, but people feel like their heads'll explode.'

'But Brack took it as a smartarse comment?'

'Bodyguard came first, prick king hit me. I fell onto Brack's desk, he scratched my forehead with his letter opener, bled like buggery. So now I can't see, and they both shoved me to the ground, felt a few kicks, then I passed out, woke up in an ambulance.'

'Is there a better word than scratched?' said Sandy.

Baxter laughed, 'I see where you're going with this.'

'Well, I have yet to review all the Adelong files.'

'Stabbed, I think. Afraid he'd kill me.'

'You would have been good at scrabble,' said Sandy, 'Clive I'm going to have another officer come in, record your statement and write it up...'

'I know the drill.'

'Give you the opportunity to read it over and when you're satisfied, you sign it. Hardyn Brack, attempted murder. Can we get you anything while we set that up?'

Mick Darby was on the phone, 'Sandy, how did that go with Baxter?'

'We have a statement. He's pressing charges against Brack and his bodyguard, attempted murder. I need to get hold of a letter opener Brack keeps in his office, probably in or on his desk.'

'Wait one. I've got a few officers stationed there.'

Sandy waited, doodled, geometric shapes, aligned, every second one shaded.

'Sandy, got it, in an evidence bag, labelled and waiting with everything else left there to be collected, why?'

'According to Baxter's statement he was assaulted in that office by Brack and his bodyguard. Does that guy have a name yet? Brack stabbed Baxter in the forehead with it. Need to get it to forensics.'

'Really? He didn't look that bad, those forehead cuts bleed heavily. I'll sort the forensics.'

'Yeah, he was lucky, could have been much nastier. I'll get the statement to you.'

'Look forward to it Sandy, and thanks.'

Baxter looked up as Sandy came back into the interview room, signed his name, and handed him the statement.

'You know what to do with this?' Sandy said to the officer who'd processed the paperwork, 'where to send it?'

'Yes sir.'

'OK, good, thank you,' and shut the door after him.

'Where's it going?'

'To Mick Darby, anti-terrorism, he's handling Brack.'

'Hmmm, anti-terrorism, should be worth something for me.'

'You know Clive, with your being held here, the officers upstairs, not really upset about your beating, you realise that? They don't call you Clive. You know that?'

Sandy shrugged, took a drink of water, screwed the top back on.

Clive sat up straight, scratched his palms, first one then the other, bumped his fists on the table.

'Do I know? I've known for years, known all along.'

'Years,' said Sandy.

Baxter waved his hands towards Sandy, shooing flies, 'these idiots, wouldn't know where to start. Arseholes. The sneaky shit, that's what I couldn't stand.' He slumped in his chair, folded arms on his chest, quickly unfolded as his ribs objected, chin down.

'The sneaky shit?' asked Sandy.

Baxter, firing up, leaning across the table, ribs forgotten, fingers inches from Sandy's face, pointing, 'envelopes on my desk, in my car, left for me at the club, in my letter box at home. Want to know what's in them? Socks. Ankle socks. Clever, eh? Gutless. Ankles. Of course I knew. Known all along.'

'Bother you?'

'Sure,' smiled Baxter smoothing down the end of a steri-strip on his forehead, 'but the joke was on them, right? Got more in a month, every month, from Lucas and from Brack than a carload of coppers.'

'Lucas and Brack? What did you see in Lucas?' asked Sandy.

'Always paid what I asked for, never quibbled, I never met the guy, tried to follow him a few times, not even sure it was him.' Baxter looked up, remembering, 'bloke could just vanish.'

'What did you do for him?'

'Me? Do for him? Fuck you've got that wrong haven't you.' Baxter looked at Sandy, smiled, 'nothing new, nothing flash, just information from a source, leading to arrests.'

'Arrests for what?' said Sandy.

'Using, shoplifting, dealing, counterfeit goods, stolen property, check the files, Pelham,' Baxter drum rolled the desk, 'check the files, outstanding conviction rate.'

'The detective from Cootamundra station, one of yours, was he? How did Lucas react to him stealing ten grand?'

'No, he wasn't one of mine, freelancing bastard. Hear you've got IA onto him.'

'I'll want a list of the officers you corrupted, and a record of what you did for Lucas. I'll have an officer get your statement when we're done.'

'Told you all I know,' said Baxter.

Sandy took a bottle of pills from his shirt pocket, rattled them in front of Baxter, 'pretty sure you haven't.'

'Brack,' said Sandy, 'stayed with him a long time?'

Baxter frowned, 'Brack, Hardyn Brack, never shook a hand he didn't bite.'

'How'd that start?'

'Usual way, minor shit, anyone'd do it, any of us'd do it, small things. Private phone numbers of the anti-irrigation protest leaders, could I have a quiet word, maybe an arrest or two. Then one day I found myself at a farmer's place. He'd shot himself, suicide note, couldn't afford the farm, so many bills, no water, note blamed Brack, reckons he'd left him threats, voicemail, phoned him day and night, texts too. I rang Brack, he told me to destroy the note, report the suicide as accidental discharge, wipe the farmer's phone. He'd called Brack just before he did it, shot himself, had the phone recording it all, everything he said, the shot, fucking nightmare stuff it is, snuff film but just with the sound.'

'Brack, say anything else?'

'Yeah, said the farm'd be even cheaper now. He had me of course. Fuck him,' voice raised, winced at his ribs again, 'I kept the phone.'

You've had a boy's look.

Even though he had his permission, Sandy arranged for a warrant to search Clive Baxter's premises.

'Search it,' said Baxter, 'don't let them ruin it though, might get back there one day.'

'One day,' said Sandy.

'Look, there's cash in the kitchen, under the cutlery, do me a favour eh Sandy, would you get the place cleaned once every few weeks.'

Tassie supervised as his team executed the warrant, checked they had their body cams on for the duration.

'There's bound to be more cash than he's letting on. Don't want anyone playing finders keepers, just because it was Ankle's,' he'd told Sandy.

'Let me know when you've got the phone,' said Sandy.

The trawl through Baxter's police career had stopped when he agreed to talk. Sandy had the officers resume the probe. 'I want to know when Baxter was in the same area as Hardyn Brack, go right back to when Brack was a juvenile, there's a twenty-year age difference between the two.'

'We already have him saying he's been on Brack's payroll,' one protested.

'You're right,' said Sandy, 'we do. And it's all too predictable and too recent, both men have been crooks for years, probably since puberty, so let's see when they could have first met.'

They probed into Baxter's career, searched his house and a factory unit he owned. Sandy waited until the searches were completed before resuming the interview with him. Forensics were revealing the secrets of the phone, easily, given they had the password. Cash found in nearly every room in his house was still being counted. Baxter hid meticulous paperwork; conveyancing records and estate agent correspondence for properties he owned and rented out. Detectives would be at his banks for financial records, property titles and deeds for days.

Directed to search the front and back yards officers came back to Tassie empty handed. He sent them back out.

'You've had a boy's look,' he told them, 'of course he's got stuff hidden out there, same as he has in every room and the roof.'

They came back with a heavily wrapped parcel, tightly bound in plastic and invisible, high tensile fishing line.

'In a drain behind the garage, Sarge. A downpipe goes into the ground, this was in a small concrete box a metre from the downpipe, buried, a meter deep, grate on top. The yard slopes away from the garage so we lifted the grate, it couldn't have been a drain, this came up too, fishing line tied to the grate.'

'Nice work boys,' said Tassie, 'keep looking, there'll be more possies I reckon. Don't destroy anything though. I'll see if Sandy will release Baxter to show us around.'

Sandy led Baxter into the interview room with electronic recording, a video screen, two chairs, no table. Small cameras on each wall fed a split screen monitor in the next room.

'An upgrade,' said Baxter, 'business class,' he grunted. 'Only right.'

'Where would you like to sit?' asked Sandy.

Baxter gestured to the screen, 'near the door,' he farted, the two detectives in the next room watching the video feed grunted, recoiled in their chairs, 'so I can escape,' another fart, louder, 'just like that one did.'

Sandy sat and clicked a remote, the screen lit, 'just to be clear, Clive, we're about to see on screen what we'll cover this afternoon, in no order, we'll go through them all. You've already declined a lawyer, that still the case?'

Baxter leaned towards the screen, 'can you make it any bigger?'

Sandy thumbed the remote. Baxter leaned back, folded his arms, sat still as photographs of the properties he owned came and went, luxury apartments, houses. Bank account numbers and statements, telephone records, title deeds, statements of rental income, photographs of bundles of cash, and a heavily wrapped package, tightly bound.

'Where would you like to start?' asked Sandy.

'It's your office, no,' Baxter shook his head, 'you tell me what you want to know.'

'Where would you like to start,' said Sandy, holding up the remote, 'we can go through them again.'

Baxter scratched at his forehead, lifting more of the steri strip, frowned, folded his arms, 'the package,' he pointed to the screen.

'OK,' said Sandy, 'where would we have found that on your property?'

'That cunning shit, Tassie,' he spat the word, 'was he out there, at my place? Shoulda been a bloodhound, always sniffin' around finding shit.'

'It's yours, you recognise it, where would we have found it?'

'There's a small pit,' said Baxter straightening, 'alongside the garage, waterproof, that,' he pointed to the screen image again, 'was in the pit. The bottom of the pit is false, waterproof too, don't see that here.'

'I didn't show all the photos we took, Clive, unless you'd rather?' Sandy was sure the two watching would be onto Tassie by now, more to that fucking pit.

'And the package?'

'You can open it you know, won't go off.' Baxter shrugged.

'You thought about it?' said Sandy.

'Nah,' said Baxter rubbing his neck, straightening, voice high, constricted, 'two pistols,' He coughed, winced, a hand to his chest, 'every cop has a throwdown or two, Pelham, even you I reckon.'

'And underneath the guns, under the gun pit?'

'Rest of the stuff from Adelong, USB, laptop from the Ink Well. Just the usual stuff,' he smiled, 'usual stuff a copper'd keep, insurance, safekeeping.'

'Lucas?'

'Told you. Never met him, no idea what he looked like until I got that photo from Deni, on a mission though. Here am I, on the take from him and from Brack. Turns out Lucas wants Brack so hard and Brack thinks he's a nuisance. I couldn't believe my luck when I got him after that prick nearly broke my knee. I wanted him to help me get out. He's a very quiet bloke, stay another day or two he said. Got something coming up.'

'Lucas?' said Sandy, 'when you rang Lucas?'

'Yeah, I had to let his blokes in, the first truck, they'd be in the first truck.'

Texas hold em.

Cindi's door was open, she was staring down a whiteboard, rearranging Post-it notes, erasing column headings and lines, only to draw them again somewhere else on the board, connecting names, places, file references. She turned around with a marker between teeth and one behind her ear, hands full of post-it notes.

'Cindi, can I interrupt you?' the young analyst began.

'You've done that,' said Cindi, holding the marker like a cigar, dropping yellow papers. The young woman shrank.

'Look, this is me being patient,' said Cindi, 'so tell me the punch line, last thing you want to say.'

'One of Hardyn Brack's companies leases cars for three people in Water. I've the records here,' she held out a sheet of paper, her hand a fist, knuckles up like you'd reach out to an unfamiliar dog.

Cindi smiled, took the paper, and ushered the woman inside, 'take a seat,' Cindi said, 'you'll want an audience for this. Or I do anyway.'

Sandy Pelham was on Zoom with Mick Darby, Cindi Rios, and team leaders, wrapping up his report on the interviews with Clive Baxter, 'he's been bent all his life, and got away with most of it, his real importance here is the connection to Brack. He knows he can't trade his way to a lighter sentence. He'll die in prison one way or another.'

'We're not getting too far with Brack,' said Darby.

'Why is that do you think?' asked Sandy.

'He's arrogant, boastful. My interviewers so far have fallen for that. Brack says we've nothing on him. Our people go all cold and snooty, "we know better" kind of body language leaking out of them in buckets. Just a cycle, bluff and threat, mediocre interviewers getting nowhere.'

'Sandy,' said Cindi, 'we've interviewed a couple of senior bureaucrats in the Water agency. They've been taking money from Brack for years now to disguise his water holdings. Nothing new there except he spun them a story about wanting secrecy so his American ex-wife couldn't come after him for more child support. Thing is, he has no children, we checked. So, it could just be a plausible excuse or, he's not wanting his ex-wife, and the company she runs to know. She's President of the Texan multinational that has a stake in Delaney Holdings.'

'If we assume he's holding out on the Texan company, where would that take us?'

'To Texas,' said Cindi, 'well, remotely anyway. Let's get their account on what they own of Delaney Holdings.'

'Thought you'd have that. Wouldn't they have to file as a foreign investor?'

'They would, Sandy,' said Mick, 'and they do, except the filing is done by Brack. Cindi wants to ask them direct.'

I want that, I'm entitled.

Clive Baxter was talking again. 'I was a good copper,' he looked up, staring at Sandy's forehead, 'you know that.'

Sandy, 'no, I do not know that.'

He opened a file, yellowing papers, photographs, reports, statements, the room smelling now of decay, of betrayal.

'Here we have a complaint, your second year of service, local publican. Remember the story, Clive?'

'I was never charged.'

'Good as in those days. You were moved way out west, away from the city. Missus couldn't handle it, so she went back.'

'Nothing to do with her,' Baxter stood, face red, fists by his side, one of the watchers next door picked up her phone, asked her colleague, 'call Tassie?'

'No, not yet.'

Sandy shrugged, 'you are right Clive, absolutely nothing to do with her. It's all to do with you.'

Sandy turned each yellowed page, some transparent almost, old faxes, 'smacked on the bum by an angel when you were born, Clive. This is not your regular, sanitised, service file - this is the file of coverups, cautions, transfers, reports, write-ups. Blokes who let you off covering their arses.'

Baxter held his hand out, 'I want that, I'm entitled.'

'Bad choice of words, Clive. Sit.' Baxter sat; the watchers grinned at their screen. 'Tell me what else you did for Brack?'

'You know it all.'

'Clive, all this material has been referred to ICAC. You're retired so that's why it's going to ICAC, won't be an internal investigation, like these ones,' Sandy put his hand on the file, 'where nothing was found. Now, you want to go down for all of these, alone, public hearings? The people in these files, retired, left the Force, many on compo, the civilians will go to ICAC. Serving officers, internal affairs. These mates of yours, they'll let you down, you reckon they'll stand by you?'

'Cops,' said Baxter, 'always protect our own, except undercover,' he looked up at Sandy, 'they'll get nowhere, Pelham, you know it.'

'Serious this time, Clive. My old boss, Deputy Commissioner now, inside running for Commissioner, giving evidence at the public hearing, do you think he'll be there for a whitewash?'

Baxter rubbed his eyes, scratched his forehead, 'I could do with one of my pills.'

'So, let me ask you again. What else did you do for Brack?'

'Read your fucking files.'

'Pages don't talk,' said Sandy.

'I told you; you've got it all there,' he pointed at the papers in front of Sandy.

'Well, we have gone through every charge sheet you signed off on in the District while you were here, I'm interested in the charges you downgraded, specifically these ones, the list is on the screen now, and we'll go through them one by one. Which ones were influenced by Brack, and don't forget we have a record of all your phone calls around the dates of each of these charges.'

Sandy passed a pill to Baxter; he swallowed it with water.

'The fourth one, there, that was for Brack. Hated doing that one. Bastard worked for the Tax Office, who wants to do them a favour?'

'What happened?'

'Bloke ran off the road, well pissed, woman driving along behind him called the ambos. Weren't needed. He was blood-tested at the station, Talbingo, then charged. I got a call from Brack saying the guy was important to him, well, you've seen the file. Cost Brack a lot that did, bloke at Talbingo, nurse who did the blood tests.'

Sandy and Mick Darby were on speakerphone, 'there were another three like that.' Sandy's summary of the information from Baxter, 'senior public servants, one retired and the other three now more senior, protected by Baxter and paid for by Brack. Question is, isn't it, why?'

'Sandy, thanks, your email's here now, I've got the interview record. We'll do some digging around and then go and see them. Mate, how do you get all this out of him?'

'Well, I have nothing from him about Lucas, nothing we were not onto, but Brack,' said Sandy, 'I can't shut him up about Brack.'

'I do need you to interview Brack.'

'Yeah, Brack. Anything from the US?'

'Yes, Delaney Farms.'

'Delaney Farms?' said Sandy. 'Sounds like a hobby farm, llamas, bees, truffles, ten hectares on the south coast, seriously?'

'Well, just out of the top one hundred US exporters. Let's stick to their cotton interests, their paperwork shows they have a sixty percent stake in Delaney Holdings. Brack's filing gives them a twelve percent share. That's a big difference. Cindi's getting their records, maps etc. We've software that consolidates all these different accounts of what Brack owns. This is going to take months. I reckon we charge him with conspiracy for now.'

'Oh, we've more than that, Mick. We've got the bodyguard talking.'

'That bastard doesn't have a name, still,' laughed Mick.

'Jack Parker. Believes some talk he's heard that the million dollars Brack paid his fine with is proceeds of crime. That means the fine is outstanding, with interest, punishing interest rate.'

'You have some scary powers,' said Mick.

'Perception, mate. Alter the perception, remand centre gossip. Powerful beast.'

'Oh shit.'

'So, old mate Parker, he's looking at five years, and a million dollar plus fine. And he's been trading on futures, wheat, and rice. Again, insider trading using what he learns about the water market. He does this with Brack. Gave us the accounts. Gave us Brack.'

'And the dead chief of Brack's Security?'

'Taped his conversation with Brack on that. Admitted killing the guy. Brack ordered it.'

'Too easy?'

'Evidence of a convicted crim, given a lifeline, a second chance, biting the hand and so on. He's an insider trader, not a gambler, so no, not too easy. Parker's done his homework.'

'We need to know a lot more about this guy. Brack's lawyers will go through his life. We must be prepared. Enough do you think?'

Sandy listed it all again; forensics on the letter opener, bodyguards' testimony, phone records, Brack's voicemail about the farmer's suicide voicemail to him, enough for attempted murder of Baxter and accessory to murder his former security chief, accessory after the fact with the backpacking couple.

'Been a long day, Sandy,' said Mick, 'where are you going with that ICAC story? Did Ankles buy it?'

'It's no story, Mick. It's with ICAC. Baxter's still talking to my Chief of Detectives, names, dates, rorts. He wasn't working only for Brack and Lucas.'

'So,' said Mick, 'you're finished with Baxter then?'

'No, I've got another station record coming through, should have it in a day or two, covers a two-year gap in his paperwork. In that two-year posting he bought his first commercial properties, cash. There'll be an answer in there.'

We can freeze the assets.

Mick Darby and the Minister sat in her office, pale Canberra sun making it to the furthest corner of the room. She'd approved the proposal to bring water trading under ASIC regulation. Traders, brokers, and lobbyists temporarily blinded by Lucas's attack were keen to have the protection that would provide. Darby brought her up to date with the attack on Brack's water.

'So, that's the eco-terrorist piece, Brack's infrastructure. Let me take you through the other three pieces in play,' said Darby. 'There's a more complete report being finalised now. So, environmental damage, good material to fine tune for the ecocide test case, fraud, murder related.'

'Murder? Brack? Better start with that one, Mick.'

'We know Brack solicited his bodyguard to murder his security chief, conspiracy to murder, maximum is twenty-five years in NSW.'

'Others?'

'Yeah, Superintendent Sandy Pelham will be charging two of Brack's security guards with the manslaughter of a couple, casual cotton workers for Brack. Complicated, an element of the violence resulting in the deaths may be attributed to Brack. The murdered couple were NSW residents, and the guards charged under NSW jurisdiction. There's enough to have Brack charged there too, conspiracy.' Darby looked up, 'at a minimum he helped arrange where the bodies would be buried.'

'Let me get this straight,' said the Minister, 'couple of Brack employees charged with manslaughter, in NSW. Brack and his bodyguard charged with conspiracy, this the couple, backpacker couple?' Darby nodded.

'Then we have the bodyguard charged with the murder of the ex-security chief, and Brack on conspiracy to murder him. He asked for that murder?'

279

'Yes,' said Darby.

'He's being charged. Brack?'

'Yes. Suits us, Minister. We need more time for the investigations into suspected ecocide, and the financial crimes. And there's the ongoing investigation into the destruction of Brack's water storage.'

The minister looked up, 'Brack's lawyers are going to want separate jurisdictions, aren't they?'

The Minister poured water. Darby consulted his notes.

'What do we think?'

'My take,' said Darby, 'my take only, is that once we complete the asset freeze and forfeiture on Brack he'll have to apply for legal aid. He'll not be able to afford lawyers able enough to successfully argue jurisdiction.'

The Minister tapped her fingers on her desk, 'if he raises the money?'

'That takes me to the last item,' said Darby, 'Environmental degradation caused by water theft, illegal storage, illegal diversion of water courses, illegal land clearing, destroying of native habitat, and now illegal fracking.'

'Brack the only one you're investigating?'

'No. He's just the most well-known. We're going after the other directors of the Cotton Federation. We're getting enquiries from lawyers acting for nut growers and the Queensland cotton industry about amnesty. We're getting there.'

'This guy,' she searched her device, 'Lucas, not on your payroll, is he?'

'I think that list of charges would deter even the most criminally altruistic from any public support of Brack.'

'Yes, but there's always the Americans, his Texan connection. They'll want to fight the seizure.'

'They do have an interest in the assets, Delaney Holdings. But the extent of their interest is unclear.'

'Delaney Holdings, maybe does not have part foreign ownership? Mick, you'll have to take me through that.'

'We're not fully across it yet, so,' held up his hand, 'if the Texans still have an interest in Delaney Holdings, we may have a case for seizing their assets here and in Texas. They've not filed a return to Foreign Investment for three years, Brack's filed them.'

'I don't see the problem. Brack filed the reports?'

'Brack is not the one responsible for filing the reports, the owners of the Texan share in Delaney are responsible. Litigious people, our American friends, they might come after Brack as creditors, victims of fraud, claim a percentage of the assets.'

'I'd be confident we can freeze the assets,' she mispronounced, 'of a terrorist.'

You could leave it with the Land Councils.

Sandy, Tassie, Mick, and Cindi had finished, sprawled in chairs, half glasses of wine in front of them, each with their own thoughts. The waiter misread the table, and they brushed off dessert.

'Shop?' said Cindi and started talking.

'I've told you about the Land Council meeting I went to where the women asked me about being one of them. Vasco Da Gama motherfucker?'

'Yep, been in touch again, have they? You haven't talked about the land have you, Brack's properties?' said Mick.

'Mick?' asked Cindi, rousing Sandy and Tassie with the sharpness in her voice.

'We've seized Brack's properties. All his assets,' said Mick.

Sandy whistled, 'so, he's broke now?'

'Early days,' said Mick, 'we're not sure we have it all, and there are some financials to untangle to prove the acquisitions came from proceeds of crime. Cindi's putting together a list of the Land Councils we would invite to decide how to reinstate land rights title.'

'Shit,' said Tassie, 'bit sensitive.'

'Yeah,' said Mick, 'sorry Cindi. I'm a bit jumpy. We're pulling it together by stretching the secrecy provisions of Ecological Intelligence, Security and Terrorism, quite a mouthful, we need an acronym,' he laughed.

'And the elders you met,' asked Sandy, 'wanted to meet you again, Cindi?'

'Let me get there,' she said. 'Under our new legislation we've started to get at water trading and ownership records. Who owns water, entitlements, rights, allocations. I found a dozen water holdings gifted to Land Councils throughout the Riverina.'

'A dozen,' said Sandy, 'how many, which ones?'

'New South Wales, from Western and Wiradjuri, not all of them, twelve. The holdings are all in women's names. So, I rang Glenda, she knew all about it. Donations, all, we don't know the donor or donors, we don't know how many. The holdings are entrusted to the Land Councils to use for their communities.'

'Cindi,' said Mick, 'not sure why you're telling us this. What does your team think?'

Sandy looked away and back again, fingers turning the bottom of his glass.

'Haven't told anyone else,' said Cindi, 'it'd be hard to find among all the data we have, I just saw one name, recognised it as one I saw on the poster of indigenous women when I met Glenda, just went looking. These twelve are the only gifted water holdings, ever.'

'Sandy? Something? Or nothing?'

'No,' said Sandy, 'nothing?' he looked at Tassie.

'Might have something,' said Tassie and summarised the progress with the accounts set up for Lucas, Mike Nelson, Clive Baxter among others. 'Twelve rings a bell,' he said, be back in a minute and went outside, phone in his hand.

'A new man your Tassie,' said Mick, 'financial crimes now, money laundering?'

Tassie sat down, 'twelve of the financial entities that Lucas had the lawyers set up, let's call them accounts, are empty, the money's gone. The money from the twelve accounts transferred to one account, then it was closed too.'

'You're telling us,' said Mick, 'the assets you've seized? Those accounts are worthless?'

'No, not all of them,' said Tassie, 'one of the accounts was used to buy water,' he looked at Darby, 'same process, money transferred to the one account. That account was used to buy water, millions of dollars of water. We don't have jurisdiction,' he looked to Sandy, 'the trades were made in different states, water bought from valleys all along the Murray Darling Basin.'

'Were the transfers and the trades hard to find?' asked Cindi.

'No. We would have uncovered it quickly once we had the accounts, getting them would have been the hard part. Once the law firm gave them up without a court order, getting the rest was easy.'

'Jurisdiction', said Mick, 'NSW police would have jurisdiction. Proceeds of crime is about where the crime is committed.'

'Hmmm,' shrugged Sandy, 'where the Commissioner for Ecological Intelligence, Security and Terrorism is involved the proceeds of crime are undisclosed. The states have full disclosure so the proceeds can't be used for political purposes. That's the good part, the bad bit is that proceeds of crime money attract all sorts of appeals for money, bit like the bloke who wins the lottery finds dozens of cousins. So, if these water trades, like Brack's, are seized by you, Commissioner, it doesn't attract that attention.'

'Never have enough water,' said Mick saluting Tassie.

'Lot of water, you could leave it with the Land Councils,' said Sandy, 'land titles, water, and no disclosure.'

'Cindi?' said Mick.

'Ecocide reparation,' she said.

'That would work,' said Mick, 'moving on, Sandy, you still want Ankle's record for that missing two years?'

'I have it,' said Sandy. 'I'll get to it first thing in the morning.'

'What do you think you'll find? I mean how much more is there to know about Ankles?'

Mick, Cindi, and Tassie stared at Sandy. Obsessed with Baxter? He wondered too.

'I think I'll find out how he financed his first properties.'

'Sandy,' Mick sighed, 'how important is Baxter now? Thanks to you we have him and Brack, never seen a tighter case. Mate they'll never be released. It's done. And with the proceeds of crime, the dollars are huge, millions, together we've recovered more money from these two than you spent on Operation Marinya and more than enough to cover what I've spent. It's over.'

'What, we stop when the crime's been paid for.' Sandy stood and edged his chair back under the table. 'What if it's never paid for How do we know when to stop then? A set of mysterious criminal fucking ledgers?'

'Yeah,' said Mick, 'ledgers called politics.'

'I'm out,' said Sandy, 'there's something in those two missing years, I know there is, Brack, Baxter and his protector. I'll find it.'

'Sandy, no, not like this.' Sandy was moving.

'Talk tomorrow,' Sandy's words lost on them as he turned and left the restaurant.

Sandy elbowed open the restaurant door and turned right, patted his pockets, patted them again. He needed to buy more cigarettes; he wasn't going back for them. Childish? Much, but I'm not going back. He slung his hands in his pockets, fist closing over a wad of notes. He hadn't even left money for his share; well, I'm not going back for that either. I'll see Tassie right in the morning. The 7-Eleven didn't have any of Sandy's brand left.

'Do you want to check out back, your storeroom?' said Sandy.

'These are what we have,' said the attendant.

Sandy opened the pack while his change was being rung up only to be told he'd have to smoke outside the shop. He waved the change away and lit up after closing the shop door. This is ridiculous, a grown man. Part of him knew that his reaction didn't mean that Mick was right, but he needed a walk so he could turn over the idea. Tassie and Cindi had not disagreed with Mick. Number of dissenters had never meant a lot to Sandy.

I had a system.

Sandy closed the file he'd been using and picked up another, internal police file, set it down on top of the closed one. Baxter tried to read the cover.

'Come on, Pelham, I need a coffee and a smoke.'

'I don't think this will take long. For years now you've been taking money from two of the biggest players in the Riverina, Lucas and Brack. But, before then, who did you party with, who paid you?'

'Luck really, horses, dogs. I had a system.'

'This system,' Sandy opened the file picked out a photograph and laid it gently on the table.

'Never seen her before,' and turned the photo down.

'Never?' Sandy turned the photo over and picked up another paper from the file, 'you were the attending officer.' He hit the table with the next page, 'and the officer present at the autopsy.' Another hit, 'officer giving evidence at the inquest.'

Sandy spread the pages out, 'so this time,' he leaned in very close to Baxter, 'answer my fucking question.'

Sandy thought Baxter had fainted or worse, pale, he'd slouched, breaths now erratic and shallow, and decided he didn't care. He smacked the table flat handed, hard. Baxter jumped. The officer standing with his back to the door started.

'Tell me what happened.'

'Water,' said Baxter, 'I need a drink of water.'

'No,' said Sandy.

'Thirty years ago, I got a call from Brack's father. He was a stock and station agent, and we knew each other.'

'What happened?'

'He said his son, Hardyn had been in a car accident, all a bit unclear, he was upset as you would be.'

'What happened?'

'Could I get his son off, a girl's dead, Aboriginal kid, wrong place, wrong time.'

'This her?' said Sandy picking up the picture.

'Yes, very sad, Helen. She'd won a Rotary scholarship. With the girl dead Hardyn was next in line, his father wanted me to massage the accident, autopsy, inquest, all so Hardyn could take up the scholarship. He was going to Texas.'

'Massage?'

'You know I never figured out what happened, I was pissed most of the time back then. But the car was a write-off, dead girl, not a scratch on Hardyn.'

'So, you get a call from Brack senior, turn up at the scene, the bad Samaritan. Accident report says evidence of two separate accidents to the car, two single vehicle accidents,' Sandy looked up, 'know anything about that?'

'I interviewed the assessor. He ended up saying that finding was inconclusive.'

'Ended up saying?' said Sandy.

'Little bit of encouragement,' whispered Baxter.

'Pissed most of the time, not too pissed to keep everyone else out of it, though?'

'No, you're right,' said Baxter, 'massaged it all right though. The kid got off and we were rich for the first time. Woulda been murder, no way he'd have got it beaten down to manslaughter, so it paid well, very well.'

Sandy shrugged, 'we were rich...'

'My missus and me.'

'You had no missus. Who is we? You had some help, didn't you? Your boss?' Sandy flicked over a page, looked at Baxter, 'well?'

'He was younger than me, one of the first fast-tracked graduates. I didn't know whether to call him son or sir. He soon put me at ease, reckoned we could clean up in the bush, no one would question him. This was our first massage.'

'And Hardyn Brack?'

'Got the scholarship that week, Rotary. Left for Texas straight away. His old man died six months later. Young Hardyn didn't fly back for the funeral, phoned me to help him find a lawyer sell the family business, and since then...'

'Clive, time for your meds,' said Sandy. 'I'll get you taken back, your pills, water, something to eat. I'll come and get you later this arvo, we can pick it up then.'

'I need the pills. Really.'

'Yeah well, don't take them all at once, we're not done here.'

'Bastard,' said Baxter.

'This officer will walk with you, keep you out of temptation,' said Sandy opening the door.

Sandy leaned against the door when they'd gone, deep breath out, slumped a little, felt for his smokes and stood.

'You're not smoking that rubbish,' said Tassie. 'Lucky, I have mine, c'mon,' and opened the fire escape door.

'I want someone with him the whole time, suicide watch,' Sandy pulled out his phone, 'there's a guy at the uni who does risk assessment, suicide risk,' scrolling, 'now what's his fucking name?'

'You think?' said Tassie.

'Mate,' Sandy looked up, 'with what we have on him, guilt, fear, and no hope. It's caught up with him, it's on his mind. I want him assessed.'

'On it,' said Tassie.

'Thanks,' said Sandy, 'and now to the 'Gong, gotta brief the boss in the morning. Tell her what I found in the weeds.'

'About that,' said Tassie, 'last night.'

'Forget it mate.'

Writing his memoir.

Sandy drove to Wollongong, he stayed on the M31 to Wilton, used his lights and sirens a few times. They were waiting for him, one of the young officers parked his unmarked and another took him to his boss.

She checked her watch as Sandy closed the door to her office, 'good time,' she said.

'Not going to nick me for speeding.'

'Don't you have a scanner?'

'Had it off, was on the phone most of the time. How many cameras?'

'Three,' she said, 'Don't worry about them. Where are we?'

Sandy referred to his tablet as he detailed the highlights of Operation Marinya and his collaboration with Mick Darby. His boss listened, jotted a few notes.

'Is there anything else you need?'

'Yes,' said Sandy, 'I'll need some help with the media, keeping them away from me. Darby's Minister is ah, overexcited, and Canberra wants to be all over this.'

'Step ahead of you there Sandy, they don't want to touch it. Brack has had his claws into pollies of both sides, senior bureaucrats too, ATO is embarrassed about what he's done to them as well as the Foreign Investment Board. They want Brack put away forever and they'll all be shy, Darby will front any media.'

'That's a relief.'

'NSW pollies don't want the publicity either, happy for the Force to front the media and take the credit, you'll be with me and our new Commissioner on that.'

'New Commissioner?'

'Not official yet, he'll be sworn in Friday morning. The vacancy was down to two candidates. One of them was all over your reports on Clive Baxter. Our now Commissioner ran his own investigation and discovered his rival for the top job was Ankles' mentor.'

'Two candidates, one gets the nod because the other's found to be corrupt, on what - the day of the interviews. That file,' Sandy paused, 'the one that miraculously appeared for me, the new Chief, he had it didn't he, he had it before me. I should have fucking known, an old file so neat, not a speck of dust, not a page out of order. He knew he couldn't ask for it, he was waiting for me to, then he'd have to approve me having it.'

'Didn't take you for a conspiracist Sandy.' She felt Sandy looking at her as though he knew she had something to hide. She looked up, dismissed it, every copper was taught that look at the Academy.

'Mentor,' said Sandy, 'misuse of the term.'

'Well,' she said, 'he's now retired as of,' she checked her watch, 'fifty minutes ago.'

'Retired? Not suspended?'

'Too soon,' she said, 'suspend his rival for twenty years on his first day, bit political.'

'Retired,' said Sandy, 'family reasons, spending more time with the grandkids?'

'No,' she said, 'he won't have time for that, he's writing his memoir, journaling his corruption. Our Commissioner is not finished with him yet. And he's not done with you.'

'Ma'am.'

'No, it's all good. He approved Operation Marinya and wants to make sure he gets some credit when you close it.' She reached behind her to open a low cupboard and pull out a bottle and two glasses.

'Relax Sandy, you're not driving back to Wagga tonight,' she poured, 'you're flying. Police helicopter, your vehicle will be there for the morning.'

'Brilliant,' said Sandy.

'Marinya,' she sniffed her whisky, 'flushed out a corrupt Deputy Chief Commissioner, only that wasn't its objective, was it? Marinya, not a lot of results to celebrate are there?'

'A result's a result,' said Sandy.

His boss opened the Marinya file, 'meth manufacturing and distribution in the Riverina? Lucas, Harry, Trevor Thurlough, Gino, Chip. Where are you with these,' she paused, 'characters? Did you invent them?'

'They're real, Thurlough is in jail,' Sandy was yet to taste his whisky.

'On a drink driving charge. The others, where are they?'

'I do know from the water testing and the sewerage testing that there's little meth in the Riverina now. Marinya's objective was to close it down, it's closed. And we solved a cold case murder, Hardyn Brack.'

'He's yet to be charged with that,' she said. 'Operation Marinya appears to have solved Mick Darby's problem with Hardyn Brack and Lucas the eco-terrorist, and you're correct, meth use is negligible. Where I struggle is in finding any result related to the objectives of Operation Marinya. And you're yet to answer my question about these names,' she ran her finger down the page. 'Lucas, Chip, Gino, and Harry, for fuck's sake – did you make these up?'

Sandy stood, put one finger on the desk.

'Oh, don't bother Sandy,' she said, 'you don't miff convincingly. You're our new Commissioner's first catch of the day. You got Clive Baxter talking after forty years. He exposed his protector, who may have been Commissioner if not for that,' she sipped her whisky, 'perfect timing, never crossed your mind? Serendipity? No, I thought not,' shook her head, 'but you know me and coincidence.'

'Now who's the conspiracist,' said Sandy.

There was a knock at the door and a woman in flight gear came into the room, 'Ma'am,' she said, 'I've the car for you now sir,' she looked to Sandy, 'the heliport is ten minutes away.'

'Right,' said Sandy as he put down his glass.

His boss stood, 'the ecocide bill is being introduced into the House of Reps tonight, Darby's minister will want Brack for ecocide, she can have him – after I have him for murder. Here's some light material for the flight, homework. Make sure of the murder charge,' she handed him an envelope, 'I don't want to be bothered by,' she paused, 'coincidence.'

Sandy was strapped in, fitted with a headset and after looking out over the south coast lights for ten minutes he opened his homework. He shook his head, a NSW Police Force file on a Federal Cabinet Minister. He looked up to see the pilot watching him, 'sick bags in the pocket, back of the seat', she said.

'Thanks.'

We've a bit on.

Sandy Pelham looked around him, coffee table littered with papers and files, bragging wall of photos of the Minister with even more important people, many of the photos crooked, he wondered if Darby had misarranged them deliberately, shuddered, dragged his eyes away, pictured himself in his own home.

Other than for the clutter Sandy was finding it hard to fault the Minister.

'None of that,' she said, 'call me Kerry,' shaking hands. 'Hope you don't mind me saying, you do look tired, and I want to thank you for coming in, join me in coffee, tea?'

Sandy settled for coffee, tried to relax while Darby did the run through. He'd covered Brack's property crimes, financial crimes, corruption and bribery, water theft, tax avoidance, water insecurity, and the big gun, ecocide, saved until last. Darby hadn't mentioned murder.

He and Mick Darby had argued. Where to now with Hardyn Brack? Sandy wanted Brack tried first for the murder of Helen, the other crimes could wait.

Darby stopped talking, the monitor's spilt screen showed the major crime headings.

'That's a lot to take in,' the Minister said, finger to her chin. 'Brack is serving ten years, non-parole, on the conspiracy to murder charges. His security chief, right? He's been in for what, eight months?

Sandy had been still during Darby's presentation, now he put his coffee on the desk, looked up, how to raise enough doubt, and not offend Mick, 'Minister...'

'Again, Kerry. It's not the time to go all formal on me. Now. You've had your time to think.'

'Kerry, Mick, and I planned the presentation. We wanted to start with the criminal activities falling under your agency, and move out from there to those crimes,' he responded to her look, 'alleged crimes, more remote from your responsibility. We pictured you at the centre of a circle, core,' he used his hands, 'start there, we decided, and move out.'

'Surely you don't see me as a target,' she smiled.

'For all of that,' Sandy indicated the split screen, 'we not only have Hardyn Brack in our sights. But, the certainty of prison, he wants to talk. He could take us right to the others. Our investigations have stalled, we need a confession.' Sandy leaned forward, 'a confession to the murder which started all this,' he gestured at the screen.

'You have enough to prompt a confession to the murder?' she asked.

'Yes,' Sandy, 'the police officer who made it all go away for Brack.'

'Clive Baxter?' the Minister asked, 'the same Baxter who may be the subject of an ICAC investigation, allegations of widespread corruption, in which he's not the only player.'

'There's only one Clive Baxter,' said Sandy.

'So, you and Mick agreed the presentation. Now, where do you disagree?'

'Disagree?' said Mick.

No-one spoke. No-one moved.

'Is it a question of protocol, Sandy?' she said.

'Mick does head your agency, Kerry.'

'So, is this when boys toss a coin?' she took a coin from a drawer under her desk, 'call it, Sandy.' She flipped the coin. Sandy saw it spinning, so this is how they get things done in ecocide, eco-terrorism; or not done, 'heads.'

'Heads it is,' she said, catching and not showing the coin.

'You're up first then, Sandy,' said Mick. 'Won the toss.'

'Yeah, I did,' said Sandy, 'so I'm sending you in to bat, pad up.'

Darby shook his head and did not convince Kerry.

'Ecocide,' said Sandy when Darby had finished, 'your agency website talks about killing the planet. Kerry, it's much more personal than that. Ecocide is about where you live, it's about having your home killed. We'll get Brack on that because he killed a young woman, Helen, to do it.'

'Gentlemen,' she said, 'pursue Brack for murdering Helen first. Keep the ecocide investigations on the others parallel, Sandy gets everything he wants, all our resources. We're agreed.'

'She's right of course,' said Darby as the lift closed.

'Of course? Is that a Canberra thing? Minister's right, always?'

'How did that happen, you said hardly anything.'

'You said it for me,' said Sandy. 'She remembered headlines in the paper "murderer convicted of forging cheques". Happened a long time ago,' he put his hand on Mick's shoulder, 'one of her first cases, she got a bloke off a murder charge. He was picked up a month later, charged with fraud, back in the nick again the bloke confessed to the murder.'

The lift opened, 'you wouldn't forget a thing like that. She got it right this time. She's got Brack for conspiracy, now she wants him for murder, after that, for the forged cheques.'

'Yeah, but how did you know?'

'Homework Mick, homework, and a bit of digging.'

Sandy noticed Mick not beside him, turned, 'coming? we've a bit on.'

Don't miss out!

Visit the website below and you can sign up to receive emails whenever Joe Moore publishes a new book. There's no charge and no obligation.

https://books2read.com/r/B-A-TAIY-OTLFI

BOOKS 2 READ

Connecting independent readers to independent writers.

Did you love *The Waterboy*? Then you should read *False Reckoning*[1] by Joe Moore!

[2]

False Reckoning is an 86,000 word fictional, political thriller set in early 21st century Canberra.

The crises are set in some present-day political realities of politicians swayed by the reactionary right, and of government abandoning responsibility for aged care to the market.

Intelligence chief Mick Darby is convinced that corrupt gospel church leaders are trialling assistive robots in aged care as a lead up to surveilling politicians and senior bureaucrats. Obstructed by the politics he gets nowhere; confused he becomes paranoid and leaks details of investigations into the church by the Attorney-General's office.

1. https://books2read.com/u/mB8wwk

2. https://books2read.com/u/mB8wwk

The leaks are widely publicised, sparking outrage and sympathy for the popular pastors of Asher Ministries; the church run by Hudson and Phoebe Lang. Phoebe, best friends with the Prime Minister, is angling for a seat in the Senate. Hudson runs the nursing homes where lives are lost to understaffing, poor food and serious overcharging for the services and care denied residents. The Langs' blood money is laundered by the directors of Asher Ministries.

This intriguing, fast-paced thriller focuses the risks and conflicts in revealing the high stakes of pursuing corruption. The story's Australian setting, edgy tone and casual dialogue will appeal to readers open to a look at what actions may result from walking past corruption. It will leave them like Fagan, 'reviewing the situation.'

Also by Joe Moore

False Reckoning
The Waterboy

About the Author

Joe Moore was CEO of an international conflict management company, so he knows first-hand about corruption, conflict and violence.

False Reckoning, his debut fiction novel about government ministers corrupted by prosperity gospel pastors was published in 2023. Joe has published over forty nonfiction articles on conflict and violence and is co-author of a nonfiction book on Instructional Design.

He lives with his wife Janice in the Blue Mountains, walking, gardening and writing.